SONG OF THE SANDS

Other Books from Splinter Press

Mere Mortal by AJ Stevens

The Dissection and Reassembly of Cohen Hoard by Elesa Hagberg

Splinter's Edge by Boydell Bown

Sorry, Humans (Especially Greg) by Faralee Pozo

Between Tungsten & Gold by Taryn Skipper

Song

OF THE

Sands

by Spencer Sekulin

SPLINTER PRESS

Song of the Sands

by Spencer Sekulin

This book is a work of fiction. Names, characters, places, and incidents are the product of the author's imagination and are used fictitiously. Any resemblance to actual events, private locales, or persons, living or dead, is coincidental.

Cover art by: Charlotte Chesley

Published by:

Splinter Press,
Spanish Fork, Utah

splinterpress.com

ISBN-13: 978-1-960108-21-0

To Mom and Dad, for so many reasons.
To Lara, for your kindness and patience.
To Sam, Arthur, David, Dave, Elaine, Jennifer, Brittany, Dustin, Jason, Rebecca, and the rest of the writing gang, for your friendship.
And to you, dear reader. Always to you.

Chapter One

A muffled howl pierced the saloon's languid shadows as a steam engine departed the nearby Frontier supply depot of Anchorshaw. The sound made Lugh Ahearn wish for simpler times, times before karma had left him chasing legends in a wasteland that was doing its best to leave him dead in a ditch.

But he had burned those bridges long ago.

The floorboards rattled with the departing train. Motes of dust fell from the rafters and danced in the silvery beams of light stabbing from old bullet holes in the thin wooden walls.

Play the hand you're dealt. Play, or lose it all.

Lugh touched his chest and the outline of Grandfather's heirloom—a semilunar crystal, hidden in a secret pocket between the layers of his tweed jacket. Grandfather had called it a *Godstone*. Lugh stifled a scoff. Pagan goddesses with the power to heal, a paradise lost through bloodshed and hate, and somehow this "Godstone" was the key to it all. This journey had wits' end written all over it. He hated chasing the Uluru tribe's lost folklore, hated that it was the only hope he had left.

The only hope for his little sister, too.

And as usual, it required money he didn't have.

Lugh blinked a drop of sweat. It pattered on the hexagonal card table's green leather surface. What was with the Frontier and keeping their saloons like ovens? It even smelled like one: sour from kerosene lamps, cigars, and overflowing ashtrays. The rumble of passing trains added a fitting sense of doom.

Perhaps it's just practice for Hell. Most folks here are well on their way.

He winced. Sounded like something Mother would say about *him*. Nineteen years old and already in deep like his old man, always on the run, always in the wrong company. He swallowed hard and glanced at the circular skylight above, its lance of light, and the blue sky beyond. He wondered if Mother was watching from that peaceful blue and hoped that she understood. Then he focused on the smoothness of the cards he shifted in his hands. He'd go straight when this was over. When Sabia was better. Enough chips were on the table to cover Sabia's medicine for months. He could get one of those fancy misting machines to help her breathe at night, maybe even—

"Oi, kid." The ham-fisted man opposite Lugh kneed the table, toppling careful stacks of blue chips. His snarl was made less intimidating by his crisp white tux and little red bowtie, like a heavyweight boxer turned posh salesclerk. "Last move. Make it before I make you make your move."

Mighty proud of that line, aren't you, Jack? Lugh opted for the startled look of a daft teenager who had no idea how to play Stacks, then added a tremor to his hand as he rearranged his cards. He knew what Jack saw: a reed of a youth in ill-fitting tweed, pale face spattered with freckles, and hazel eyes tellingly wide. Easy prey. Jack loved it, sneering as he puffed on his cigar like the devil's dealmaker.

"You can still back out," Jack said. "Better men have made it this far and done the same."

Lugh flinched, then pulled his woven cap tighter over his mop of sandy blond hair to shield his eyes. He'd been seeding the entire game with nervous tells, but he was only half faking it now. The other four players had already thrown and had joined the rest of the onlookers in the hazy gloom. Their cards lay discarded on the table, and their chips belonged to Jack—or as he was known in this Frontier shithole, *Jack the Breaker*, because losing Stacks against him meant losing more than money.

Good thing Lugh intended to win.

"I'm still in."

"That's a good lad." Jack jetted smoke through his nostrils. "Now play."

Another train shrieked to a halt outside. Lugh glanced at his cards: two seers, two dukes, one emperor, one peasant. One more emperor and he'd clear Jack out, bowtie and all. It took Lugh a saintly effort to keep his lip from curling. He'd arranged his hand so that the peasant and emperor were side by side, ready for his deception.

"No stalling," Jack growled.

"I . . ." Lugh faltered, sweat trickling along his jaw. He nervously pushed all of his chips in and cleared his throat. "C-Call."

"Bull's balls, you're shit at bluffing, you know that?"

Jack splayed his cards. Two seers, two dukes, one emperor, and one viscount. He poked his tongue through his gap-toothed smile. "Best start thinking about how to pay. Maybe that lonely little blondie in your hotel room."

Sabia. Lugh grated his teeth. "That's my sister."

"Really? Always wanted one. Raise her myself, teach her a few things."

Lugh's stomach twisted. He ought to take the threat like the greenhorn he pretended to be, but he found himself growling instead. "You leave her out of this, asshole."

"Has sand gotten into your dunce brain already? You have to wager something to meet my bet if you lose, and we both know you came with empty pockets. So be a good sport and put some meat in the game." Jack's grin grew two molars wider. Two molars crueler. "That, or I kill you."

One of the ex-players, who'd taken refuge at the bar, chipped in with a nervous smile. "Like you used to kill those Uluru savages eh?"

Jack shot the man a withering glare. "Are you still in the game?"

"N-No, sir." The man focused on his mug.

"Then keep your craven mouth shut." Jack's sulfuric gaze slid back to Lugh. "Man's right though. Used to be a prospector. Was mighty good at it, too, but those clay-faced savages didn't take well to it. And I didn't take well to them killing my people. Back when I had people worth killing for . . ." He trailed off and glared at the tabletop for a few seconds. "Those days are dead, but the thing about the Frontier is it keeps part of you for a souvenir, and it kept a whole lot of me. I've lacked patience ever since I returned. So don't try anything sly, kid. I never bluff."

Lugh took a deep breath and focused his awareness on the peasant card. Out here he was just another young idiot, but back in Auklenn, his homeland, he was Lugh the Liar—and one of the few gifted with a sorcerous knack.

Sorcery was a fickle mistress who loved desperate suitors.

It started as a *click* at the back of his mind. Tingles crept along his scalp, down his arm, at last pooling hot at his fingertips. When Jack puffed his cigar, Lugh faked a coughing fit and let the tingling warmth rush into the peasant while he simultaneously envisioned his intention. A subtle white flash lit his hand, and the useless card became a perfect copy of his emperor. He called it *Doppeling.* With it he could create a fake of whatever he was physically touching. Shame it only lasted a few minutes, otherwise he'd be rich. And it came at a cost. Sorcery, like any exertion, cost metabolic energy. Or so the tabloids said. But it was worth it as long as he didn't take it too far and risk the *other* cost of his power.

Lugh coughed harder and leaned forward, just in case Jack's porous brain had registered the sorcerous flash. Nothing distracted this prick like suffering.

"Oi." Jack caught his arm, blurring fast for a man his size. "Careful. Don't want to drop your hand and mix it with what's on the table. Think you can get off that easily?"

Idiot. Lugh shook his head. Shouts echoed outside over a steam engine's grumbling, along with the thud of many boots. Jack pulled Lugh closer.

"Smoke getting to you, boy?"

"P-Please stop that . . ."

"What? This?" Jack blew smoke into Lugh's face, then laughed and shoved him back into his seat. "Show me your hand or I'll fit your lips around a chimney, see how much you cough then."

Laughter crept through the saloon's denizens. Jackals in men's clothing. Just like Lugh's late father, who'd only ever deigned to smile when Lugh had done his dirty work.

I'll show you. Lugh began a dramatic reveal.

The front door squealed open with a blaze of midday sun, and a rancid, sulfuric odor flooded the room. Lugh froze. Jack's rosy face went gray.

A tall man in a black duster sauntered in with the rhythmic song of spurred boots, hat tipped over his eyes, right hand drumming on the grip of his holstered revolver. The saloon's patrons crowded towards the walls like bats shying away from a bonfire. The closer the newcomer got, the more Jack hunched, his piggish eyes wide and glazed. Others entered, harsh men and women of dust and leather and lead. Desperados. Their expressions bore the grim coldness Lugh had often seen in Auklenn's most violent slums. The air grew hotter, drier, every breath scratching Lugh's throat. But worst of all was that rotten-egg stench.

Only one kind of sorcerer brought such an aura.

"By all the saints and bloody martyrs," Jack rasped, trembling.

Jig's up. Lugh brushed off his tweed jacket and stood. "Well, it's been fun, but the toilet's calling my name." And so was the window he'd slip out of.

"Please, have a seat," the tall desperado said. "*Now.*"

Lugh swore under his breath and sank back into his chair.

"Jack, is it?" The desperado laid a gloved hand on Jack's shoulder. "Thanks for keeping the seat warm, friend. Now step against that wall."

"Y-yes, Mister Fawkes." Jack stumbled aside like a timid schoolboy.

Eirlys Fawkes? Damnation. Lugh had heard stories of a gang of Frontier desperados led by such a man. They called themselves vigilantes, but that depended on who was on the receiving end of their steel, which allegedly changed as often as the wind. But why here? Why now? Lugh slowly dipped his head to hide behind his cards, but Eirlys's brown eyes arrested him as surely as cast-iron shackles. Cold, like a scalpel's edge, though not nearly as cold as his stubbled, pockmarked face. A killer's face.

Eirlys ignored Jack's empty chair. His voice grated like two colliding mountains. "You Lugh Ahearn?"

Lugh's tongue felt ten sizes too large. "You a lawman?"

"Of sorts." A sardonic quirk tugged at the corner of Eirlys's mouth. He bit a cigar between his teeth and snapped his fingers. Fire burst to life on his fingertip.

A Flameshot.

Don't piss off the human candle. Lugh slowly turned over his cards, revealing his winning hand. "Well, would you look at that." He forced a grin and winked. "How about we split the spoils, have a pint, and happily ride our separate ways? Fifty-fifty?"

Eirlys gave an amused grunt.

"Sixty-forty?"

Eirlys drew his revolver and rested it on the table.

Lugh's smile wilted. "You drive a hard bargain. You can have all of it."

"Do I look like the kind of man who needs permission to take what he wants?"

"Absolutely not, sir. You look like the kind of man people trip over each other to give what*ever* he wants. So . . ." Lugh showed his empty hands. "What can I do for you?"

Eirlys's mouth twitched into a sneer. "You can start by apologizing for presuming to buy me off. I take mighty offense at being told my price."

"That will be enough, Eirlys," said a female voice as precise and deadly as a stiletto. "I deputized you for your local expertise, not your theatrics."

Lugh's gut twisted. Every career criminal in Auklenn knew that voice, and those who hadn't learned to fear it had been quickly introduced to the gallows.

Puffing his cigar, Eirlys clapped Lugh on the shoulder and stepped aside. A middle-aged woman approached from the doorway. Willowy, resolute, she walked as if she not only owned the saloon, but every wretched soul in it. Her gray uniform had fewer wrinkles than a fresh sheet of paper. A fine basket-hilted officer's sword and revolver rattled on her belt as she took a seat and stabbed Lugh with her sapphire eyes. Besides a few strands of silver, her short obsidian hair made the shadows look bright, and her rusty-tanned skin bore none of the warmth of the southern borderlands it hailed from. Her hawkish face wrinkled with what was either mild disgust or bemusement. Probably both.

"You're a long way from Auklenn, Lugh."

Lugh resisted an urge to bolt and cracked a smile instead. "Fancy that. So are you, Major."

"It's colonel now."

Lovely. "Congratulations." Lugh crept his free hand towards his belt. "Colonel Lyza Vyzeryn has a lovely ring to——"

"Leave that rusty derringer in its leather. I'm not here to see you hang."

Lugh glanced at Eirlys. "Sure looks like it."

"You think much too highly of yourself if you think I'd come here solely on your account."

Lugh's neck didn't feel any safer. "I don't see why else you'd be out here."

"Hmm." Vyzeryn casually inspected her fingernails. "I see eight months behind bars did nothing to correct your attitude. How does ten years in Sablethorne sound?" When Lugh practically choked on his own tongue, she nodded and folded her hands on the table. "A lot has happened since you fled the coast. Eliminating the remnants of your father's enterprise was just the prologue. The parliament recognized my efficiency and thought it wasted in domestic affairs. I've moved on to more important matters of state." Vyzeryn eyed Jack's cards, thin lips curling. "And so have you. Gambling your way across the continent to the Frontier? You're not fooling anyone. You may be called Lugh the Liar, but this is a terribly bad ploy."

Lugh's heart raced. He glanced at the door, now blocked by Auklenn soldiers. There had to be a way out. "I don't know what you're talking about."

"Then let's encourage your memory. Kal, bring her."

The soldiers parted, and in strode another of Eirlys's

subordinates: Kal, a brown-haired woman with burn scars on her face and four revolvers on her belt. She had a large tangle of wool blankets in her arms. Blonde hair poked out between the folds. Lugh shot to his feet.

"Sabia!"

The bundle shifted, and his sister's pale, freckled face peered out. Nine years old, yet smaller than six, a consequence of the rusted lung.

Her wheezing breaths caught with worry. "Lugh? What are they . . . ?"

"Shh." Eirlys took Sabia from Kal and bobbed her like a baby. "We're friends of your brother's."

Lugh lunged forward, and Eirlys readied his fingers, his sneer daring. Lugh's knees wobbled. He swallowed hard. Hating them. Hating himself. "Yes," he said to Sabia. "They're . . . just friends."

Sabia blinked slowly, already half asleep. In her frailty, she slept often.

Vyzeryn motioned to the chair. Lugh sank down, dizzy and chilled to the bone.

"What do you want?" he asked.

"I want you to redeem yourself," Vyzeryn said.

"Now who's the liar?"

"I deal in facts, something you can't seem to stomach. Despite every opportunity the system provided, you turned out a criminal like your father. He with his opium dens and trafficking. You with your petty thievery and fraud." Vyzeryn's mouth quirked. "Your mother died ashamed of you, I hear. Now your sister is dying too. And here you are, gambling. Desperate for second chances? Or just whetting your old appetites?"

Lugh clenched his fists. "If I'm such a stain, why bother coming to find me at all?"

"Because we have the same objective."

"I don't think you're—"

Steel sang, and in a blink, Vyzeryn's sword jabbed into Lugh's coat and clinked against the stone. "The Godstone. Show me."

Gods dammit, how does she know? Lugh hesitated until Eirlys sparked a flame on his middle fingertip. Lugh reached into the hidden pocket, hands shaking. The Godstone, about half the size of a poker chip, warmed his fingertips and sent tingles up his arm. His last desperate hope.

If only he could do something. If only he could fight! Not for the first time, Lugh wished his sorcery was different, that it wasn't so limited.

"Well?" Vyzeryn said. "Don't make me carve it out of that secondhand tweed."

Lugh bit his lip, hand still in the hidden pocket. Maybe if he Doppeled a fake . . .

"And spare me your anemic excuse for magic." Vyzeryn's lips curled into a sneer as Lugh balked. "Don't act so surprised. Your father sang like a bird when I dangled the prospect of clemency. Not that it abated his well-earned appointment with the hangman." She dragged her blade upwards, its fine point tickling Lugh's throat. "Poor Lugh Ahearn. Born with a knack that's only good for falsities. And with aversion sickness, no less."

Cold spread through Lugh's chest. "I never told him about that."

"I pulled your mother's medical records, and we both

know aversion is hereditary." Vyzeryn's sneer deflated into a grim frown. "A tragic case, hers. Aversion is cruel. She was a healer, a much more useful sorcerer than you. It's a terrible shame to die from overusing a power so good, but I suppose we have your father to thank for that. Meanwhile, you stood by. And. Did. Nothing."

The words pierced deeper than any blade could. Lugh clenched his teeth, shutting out memories he wished he'd forget yet he knew he deserved.

"So . . ." Vyzeryn tapped Lugh's cheek with the flat of her blade. "Was all that sufficient to remind you of the folly of delaying the inevitable? Or would you like me to recite the coroner's report verbatim?"

Lugh gripped the Godstone tight. The mention of Mother's death was enough to drain the fight right out of him, like blood from a sliced jugular. Even if he tried something, Vyzeryn's blade would be in his heart before he could move, and Eirlys had Sabia as collateral to boot. This wasn't a game he could win. Sick to his stomach, he placed the semilunar stone beside his cards. Translucent, like crystal, but veined with fractured patterns of sapphire and gold. It glowed with a life of its own, an inharmonious crimson. The longer one stared at the pattern, the more it seemed to move in a clockwise dance.

"There it is." Vyzeryn rested her sword across her lap. Her eyes narrowed, the Godstone's light dancing in her blue irises like blood on water. "To think your grandfather left this to *you* of all people. Perhaps he wasn't thinking so clearly in the end. Even a brilliant mind can lose perspective as the curtain draws."

Lugh set his jaw but kept his vitriol to himself.

"Goes to show how it only takes a generation to soil a family name." Vyzeryn frowned. "Amon was a respected archeologist, before his reason gave out. He had many . . . intriguing theories."

Of those theories Lugh knew only fragments. Grandfather had fallen ill shortly after returning from a yearslong expedition that financially ruined him, and on his deathbed had given Lugh a tin, warning him not to let Father have it. Inside, the stone and illegible, moisture-stained notes. Grandfather's fevered mumblings had gone on about a power in the west, beyond the Frontier. A power guarded by the Uluru tribes, capable of healing land and body, and some nonsense about saving the world. His last words had been nigh as confusing.

"Unite them. Return them. Open the eyes that bloodshed closed. Prove . . ."

Grandfather had died before he could finish. Years ago. Before Mother's death. Before prison. Before . . . so much. What the hell had he meant?

"Look at me," Vyzeryn said.

Lugh realized he was staring at the fake emperor card, which had morphed back into a peasant. His throat scratched, dry as desert bones. "I just want to save my sister. She's all I have left. Please."

"Help me and you will," Vyzeryn said. "Your crimes will be forgiven. You can start anew, live a life your mother would be proud of. That's what you've always wanted, isn't it? A second chance."

Lugh scoffed. "You think I'll fall for that?"

"The alternative, then." Vyzeryn gave Eirlys a nod. The Flameshot pointed at Jack, who still cowered against the wall. A palm-shaped light flared on Jack's shoulder—right where Eirlys had clapped him earlier—and burst into flame, engulfing the big man and bursting him into a shower of cindery bones. Lugh yelped and fell out of his chair, grasping at his own shoulder, feeling the tingle of latent magic where Eirlys had touched him moments ago.

"So . . ." Vyzeryn brushed ashes from her uniform. "Do we understand each other?"

The smell of charred flesh crawled to the back of Lugh's nose. He retched, nodding vigorously between heaves, hoping Sabia was still asleep, praying she hadn't seen a man die. This was the last place she deserved to be, yet he'd brought her right to it. *Damnation,* would his past never stop coming back to haunt him? Two of Vyzeryn's soldiers pulled him to his knees. He didn't fight it. Vyzeryn stood and sheathed her blade.

"Sabia will stay under my wing. She'll be well cared for, provided you follow orders."

"What kind of orders?"

"Nothing you haven't done before. I want you to deceive someone. You see . . ." Vyzeryn touched his chin, tilting his gaze into her eyes. She smiled gently. "There's a second half to the Godstone, otherwise it's useless. An Uluru outlaw has the other. A blood sorceress, and a female. So very few of that combination anymore. She was last seen near Capstone, at the train line's end. So, Lugh the Liar, do what you do best and bring me the other half, and the outlaw. Alive. Otherwise, your ashes will feed the crops, and little Sabia will suffocate in her sleep."

"Can't you just do it yourself?" Lugh asked, grasping at straws. "You have an army. Take the stone and let Sabia—"

Vyzeryn pinched Lugh's chin. "You don't think I've tried? All I have to show for it are dead bodies. This isn't going to happen with force. Lucky for you, subtlety and trickery are your specialties. Are you questioning me?"

"N-No . . ."

"Good." Vyzeryn looked to the saloon's pudgy keeper, who huddled behind the grimy bar. "Give the lad his winnings. He won the Stacks, after all." When Lugh balked at the wad of bills the keeper put on the table, Vyzeryn smirked. "A lesson for you. It doesn't matter how much you cheat, as long as you win." She leaned close, smelling of tea and lilac perfume. "Victory is *everything*."

A rumbling shook the saloon, and through the skylight, Lugh glimpsed armored airships descending from the blue. Auklenn's iron might.

"The world is changing, as it always does." Vyzeryn pushed the Godstone towards Lugh. "Do the smart thing and be on the winning side."

Lugh blinked at the Godstone. "You're . . . letting me keep it?"

"Of course. Your grandfather made his choice, and a gift is a gift. Besides, you will do everything I want you to do." Vyzeryn stood up and gently caressed Sabia's hair, eyes like chips of ice. "You can't afford not to."

Trapped. Lugh realized he'd never truly understood the meaning of that word until now. All he could do was nod. It made him sick—and made Vyzeryn smile.

"You're finally learning to stomach the truth." Vyzeryn

strode for the door as the landing warships rattled the shutters. "There's a train bound for the line's end. It leaves in ten minutes. Be on it."

Lugh wiped his burning eyes. "Why are you doing this?"

"It's simple," Vyzeryn said. "To kill a god."

Chapter Two

Lugh boarded the train with a crushing urge to steal something.

So he did.

A dusty, long-haired man stooped out of the latrine in the train car's narrow foyer. *And we have ourselves a volunteer.* Lugh squeezed past him, getting so intimate with the man's weathered jacket he sneezed from the sour dust it gave off.

"Bless you, lad," the man said through a scraggly beard, breath rank with alcohol.

"Thank you kindly." Lugh didn't meet the man's gaze. Him? Blessed? Yeah, and rats could fly. He walked on, shoulders hunched, hands in his pockets. The train car was empty, the rows of rough wooden benches reminding him of the vacant churches back in Auklenn. Lugh chose the bench that looked least likely to leave a splinter in his backside, slumped down, and took out the man's leather coin purse. Battered to hell. Heavy, too.

Turned out a pocket full of gambling money couldn't change a man. Spend a lifetime getting a thrill out of theft, and you built a vicious cycle. He tried to smile at the purse anyway, but the nervous urge in his chest only worsened, eating at him like a thousand nibbling lice. He muttered several curses that would have made even Eirlys blush.

Committing petty theft in hopes of feeling a semblance of control? Stupid. The last thing he had was control. Vyzeryn held all the cards, and the game was rigged.

Still, old habits die hard.

Lugh opened the purse and tipped it over onto his lap. Sand poured out, topped with a rotten molar with a silver filling. King's ransom. He'd really hit the big leagues. Lugh rolled his eyes and tossed the empty purse out the window. The train jolted into motion. So did the dreary to-do list in Lugh's head.

Get to the Frontier proper. Find the outlaw. Get the stone. Save Sabia.

Thirteen words that pounded between his ears like a thousand.

An hour later, they still pounded.

Lugh thumbed the molar. Disgusting, but silver was silver. *Click.* Warm tingles rushed to his palm, and the molar winked into a copy of his wrinkled train ticket. The squeal of wheels on rusted tracks needled him endlessly, and the patter of sand on the windows mocked him for getting sick of his own reflection. He'd fooled many people with that youthful face. He could never fool himself.

He reversed the Doppeling, then did it again, back and forth, each time feeling angrier. Of all the knacks he could have been born with, why this one? Only good for cheating. It couldn't heal Sabia. It couldn't make Mother proud.

Perhaps I was just born this way, and the magic mirrors what I've always been.

Lugh magicked the molar into a ticket again. His throat still itched where Vyzeryn's blade had touched, but her words dug at him harder, lurking in the back of his mind. That holier-than-thou lunatic was right. Mother's power had been far better than his, and he knew he could say the same about her heart . . . yet they both shared the same weakness. Aversion. While most sorcerers didn't suffer ill effects unless they used their powers to extremes, those with aversion had a lower threshold, some so low that even tapping into their powers stopped their hearts with fatal dysrhythmias. A phenotypical variance—academia's fancy word for inferior. While Lugh could use his power, he could only Doppel small objects. Only once had he tried to use his knack in a fight to Doppel a rival's shotgun into a penny. He'd woken up hours later, in a ditch, covered in his own piss and vomit. The aversion had hit him so hard his enemies had assumed he'd died—a silver lining that did nothing to diminish the terrifying lesson he'd learned that day.

One careless overstep could kill him.

Some gift. Lugh clicked his tongue as he Doppeled the molar a few more times. The repeated effort only brought a twinge to his chest. Nothing like the palpitations that came when he overdid it. Gods, he'd pulled the short straw, and his gut told him he deserved it. *But you didn't, Mother. You didn't.*

As a healer, Mother had never been one to withhold

her gifts. As careful as she'd been, she'd danced on the edge far too often, taking her past the tipping point into aversion sickness. Unlike regular aversion, full-on sickness was irreversible and set the body against itself—an incurable ailment that slowly ate away all the nerves in her body.

Not that Father had cared.

Not that Lugh had done much to prevent it.

If he could do it all over again . . .

The train shifted and rattled as it took another bend in the track, making the rough wooden bench more torturous with every passing second. His backside felt like it would fall off. Lugh gritted his teeth and glanced out the window, ignoring his reflection as best he could. Fields of dust and dead crops. Roads sprinkled with wagonloads of settlers returning to Auklenn. Abandoned farmsteads. Dried rivers. Hopelessness. Loss. Ruin. Why had these people tried to settle this land in the first place?

"Land of death," slurred a leathery voice. "First time?"

An eye-watering stink of alcohol assaulted Lugh as the dusty, bearded drunk he'd just stolen from plopped onto the bench opposite him. Dressed in a faded cavalry jacket with army insignias rusted to oblivion, he looked like a relic dug up after a century—and smelled like it, too, redolent of fifteen shades of shit.

"I'm not giving you money," Lugh muttered.

"Not looking for any. Just company. Ah . . ." The man kicked his muddy boots up on the bench and fished his hand into his pocket. "Now where is it . . . come here you little . . ."

Lugh winced. They were the only two people in the car, and even a drunk could do the math. He silently thanked Lady Luck when the man fished out a tin flask instead.

"Why's a young lad like you going to the end of the world?"

"Business," Lugh replied.

"If your business is dying." The man took a swig. "You ever heard of the Clysm?"

Lugh rolled his eyes. He would be rich if he had a silver coin for every time people whispered about that stupid storm. The Clysm was supposedly a vast sand cyclone deep in the Frontier, what had once been the heart of the Uluru people's domain. Probably an exaggeration, like most tales these days. Nonetheless, it reminded him of Grandfather's ominous ramblings. Wouldn't be the first coincidence.

"Well?" the Drunk asked.

"Yeah, everyone from you to the rats in Auklenn knows about it. Bad weather."

"Wrath of a goddess, that's what it is." He knocked on the wooden bench. "Did you know it's expanding? This desert, too."

"News to me."

"You're criminally uninformed, lad."

Lugh glanced out the window at the passing settlers. Is that why they were packing up in droves? "Don't you think everyone in Auklenn would have heard about that if it was true?"

"Ah, see that's the thing about most people. They like to ignore the subjects that terrify them. Ignorance is armor, they think, rather than the soggy paper it is." The Drunk winked and knocked on the bench again. "Last two centuries the storm and the desert's been growing, ever since the Uluru tribes and their blood sorcerers were massacred by us intrusive colonials. Angered their goddess, Ehekahl, and rightfully so. I'd be fuming too if my worshipers were snuffed out. Who doesn't like a little worship?"

Lugh cursed under his breath, wishing the man would pass out already.

"Another unbeliever. Oh well. Those poor settlers certainly believe it. As do the bigwigs back in Auklenn, although it's their modus operandi to hide such things from the excitable masses, eh? Panic is bad for the markets." The Drunk leaned back and stared at the ceiling. "Used to be pretty in this land. Full of lakes and meadows and flowers. A true paradise."

Lugh wrinkled his nose. His grandfather used to say something similar, long ago. He recalled the man's deathbed. The smell of urine and feces. The rattle of his breaths. The brittleness of his voice as he spoke his final words in a fevered delirium.

"*Unite them. Return them. Open the eyes that bloodshed closed. Prove . . .*"

Unite the halves of the Godstone? Return them where? To whom? And whose eyes had to be opened? What had to be proved? It could all be nonsense, a hallucination of a dying man. Lugh had certainly thought so for the last three years, though he'd kept the stone hidden nonetheless, buried on the city outskirts. He'd only dug it up a few months ago out of sheer desperation, on the one-year anniversary of Mother's death and after a year of barely keeping himself and Sabia alive. Why did things always have to get worse?

Lugh stared at the molar, still conjuring it back and forth. The Drunk either didn't notice or didn't care. Maybe the Drunk's information was more lucrative than his purse.

"What do you know about the Uluru?" Lugh asked.

"Curious *now*, eh?" The man grinned like a piano missing half its keys. "The tribes have been rallying, nettling the garrisons at the diamond mines. I hear there's a new colonel come to bring them to heel. A dapper lady from the coast."

Dapper wouldn't be the word I'd use for Vyzeryn, Lugh thought.

The Drunk belched and took another swig from his flask. "Colonel Vyzershit or something like that. People say she's brought a miraculous contraption. An armored train that lays its own tracks. Airships won't work out here, not with the Clysm's wind eating them alive. But this colonel found a way. She's on a warpath, just like the Uluru."

"War over *what?*"

The man's smile faded. He gazed out the window, eyes suddenly clear. His voice became somber. "Legends, mostly. From an age when gods walked the earth. Some say lost in all that dust is the home of Ehekahl. The heartland of all creation." He made a bitter sound at the back of his throat. "Power. Turns men mad."

You're using the drink to forget. Lugh leaned forward. "Who are you? A soldier?"

The man's eyes flashed, then lost their focus. His gap-toothed smile returned. "Just a drunk."

"Well, *just a drunk*, I'm looking for someone. An outlaw."

"Everyone's an outlaw out here."

"An Uluru outlaw. She's a blood sorceress."

The Drunk's eyes narrowed. "Did you leave your wits back in the city, lad?"

"What?" Lugh asked. "You know this outlaw?"

The Drunk tottered from the bench as if Lugh had the pox. "Word of advice. Some things aren't worth it no matter how much they glitter."

"But—"

"No matter how much they glitter. That is, unless you like flirting with death." The man wiggled out one of his rotting teeth, reached into his pocket, and pulled out a coin purse. With a wink, he plopped the tooth inside, and then stumbled away, muttering to himself and knocking on every wooden bench he passed, as if he could stack luck like chips.

Lugh glared after him, trying to wrap his head around what he'd just seen. Probably had two purses. Yet when he looked down, the molar was gone. Only wisps of sand remained. *Must be all the sleepless nights. That's it. That's all this is.*

He set his jaw against a flutter of anxiety at the Drunk's ominous words. It didn't matter how dangerous this was. He gripped his shoulder where Eirlys's curse tingled, thinking of Sabia, remembering her smile, her staccato laugh, and the brightness of her eyes whenever he brought her toffee. He'd do anything for her. He'd done *everything* for her. Protecting her from Father's drunk rages, taking up that bastard's demands to work in the gangs instead of fleeing home so Sabia wouldn't be left behind. Saving what he could to pay for her tuition at a good school in a safe community.

Her illness had ruined that plan.

Mother's death had driven a final nail into it.

What he wouldn't give to see her run and play again.

Hold on, Sabia. You deserve a better brother, but please, give me one last chance.

That last chance began where the tracks ended.

As the final stop on the Frontier railroad, Capstone had a *glowing* reputation. Lugh disembarked at a station riddled with bullet holes and sandblasted wanted posters. The town looked no better: a ramshackle orgy of wooden houses and barns, with a rusty weathervane shrieking in the wind. Lugh shielded his eyes from the sandy gusts and squinted over the rooftops—and felt as if Vyzeryn's blade was poking against his chest yet again.

A towering wall of reddish sand dominated the shimmering horizon. Its cyclonic whirls engulfed the sun, leaving the sky a rusty, septic brown. Sickly veins of green lightning flickered and danced over its churning chaos, and the longer Lugh stared, the more he heard it over the breeze, a deep rumbling that gnawed at his nerves. A sound befitting divine rage.

The Clysm.

Gods, it's everything the rumors said it was. Lugh took a step back. Part of him wanted to get right back on that train and never see the horrific storm again, yet a surprising thrill fluttered in his chest, and he stepped forward again. If he was wrong about the Clysm, what else was he wrong about? Had Grandfather's fevered mumblings been true? The Drunk's prattling bubbled at the back of his mind. So did Vyzeryn's ominous words. *To kill a god,* she'd said. And the Clysm was growing. Was she aiming to stop it? And if someone like Vyzeryn was taking a pagan goddess seriously, then that added even more credence to the legends.

He'd started this journey in search of a power that could save Sabia's life.

Maybe this wasn't a fool's errand after all.

I suppose I'll find out. One step at a time, Lugh. Play your hand, however rotten it may be. Lugh tore his gaze from the storm and focused on the town. He felt eyes on him, saw pale faces in the windows, even smelled their fear over the stench of horse dung and oil. He touched his jacket, rubbing the Godstone's outline. Sand already chafed in his underwear.

Welcoming place. Now, where to find an outlaw?

May as well start where everyone got drunk.

Chapter Three

Lugh sidled up to the train station's tiny office kiosk with all the casual disinterest he could manage, but the man behind the dusty window made him work hard at it. He reminded Lugh of a bulldog—bald with massive jowls, and so thick it looked like the booth had been built around him rather than have him squeeze through its tiny doorway. Lugh tapped on the glass. The man ignored him. He tapped again. Still ignored.

World-class customer service. Lugh raised his hand to tap again.

The window slid open with a shriek, assaulting Lugh with a shower of dust that tasted like coal smoke. The man at the counter didn't even look up, scowl directed downward at an old chessboard crammed between stacks of crumbling papers and unused tickets.

Lugh cleared his throat.

"What you want?" the man asked in a slow, bored tone.

Lugh eyed the man's weathered placard. Most of the letters had worn away, but the remnants spelled *Dolt*. He smiled. "I'd like to ask for directions, in particular the—"

"Train's leaving in ten minutes," Dolt said.

"Excuse me?"

"Train. Ten minutes. *Leaving.*"

Lugh blinked, then laughed it off. "I'm not going back. I'm here on business."

"And I'm here doing you a favor."

"I don't need that kind of favor, sir. I need directions to your saloon."

Dolt moved a pawn, grunted, and then looked up, narrowed eyes flicking over Lugh as if he were a piece of secondhand furniture. His scowl doubled. "You won't last twenty seconds in this town."

And you look like the reason the town's starving. Lugh swallowed the remark and ghosted a pebble into his right hand, eyeing the cheap watch sitting beside the chessboard. "Oh . . . I see. That's a fair cop. May I ask the time?"

"Check it yourself." Dolt tossed him the watch.

Gladly. Lugh counted out a full minute. Aloud. Dolt flushed red, and the kiosk's plank walls groaned as if the man were puffing up like a southland swamp toad. Lugh finished with a whistle. "Well, would you look at that. Already lasted *sixty* seconds." He handed a Doppeled watch back while pocketing the real one. "Ever heard the saying, don't judge a fruit by its peel? Or has that bit of wisdom not yet made its way into this sandy armpit of the world?"

Dolt muttered something and resumed his staring match with the chessboard, oblivious to the trick. Most non-sorcerers couldn't sense magical auras, and even among sorcerers it depended on one's intuition and the magnitude of the sorcery. Clearly Dolt had as much sorcery-sense as a doorknob. After interrogating the chessboard with a constipated expression, Dolt moved a rook on his side, nodded to himself, then waited. A few seconds later, he moved an opposing knight, then squinted as if the move had been a surprise.

"Who's your opponent?" Lugh asked, craning his neck to see the pieces.

"Garin," Dolt said. "Now piss off."

"I'll gladly piss off to the nearest saloon. Thirstier than a man trying to eat his way out of a salt mine. If only someone could point me in the right direction."

Dolt moved his rook to counter the knight, then jabbed a meaty finger to the left.

"Thank you kindly, your largeness." Lugh reached into the booth and moved the knight. "Checkmate. Garin wins."

Lugh was strolling down the wagon-rutted street by the time Dolt shouted a curse after him. He smirked and slid on the new watch, only to find it didn't even fit his skinny wrist. A child's watch. No wonder Dolt hadn't worn it. Maybe Sabia would like it . . . He stopped, boots grinding to a halt on the bone-dry earthen street. Dust skittered past, along with dead grass and scattered bits of outdated tabloids.

A stolen watch. Can't you do better for her than that?

Lugh clenched his hand, watch digging into his palm. He had to do better. Starting here, in this dump of a town. He had to get through this. For her. And that meant he had to stop letting his ego get him into trouble. Gods knew he'd made enough enemies back in Auklenn.

If he wanted this time to be different, *he* had to be different.

Easier said than done.

The main street looked like any Frontier town. Slapdash plank houses with facades and painted signs, cracked shutters, and sand-weathered glass. The Clysm loomed beyond the street's end, its whirling chaos blotting the sky, ever rippling with that sickly green lightning. A smaller storm spilled out from its edges, tumbling over miles of barren land. Another came shortly after that, and though smaller, it looked plenty big enough to flatten any Frontier town. It reminded Lugh of water spattering from a boiling pot. No wonder everyone was fleeing the Frontier. Capstone was a ghost town in the making. A faded banner hung between the post office and a boarded-up hotel that likely hadn't seen a guest in years: *Welcome to Capstone, gateway to paradise.*

Lugh snorted and kept walking down the street. Someone ducked into an alleyway. A woman on a porch, beating a depressing rag of a rug, saw Lugh and went inside, and he didn't miss the muffled thump of a crossbar dropping in place. The same sound followed him down the whole street. Shutters closing. Muffled voices. A baby wailing somewhere. A dog bark followed by its owner hushing it.

And a man whistling a discordant excuse for a tune.

Lugh stopped and shielded his eyes against the dusty wind. A well sat at the street's end, made of cobblestone and cracked planks. A spindly young man in threadbare trousers and boots sat on its edge, shirtless and whistling as he worked its crank. A tingle down Lugh's spine told him to turn around, and a glance left and right showed no saloon, just battered houses and derelict shops. Had Dolt pointed him in the wrong direction? Maybe Lugh shouldn't have spoiled his game. That was probably the first *real* loss the man had suffered in eons.

Oh well, on to the next local weirdo. Lugh approached the well, hand in one pocket near his derringer, the other snapping a casual wave.

"Good afternoon. Need any help with that?"

The young man stopped whistling and leaned against the crank's frame, panting. His skin was sunburnt red. "Rare thing, the kindness of strangers, but a man's gotta finish what he started." Whistler pulled the bucket out and turned it over, adding rusty sand to a growing pile at his feet. Then he flashed a yellow smile at Lugh. "Just got off that train, did you?"

Lugh took one step back and nodded. "Looking for a place to get a drink. The gentleman at the station pointed me this way, but I don't see a saloon."

"Oh, that's a crying shame."

Footsteps crunched behind Lugh, and before he could turn, someone tackled him from behind. He stumbled towards the well, and Whistler dodged to the side, unspooling a length of thick rope. Everything happened at once: hand on his back, rope hissing around his right leg, the well's hard edge, wind in his ears, world turning upside down then snapping to a painful halt. Lugh blinked sand and sweat, then yelped when he found himself staring at the bottom of a dried-up well from some fifty feet up, suspended by his right ankle. Pain shot up his leg. He didn't think it had dislocated, but it still hurt like a prison guard's *gentle* discipline. Lugh's cap lay at the bottom, far out of reach. He quickly patted his chest, making sure the Godstone hadn't fallen out, too. Dry laughs mocked him from above. Suddenly Dolt's shoddy directions made perfect sense.

Oh. Great. I've been played like a fopdoodle.

Perhaps someone else might have wondered if counting to sixty had been an affront to Dolt's arithmetic capacities, but Lugh knew a well-oiled racket when he fell into one. Literally. These sand rats probably did this to any clueless newcomer. Nonetheless, Dolt had tried to give him one chance to leave town. Was he such a sorry sight that even criminals pitied him?

"How you doing down there, city slicker?" called Whistler.

Dust showered down. Lugh sneezed, then took in the fatal drop below. His heart pounded, thoughts of Sabia rushing through his head like hailstorms. Done in by two goons and a well? That was low, even for him. He took a few deep breaths and hoped he didn't sound as terrified as he felt. "Oh, you know, hanging around. Nice clay walls you have down here."

"Very funny."

"My compliments by the way. How'd you get so swift at hanging poor blokes?"

Whistler rasped a chuckle. "Trial and error. You're lucky."

"Oh, thanks."

"Shut up!" The bucket lowered into view. "Now empty your pockets into the bucket, like church tithes, you know? Tourist tax, since you didn't take Grom's offer to feck off. Else we'll cut the rope and see if you break that chicken neck of yours."

Chicken neck? Lugh huffed and fished through his trousers. The money he'd won in Anchorshaw lurked in a dozen hidden pockets, but he always carried mugger money, just in case. He dropped a wad of counterfeit bills into the bucket, along with a few foil candy wrappers for good measure. The bucket disappeared. Whistler spat into the well.

"That all you got?"

"I have more. I just can't reach it."

"That so? We can drop you and fish it out later."

Sob act it is. Lugh sniffled. "Really! I won't try anything! Please!"

Whistler conferred with his partner in hushed tones, and true to Lugh's gamble, they weren't coldblooded killers. Few thieves ever were—after all, he was one of them. They hoisted him up and manhandled him until he was sitting on the well's edge. Whistler's partner was a brunette woman twice his age, desolate gown cut up to the knees, black eyeliner smeared down her face. She held one of the bills to the sky and shook her head.

"These are fakes."

Lugh's stomach dropped. Smarter than they looked.

"Huh." Whistler pushed Lugh back, holding him over the well by his collar. "So you're a con man, too. A stupid one, coming out here. Not much to go around. We don't need the competition, see?"

Lugh dug out the watch and pasted on a servile smile. "How about partners?"

The woman grabbed the watch and squinted. "That's Grom's piece."

Whistler snorted a laugh and pulled him back. "Not bad."

"Tell you what . . ." Lugh slowly reached into his tweed jacket, unfastened a hidden pocket, and pulled out a small portion of his winnings. "Genuine article this time. You get your money, I go get drunk, everyone wins."

Whistler snatched the bills, held one of the sky, then licked his lips. "That sounds good and all, but getting drunk implies you still have money on you."

Lugh huffed a sigh and fished out another stash. "There. Happy?"

"Not until you show me why your collar looks like a snake trying to swallow a rat."

"Damnation . . ." Lugh adjusted his collar, then fished another roll of bills. This time he snarled. "Want all the lint in my pockets next?"

"*That* you can keep." Whistler ran his thumb through the stack of bills and sneered. "Think of it as our generosity. Welcome to Capstone."

The woman laughed and took out a cigarette.

"So . . ." Lugh positioned himself on the edge, feet over the pile of sand. "Where's the saloon at? Really."

"Why does your broke ass even care?" the woman asked.

"I'm looking for somebody."

Whistler blinked, then shoved the bills into his pocket. A sheen of sweat broke out on his forehead. "You . . . meeting someone there?"

What's got you scared? Lugh nodded. "I'm here on personal business."

The woman choked on her cigarette. "Shit, you think he's with—?"

"Shh!" Whistler glanced over Lugh's shoulder. His anxious expression doubled. "It's on the other side of town, kid. Sorry for this . . . uh . . . misunderstanding."

Lugh stepped off the ledge. "Does that mean I can have my money—?" He slipped on the loose sand and fell into Whistler's sweaty chest. The man cursed and pushed him away as if he had the pox, and Lugh pretended to fall hard, groaning. By the time he got up, both thieves were fast-walking into an alleyway, arguing under their breaths and stealing glances to the horizon. They'd even dropped the watch in their hurry.

A cloud of dust marred the distance. Riders on approach. Was that what spooked them? Or was there something dodgy about the saloon? Lugh brushed himself off and glanced at the dust cloud. Whatever was going on, he'd best make fast like the locals. He had an outlaw to find . . . and something still felt wrong. Nonetheless, Lugh took a moment to count the bills he'd ghosted up his sleeves. Whistler hadn't even felt the snatch. Sun-toasted amateur. Compared to Vyzeryn and Eirlys, these local crooks were clowns.

Grom was still in his booth, hunched over a fresh chessboard. Lugh made sure to drop his watch back on the counter and snap in passing, "Like I said. Fruit and peel."

Grom eyed the watch, then shrugged. "Don't say you weren't given an out. What happens next, that's all on you."

Story of my life. Lugh turned the proper direction and stuffed his hands into his pockets. Every step tweaked his ankle something fierce. Now he *really* needed a drink.

Chapter Four

Lugh steeled himself for the usual saloon greeting of smoke, sweat, harsh glances, and fistfights. Instead, when he pushed through the squealing wooden doors, he was welcomed by the earthy aroma of flowers.

Clay flowerpots crowded the deserted tables, aglow with blooms. Lugh blinked and rubbed his eyes to be sure. Marigolds, like in Mother's little townhouse garden. Who the hell brought marigolds all the way to the Frontier? There was no barkeep in evidence either. A sole occupant sat hunched at the bar, wearing a battered brown duster and brimmed hat to match. Lugh sat two stools down— and realized there *was* a barkeep, a man so short his chin barely scratched the counter, with eyebrows like overused mops. The man looked dazed.

Lugh tapped the countertop. "Good afternoon."

"Bar's closed, sir," the barkeep said, his voice a strangled rasp.

Lugh sighed, but it came out like a growl. "I've been lied to, hung upside down in a well, robbed, and sand's chafing me worse than a prison bed's lice. I need a drink, my good man. Something strong."

"Afraid there's none of that."

Lugh eyed the full rack of whiskey bottles and frowned. "Right. I'll have water, then." Something was definitely off.

"W-Water's not safe here."

"Then I'll have what he's having." Lugh glanced at the other patron. Thin, with a mess of wavy gray hair hanging over his face as he stared into a blotchy tin mug. He had multiple braids, each decorated with amethyst beads. His skin was gray, like his hair, not from age but as if he'd risen out of an ash heap. An Uluru.

Lugh stared at the knife-marked countertop, thinking hard. He cleared his throat and pushed a wad of bills towards the barkeep. "Any word on an Uluru outlaw in town?"

The barkeep flinched, eyes darting between the money and the door. "You a lawman?"

"A prospector."

"You look a little young."

Lugh shrugged. "Everyone says that. Took over my dad's business after he died of the rusted lung. Debts have to be paid. I need some muscle. May as well hire the best."

"You're shit at lying, you know that?" grunted a distinctly female voice beside him.

Lugh turned to find the Uluru drilling into him with big emerald eyes striated with gold. A girl, not a man. Had he just taken a seat next to his target? Was that why those goons had been scared?

Ha. Impossible. Even his luck wasn't *that* bad. Or would that be good luck?

Red-gray freckles crowded her face, and her stern

eyebrows were notched like bayonets. No older than him, and pretty—in an *I'll-stab-you-if-you-touch-me* sort of way. She had a small nose, high cheekbones, and a little white scar across her chin . . .

"Hey, outlander, you deaf?"

Lugh blinked, realizing he was staring. "Excuse me?"

She clicked her tongue and went back to pondering the bottom of her mug. "I said you're a shit liar. You smell like dirty money, not a city dandy."

Indignation ignited Lugh's face. He played it off with a chuckle. "That's my old man you're smelling. Clings to me like cigar smoke."

The girl wrinkled her nose.

Is she the outlaw? Lugh licked his lips, neck tense. Time for a gamble. He took out the Godstone and tapped it on the countertop three times, but the girl didn't react. His nerves eased as he pocketed the stone. *No dice here. Though she looks like she's got a few screws loose in her head.*

The doors burst open with a racket of footfalls, rattling steel, and whispering sand. Lugh twisted around and nearly fell from his seat. Thirty men and women stormed in and spread out in a semicircle. They wore dusters and riding boots, had the scarred, weathered faces of seasoned bounty hunters, and held a whole lot of rifles, revolvers, and machetes. Lugh noted the faces. Not Eirlys's men. Locals? The lead man, a spindly, weasel-faced graybeard, whistled and aimed two pistols with a dual *click*.

"You. At the bar. You Ku'Adsila?"

Just my rutting luck. Lugh hunched over the bar and stole a glance at the girl. She had put a handful of .45 caliber bullets on the countertop, along with a black double-action revolver sporting a rosewood grip. She pricked her finger on a splintered section of the bar and began lazily smearing blood around the neck of each bullet. *Yeah, lots of loose screws.*

"Well?" the bounty hunter growled. "You deaf or stupid or am I right?"

"So what if I am?" the Uluru girl asked.

The metallic song of cocking weapons filled the air.

I'm sensing a theme here. Lugh drummed his fingertips on the bar. "Well, this was fun, but the toilet's calling my name." He went to stand, but Ku'Adsila grabbed his wrist, her strength like prison manacles.

"Stay put, liar," she hissed. "I'm not done with you."

"I think your hands are full enough already."

"You're right." Ku'Adsila let go, then rammed a wicked knife through his tweed jacket's sleeve, pinning him to the bar.

"That's my favorite jacket!"

"Probably your *only* jacket, knobhead. Try pulling free and the next one's between your legs."

Lugh grimaced. Yeah, definitely a theme. The barkeep vanished. Even the marigolds seemed to shrink back. Wind rattled the shutters, and a horse nickered outside. Ku'Adsila finished her bloody artwork and plopped two bullets into her six-shooter.

"Oi!" the bounty hunter yelled. "Twenty seconds. Hands up, witch."

Lugh coughed. "Hello? What about me? Does anyone see the poor bystander in harm's way?"

"Looks to me like you were conspiring," the bounty hunter said.

"Hey, see the knife in my sleeve? I'm innocent!"

"Exactly what a criminal would say."

"Oh come on!"

"Yap all you want. I have it on good authority." The bounty hunter smirked. "The good citizen at the station said there's a new conman afoot, dresses like a city twat."

Lugh flushed. "It's called *tweed*."

"Exactly." The bounty hunter eyed Ku'Adsila, who still hadn't bothered to turn around. "Ten seconds. Surrender and we'll bring you in alive."

"For what?" Ku'Adsila flipped her gun shut and spun the cylinder. "A cozy noose?"

"Dunderheaded sand witch. You're—!"

Ku'Adsila aimed blindly over her shoulder and pulled the trigger, the muzzle flare erupting a foot from Lugh's nose. He ripped his jacket free and dove to the floor, ears ringing. He covered his head, waiting for a bullet's sting, only to hear a muffled clatter of falling bodies instead. An odd smell wriggled up his nose: coppery, like blood, but with a citric tang. *Sorcery?* So this *was* the outlaw. He cracked his eyes open, praying he hadn't pissed himself.

Thirty corpses littered the saloon. Thirty headshots. *With one bullet?!*

Lugh flinched as the revolver's smoking barrel switched to him.

"Where did you get that stone?" Ku'Adsila asked.

"I don't—!"

Ku'Adsila grabbed Lugh's collar and slammed him onto the countertop, her nose almost touching his, her eyes angry slits, her breath sour with cheap whiskey. "Spit it out before I add a third eye socket to your forehead, you lying shit sack!"

Of all the gunpoint arguments Lugh had been in, this was the worst. "My grandfather was an archeologist. He gave it to me before he died. Wanted me to keep it safe."

"Why?"

"I-I don't know! His notes were all smudged up."

Ku'Adsila bit her lip. "Why are you looking for me?"

"I heard rumors."

"Rumors are horse piss." Ku'Adsila pressed closer. "What's your name, city rat?"

Lugh blushed, looking away. If this came down to a gunfight, he had a derringer, but he'd never fired it. Would it even work? "My sister's sick. I've tried everything. My grandfather spoke about a . . . a place out here, with a power that might heal her. He said—"

"Your name, not your life story."

"L-Lugh Ahearn."

A wagon rumbled outside, followed by shouts. Ku'Adsila muttered a curse. "Do they ever learn?"

Bullets tore through the walls and sent the saloon door twirling from its hinges. Lugh jumped over the counter, knocking his head against the wall. Despite her drunkenness, Ku'Adsila joined him with fluid grace, revolver in one hand and a bottle of whiskey in the other, the latter of which she finished in one go before loading her revolver with blood-smeared bullets.

Soil, splinters, and tattered marigolds rained upon them, followed by a bar's worth of gin and whiskey and shattered glass. Lugh chanced a nervous smile. "I guess these ones are on the house?"

Ku'Adsila rolled her eyes and flashed her free hand. The Godstone glinted between her fingers.

"Give that back!" Lugh said.

Ku'Adsila fired a shot over the countertop. A high-pitched zipping sound tore through the air, joined by that metallic, citrusy odor. The gunfire paused, and shouts and curses erupted from the front door. Ku'Adsila grabbed Lugh's collar and propelled him into the back door, opening it with his face.

"Don't get ahead of yourself." Ku'Adsila jabbed her revolver into his back as they spilled into the alleyway. "I want answers. Do as I say, or I'll shoot you in the ass and leave you to explain to those pricks why thirty of their pals are dead."

Convincing argument.

Chapter Five

The scratchy rope left Lugh's wrists bloody and raw, and his patience rawer. Sabia was dying, and here he was, trussed up in a smelly barn. He chanced a glare at Ku'Adsila, who leaned against the wall and peered through a crack, absently tugging at her grey, amethyst-beaded braids. Her emerald eyes gleamed in the dusk. Was she nervous? Angry? Her stony face yielded nothing. Even though he'd spent his youth reading the faces of people he sought to trick, he couldn't scratch hers.

Not that it mattered. Only escape did.

Lugh shifted on the earthen floor. With his hands bound in front of him, Lugh had almost worked his way free, exploiting his bleeding wrists to slicken the rope. It stung worse than a policeman's truncheon, but at least this pain was useful. Compared to the cast-iron manacles he'd worn in prison, rope was a joke. She hadn't found his derringer either. If he got his hands free, he would just need a moment.

I have to, he told himself. *I need the stone or Sabia will—*

He banished the horrifying thought and kept working, hands almost free, the derringer's presence heavier and heavier with each painful twist of his wrists. Wind moaned through the tattered barn, mournful, like the hospital Mother had been in with its constant song of death and suffering. Mother . . . Lugh stopped, sick to his stomach, sicker to his heart.

He wasn't a killer. He might have been a lot of things Mother had disapproved of, but he wasn't that. Vyzeryn also wanted the outlaw alive for some reason. Still, he couldn't keep wasting precious time—he had to turn the tables somehow. Lugh stopped working his wrists and wrenched his glare into a look he practiced daily and couldn't be less deserving of: innocence.

"Ku'Adsila. Please, I'll talk. Just—"

Ku'Adsila sharply lifted a hand, cutting him off. Seconds later, a trio of horsemen pounded past. Ku'Adsila took out more bullets, smearing them with her blood before loading them into her revolver. Lugh watched, remembering the carnage in the saloon, the citrusy metallic smell.

"Blood sorcery," he whispered.

"*El-Suru* is its name." Ku'Adsila decocked her revolver, eyes narrowed. "My ancestors used it to guide their arrows. I use it to guide my bullets."

Lugh looked away, prickles reaching to his toes. This girl had slaughtered dozens in the blink of an eye, and he'd been stupid enough to think he could get the drop on her. His cheap life dangled by an even cheaper thread. "I told you the truth. My sister's dying. There's no cure."

"Shame," Ku'Adsila murmured.

Asshole. Lugh looked down at his bloody wrists. He needed to stay calm for this. With how his hands were twisted, he couldn't touch the rope with his palms, which prevented him from Doppeling the rope into something else. Even if he could, what use would it be here, against someone like Ku'Adsila? He'd always played it by ear with his sorcery, but always within strict limits thanks to his aversion. He couldn't afford to test those limits now. Not with Sabia depending on him. He wasn't some fancy elemental mage like Eirlys who could tap into his power with impunity.

Curated words would have to suffice.

Lugh studied Ku'Adsila again. She looked like most desperados did, with her duster and riding boots and heavy belt, though her hat was a little large. Besides the amethyst beads in her braids, there were others woven into her belt, and necklaces of small bones and colored beads dangled over her stained undershirt. She had a machete, too, its leather-wrapped grip adorned with the Uluru's twisting markings in black ink. A red cord, braided with more amethyst, was riveted to the handle as a lanyard. Only her hat lacked for Uluru motifs. A flower caught Lugh's eye. One of the marigolds, carefully tied to one of her necklaces. Lugh latched onto that.

"Those flowers," he said. "You put them there at the saloon?"

"Shut up."

Lugh bit back a few choice words. "My mother loved marigolds. I was just curious."

Ku'Adsila glanced through the cracks again, revolver ready. "I gave them a home. Short-lived, but better than what they had. Someone shipped those flowers out here, of all places. A mistake, maybe. They were going to throw them out, seeing as there's not enough water to keep them alive. Yet those marigolds were the most color this land has seen in generations. So I saved them." She reached to the marigold, gently touching its petals as she kept watch. "You outlanders and your priorities. As askew as an arrow without fletching."

Lugh couldn't disagree with that. He let the silence hang for a while, considering his options and digging through his memory of what he knew about the Uluru and of his grandfather's tales. The Godstone, that was the heart of it. The legends that had lured him out to the Frontier in the first place. He licked his dry lips and cleared his throat, speaking slowly.

"My grandfather told stories about your people, about your goddess Ehekahl."

"And I'm sure he was as wrong about her as the rest of your so-called scholars."

"He told me about the Godstone."

Ku'Adsila looked his way.

Lugh braved her fierce gaze. "He left the Godstone to me after he died. He told me that it should be returned. That it has the power to save the world. He *wanted* me to come out here." It sounded ridiculous; Lugh hardly believed it himself, yet the look on Ku'Adsila's face became deadly serious. She squatted in front of him, revolver casually pointed between his legs.

"Lugh, was it?"

Lugh nodded, chancing a smile.

"Stop smiling or I'll punch you."

"I'm not lying." *Just leaving out half the story.*

"Said many a liar." Ku'Adsila leaned closer, the beaded braids clacking together. "Your grandfather, was his name Amon?"

Lugh blinked. "How did you know?"

Instead of answering, Ku'Adsila holstered her revolver and drew a curved bone-handled knife. "You left or right-handed?"

"What? Right. Why—?" She grabbed Lugh's left hand and sliced his palm. He yelped and recoiled, slamming against a crate. His bonds slipped off and he put pressure on the wound with his other hand. "The hell was that for?!"

Ku'Adsila ignored him, focusing on the blood running down her knife. She dripped it onto her palm, smelled it, and then smeared it around. Lugh grimaced as he nursed his wound.

"That's . . . unsanitary."

"Shut up." Ku'Adsila closed her eyes, whispering gibberish in a lilting tongue. The blood on her palm vibrated, then shifted into an intricate pattern, like circling calligraphy. She studied it, notched eyebrows knitted together. "Says you're telling the truth."

Half of it. Lugh had mentioned nothing about Vyzeryn's plans. Good thing her sorcery couldn't tell the difference. "Does that mean you'll help me?"

"It means I'll let you live even though you were spending the last hour worming your way out of those bonds thinking I didn't notice."

Oh. Lugh smiled nervously. "That's generous of you."

"Damn right it is. I'm not as bad a person as you think."

"Well, you did shoot like . . . thirty people."

"Thirty people who had it coming. Could have been thirty-one, but it wasn't. You're welcome." Ku'Adsila poked Lugh between the eyes, then went for the door. "I don't owe your lanky ass the lankiest scrap of decency. Quite the contrary, you outlanders slaughtered my people and poisoned our land. People like *you* ruined everything. Go on. Run back to the city where you belong. It's more than you deserve."

Lugh shot to his feet. "But you took the stone!"

"Oh, and thanks for that." Ku'Adsila grinned at him, reaching into her pocket. "Now that I have both, I hardly need—" She gawked when she found an ordinary pebble instead.

It was Lugh's turn to grin. "Missing something?"

"You—!" Ku'Adsila drew her revolver. "Where the hell is it?!"

"Kill me and you'll never find—wait, not the knee!" Lugh jumped aside, but her aim followed him, as did her withering glare. "Okay, I'll tell you, just answer my questions first!"

Ku'Adsila bared her teeth. "Talk fast."

Dammit, this is stupid. Lugh licked his lips. So many questions, but only one truly mattered. "The stones, your goddess . . . can they really save people? Like my sister?"

"It's . . . not impossible."

Lugh felt a crisp rush of elation. "And my grandfather? How do you know him?"

"I don't know him. My grandfather spoke of an outlander by his name. Maybe it's just a coincidence."

"What did he say?"

Ku'Adsila cocked her revolver. "That's enough *asking*, dickwad."

"Fine," Lugh breathed out. "Someone told me that the desert's expanding. The Clysm. He said it has to do with your goddess and what my people did centuries ago."

"That's still a veiled question and you know it."

"Am I wrong?"

Ku'Adsila glowered, but she did not shoot. She lowered the gun a fraction instead. "When your people came, they desecrated Ehekahl's home, Kata-Uluru, the one place on this earth that directly connected us to the divine. We call this desecration the Ravaging. They burned her gardens. Sacked her shrines. My people, *her* people, were slaughtered. And most of all . . ." She reached into her trouser pocket and pulled out a small lockbox fastened to her belt by a chain. She opened it, revealing another semilunar stone. "They broke this and tried to spirit it back to their lands."

She really has it. Lugh swallowed his excitement, but it kept bubbling up. "What are they?"

"Do you even care?" When Lugh said nothing, Ku'Adsila sighed. "My ancestors believe it is a piece of Ehekahl—a tear fallen from the heavens. Ehekahl's Tear connected her to this world, to us. It's something mortals should never have toyed with, but your ancestors, superstitious about our ways, decided to break it. Thanks to that, Ehekahl withdrew from the world, the thread that connected us broken by your violence. Our land died and has remained dead ever since. The storm you call the Clysm is the manifestation of that undoing." Ku'Adsila closed the lockbox with a *clack*. "Now. Where's the other half? You have ten seconds."

Lugh rapidly considered his options. Lying topped the list, yet something about that made his mouth sour. She'd been unreadable at first, but the more she spoke, the more her composure rusted away. He knew the look of someone who had doubts, and Ku'Adsila had many. He could use that. A gamble, but then again, his whole life had been a series of gambles—and for Sabia, he'd wager anything. "Let me help you."

Ku'Adsila blinked. "What?"

Lugh set his jaw. "I said let me help."

"Why the hell would I need your help?"

"You're an Uluru outlaw. Everyone's painted a target on your back. Me? I'm a bland Auklenn kid no one here knows about. Think about it."

Ku'Adsila rolled her eyes. "I'm thinking about it. All that comes up is that your clumsy ass will slow me down."

"Sometimes you need to take things slower." Lugh thought of Vyzeryn, shivering. "There are people hunting you. Not the locals. Stronger ones from the coast. You've heard the rumors about Colonel Vyzeryn. She's bringing an army."

"You think I need your help so I can be subtle?" Ku'Adsila laughed, but her eyes remained mirthless and cold. "I shot my way through an army to get this first stone. I can shoot through another. I'm done with subtlety. And what's your problem anyway? Do you really think I'd trust you on a dime? Do you have the intelligence of a spoon?"

"A very shiny spoon?"

"Oh piss off."

Lugh sighed, his mind a shooting gallery of competing thoughts. Loyalty to Sabia based on love, loyalty to Vyzeryn based on fear, and a third unexpected yearning to throw everything in Vyzeryn's face by helping this gunslinging lunatic. It was giving him a migraine.

Sabia. That's all that matters. Just Sabia. And Vyzeryn has Sabia. Case closed.

A heaviness worked its way into Lugh's chest. There was no changing the inevitable, no chasing rebellious fancies. He'd been sent to deceive Ku'Adsila, and that's exactly the sort of thing he was setting himself up to do—the same old script since his days working in Father's crime syndicate. Yet this girl wasn't the insane outlaw he'd imagined. She was doing her best to help her people . . . and to solve the same problem Grandfather had worked himself to death for. Was there truth to his dying words after all? Did the world really depend on a fancy rock?

Lugh pushed the thoughts aside. Deception was nothing new to him. He'd left a trail of broken promises for years. He reached into his tweed jacket and slipped out the real stone, flinching when Ku'Adsila took a threatening step closer. "I know you've plenty of reasons not to like me or anyone from Auklenn for that matter. But I think what we both need is in this stone. If I give this to you, can you make it whole?"

Ku'Adsila stared at the Godstone, pupils dilating. "I can."

Despite his every desire not to, Lugh handed Ku'Adsila the stone. She trembled as she held it again, eyes glimmering with tears, but she quickly steeled herself and put both stones in her palm. They vibrated, blurring, an odd, tinny hum ringing in the air—and then they snapped together with a *click*, like two marbles in a childhood game. The fractured patterns of gold and sapphire melded into a unified whole. Lugh frowned.

"That's it? I was expecting something . . . flashy."

Ku'Adsila chuckled, and this time the mirth reached her eyes. "You understand jack shit." She smiled at the stone in her palm, teardrop-shaped and about twice the size of a poker chip. Its tricolored glow mirrored in her eyes. "By Ehekahl, it's been over two centuries . . ." Her voice trailed off as she stared at it, eyes dilating once more, sweat breaking across her brow.

What's gotten into her? Lugh stepped forward. "Are you all right?"

She kept staring, lips moving in silent words.

Was this his chance? Already?

Lugh held his breath and reached for the stone—and then felt the curse on his shoulder itch. Outside, dusk turned into blazing midday with a shriek of fire. He jumped at Ku'Adsila. "Get down!"

They tumbled in a heap not a second before a scythe of flame cut the barn from end to end. The upper half of the building flew off like a decapitated head. A billowing wall of heat sent them rolling in dust and smoke and ash, but Lugh still caught a glimpse of Kal, the scarred woman who worked for Eirlys, grinning as fire lanced from her right palm. Another Flameshot?! What was she doing here? How did she—?

A wooden beam slammed into Lugh's head. Everything plummeted into a drunken haze.

Lugh thrashed on the ground, gagging for breath, vision coming in chaotic blurs as the barn collapsed and burned around him. Horses charged past. A wagon clattered on uneven ground, frame groaning. Boots pounded on splintered wood.

"We got the stone!" shouted Kal. "Move out! Kos, stay here and make sure they're both dead!"

"Eirlys said not to kill the city rat."

"Accidents happen. He'll understand."

Lugh found himself crawling out of the ruins. Blood ran hot down his scalp, and he tasted more in his mouth. Eirlys, that bastard. If he wanted Ku'Adsila dead, he was working behind Vyzeryn's back. Of course he was. *Damnation!* Lugh pushed through a tangle of shattered wood and rolled into the street, coughing and wheezing—and found himself looking up as a cluster of shadows stalked through the haze. The foremost shouldered a lever-action rifle, cold eyes gleaming beneath the brim of his hat. Despite the heat, chills tore through Lugh's body.

They were going to kill him. Loose ends.

BANG!

A zipping sound sang through the air, and the gunmen dropped dead. A strong hand pulled Lugh to his knees and dragged him further into the sandy street. Ku'Adsila, coughing like a cigar parlor and seething like a boiler. She glared venom at the cloud of dust left by the departing wagon. Lugh pressed at the stinging cut on his scalp. His head spun like a carousel.

"W-What just happened?"

"They took it!" Ku'Adsila made for the leftover horses. "Those pale, mangy, piss-spawned gobshites!"

Lugh staggered after her—until she whirled and jammed the hot barrel of her revolver into his chin. Her eyes were wide and bloodshot, her face smeared with soot.

Eirlys's men must have followed me. It's my fault. Lugh held her gaze. "It wasn't me."

"First you. Now them. That's a twenty-four-karat coincidence if I ever saw one."

"They tried to kill me, too!" Lugh set his jaw. "Look, we can argue and all, but they're getting away. I did not come this far to let those pricks ruin my sister's chances!"

Ku'Adsila's face twitched, but she lowered the gun. She mounted the nearest horse with ease, clicking her tongue as the beast protested. Kal and her riders were already beyond the town limits, their silhouettes shrinking fast. Lugh's heart raced. He'd been so close! If those goons got away with the stone, both he and Sabia were doomed.

"I'm coming with you," Lugh said.

"Like hell you are."

Lugh was already hauling himself into a saddle, gritting his teeth against the flash of pain from his injured palm. He fumbled the reins and nearly fell back off. The horse huffed and shifted. Ku'Adsila snorted.

"You're so dead."

I am if I fail. Lugh gave her a determined glare. She rolled her eyes, lashed her reins, and disappeared in a cloud of dust. Cursing, Lugh wiggled his boots into the stirrups, then studied the reins. He'd never ridden before, but how hard could it be? He jabbed his horse in the flanks—and was thrown halfway off the saddle by its sudden gallop, the pounding jolts of the motion wringing his neck as he hung onto the straps. The village blurred past, replaced by dead fields, sand, and rocks, all painted bloody by the setting sun. Sand and crud caked his face and drilled up his nostrils, his shaggy, unkempt hair poking his eyes. A gunshot rang, and a dark smudge on the ground blurred past, followed by two more. Bodies.

Get up! This is an undignified way to die! He hauled himself back onto the saddle just as Ku'Adsila, only a few meters ahead, glanced back. Their gazes met. Ku'Adsila's jaw dropped.

Then more bullets started flying.

Chapter Six

The tarp-covered wagon rumbled farther ahead, flanked by ten horsemen, half of whom aimed back toward Ku'Adsila and Lugh with revolvers and lever-action rifles. Ku'Adsila veered in front of Lugh, half standing in her stirrups as she aimed her revolver. Her gun flared, and this time Lugh saw her sorcery at work—a zigzagging flash of crimson, like lightning webbing across the sky. It ricocheted between four of the riders and knocked them dead off their saddles.

Ku'Adsila pounded over the bodies and yelled back at Lugh. "What the hell are you doing?!"

Lugh gritted his teeth. The Godstone was in the wagon, it had to be. He touched the bulge of his derringer and instantly felt stupid—the lever action in the saddle holster didn't make him feel any better. Him versus a Flameshot? Suicide. And his knack was useless in a fight. Yet if they got away, his deal with Vyzeryn was over, and Sabia . . .

Lugh held fast onto the reins, squinting in the dust as he came alongside Ku'Adsila. "I'll get to the wagon! You cover me!"

"You think you can—?" Bullets whizzed past. Ku'Adsila ducked and fired again, killing two riders, but clearly, it was harder to use her power on horseback. She emptied her revolver with a shower of casings, jammed it into her saddle, and took a handful of bullets from her pocket.

"She's reloading!" one of the riders bellowed. "Take her down!"

Three riders broke off to intercept.

Dammit! Lugh held on as his horse passed Ku'Adsila, then yanked the lever action from the saddle holster. He nearly fell off just shouldering it, and the coldness of its trigger against his fingertip sent chills down his spine. He was no killer. He'd never even fired a gun before. But he aimed anyway, heart in his throat, lining up the closest horseman, whose pistol was suddenly close enough to see the dark oblivion down its barrel. His stomach lurched just as badly as his aim. Could he even—?

The horseman fired, the bullet cracking past. Lugh flinched and pulled the trigger by accident. *BANG!* The rifle kicked like a mule, twisting Lugh in his saddle. The gunman jerked to the side and grabbed at his wounded forearm, dropping his pistol in the process, and then he and the other two riders veered off, abandoning their attack.

Were they retreating? Why? Lugh racked the lever action, ejecting the spent casing, only for the next to jam halfway in. As Lugh cursed and shook the weapon to no avail, the tarp on the back of the wagon fluttered away, revealing two men manning a long-barreled monstrosity. Lugh blinked.

A machine gun. Oh . . .

Ku'Adsila's horse slammed into his horse from the right, pushing him aside just as the machine gun bullets flew. She lurched in her saddle as they hit, face twisted with pain, but she fired at the same time, the bullet dicing through the wagon. The crew flopped, and the machine gun, still firing, swiveled on its mount and raked across the other riders, sending them sprawling in a mess of limbs and dust. Lugh's hands slipped as his horse leapt through the chaos, and suddenly he was flying through the air head over heels. A hard surface welcomed his ass, and he found himself sprawled in the still-moving wagon, tangled with the gunners' corpses.

"Well, that was quite a show," said a gruff voice.

Kal stood over him, sneering as fire coiled along her forearms. Lugh shrank back from the stinging heat. The sulfuric stench of her magic drilled so far up his nose he sneezed.

"Bless you," Kal grunted.

"Th-Thanks," Lugh said. "Though I'd be even more blessed if you didn't burn me alive."

Kal pointed at him anyway. Lugh grabbed the hat off the nearest corpse and slapped his other hand against the machine gun. He stopped just shy of channeling his knack. Gods, he couldn't Doppel something so large. It would kill him! Grinding his teeth, Lugh shifted his hand to the knife on the nearest corpse's belt and channeled his knack with a click in his brain. Tingling sorcery rushed to his fingertips.

Kal snorted and shook her head, brown hair fluttering

over her disapproving snarl. "Oh? Think your party tricks can save your pathetic little—?"

Lugh threw the hat at Kal, but in the very instant he tried to Doppel the knife, the wagon bumped violently, throwing his palm back onto the machine gun.

Oh damn.

Aversion clobbered him instantly, booming in his forehead, squirming in his chest, darkening his vision— but not enough to blind him to the results. With a white flash, the hat morphed into a heavy machine gun. It slammed into Kal and crashed against the wagon floor, splintering the boards. The wagon pitched on its side, wheels twirling off with a resounding crack. Lugh flew and rolled, losing count of each painful slam, and found himself on his back, choking on sand.

What . . . what just happened? How did I . . . ?

He couldn't believe that had worked.

He couldn't believe he was still alive.

Lugh coughed, the palpitations in his chest squirming like a nest of serpents. Yet he didn't black out. Didn't lose himself. The last time he'd gone this far had left him unconscious for hours, and that was for a sawed-off shotgun, not a bloody machine gun. It shouldn't have been possible. A fluke? Blind luck? The Doppeled gun lay nearby in the sand, at the edge of a slope, and when it reverted to a hat, Lugh's dysrhythmia eased.

Was it possible for a knack to change?

The wagon's overturned wreckage lurked a dozen yards away, one of the wheels groaning as it still turned. Sand whispered over Lugh like a thousand little laughs. His forehead felt like it had been pierced with a rail spike, and his meager lunch threatened to charge up his throat. But he was alive. He coughed some more, spitting out sand, then rolled over and wiped his mouth—right in time to inhale another wave of sulfuric air.

Fire burst from the wagon's wreckage, scattering wooden fragments across the sand. Kal climbed out, hair matted with blood, right ear missing. She spat out a few teeth and limped through the windswept haze, torn duster fluttering, eyes ablaze with sorcery. "You little shit. To think Eirlys wants to keep you alive. I don't see it."

Damnation! Lugh groped at his pockets.

"Give it up," Kal growled. "Your aversion might not have killed you yet, but I'd wager my teeth one more trick will finish you off."

Lugh drew his derringer and aimed. Kal's lips curled. "Really? With a pea shooter?"

"A pea-sized hole is still a hole." Lugh's arm trembled. "Hand over the stone."

Kal barked a laugh, spit flying in the howling wind. "You have balls, I'll give you that. But it belongs to Eirlys now." She showed the stone, pinched between her middle and index fingers. "Crazy, isn't it? All this trouble for a tiny rock. You'd think a goddess would make something so important a little less easy to pocket. No wonder the Uluru are dying. Their goddess is a bloody idiot."

Where's Ku'Adsila? She was hit. Is she . . . ? Lugh's mind raced faster than his heart. He needed time. "You have balls, too. You're going behind the colonel's back."

"That's what people do," Kal said. "That woman is a tool. With the stone, doesn't matter how many armies Auklenn throws at us, we'll be *gods.* As for you . . ." She snapped her fingers, fire pooling in her free hand as she faked a pout. "You resisted, and I had no choice but to kill you. Terrible waste, but life's a wasteful business."

Lugh pulled the trigger.

Click!

Kal sighed. "Damn, you're pitiful . . ."

A horse burst through the haze behind Kal, Ku'Adsila leaning down in the saddle and swinging her machete. Kal whirled, but the blade caught her in the shoulder before she could direct her flames, sending her sprawling. Ku'Adsila leapt off, sidestepped a desperate lance of flame, and finished Kal with two savage hacks to the neck.

She pried the stone from Kal's fingers and faced Lugh, machete dripping with blood. "That was stupid." She clapped Lugh on the shoulder. Her grim expression softened. "Stupid, but it worked."

Lugh almost collapsed from relief. "I thought you were . . . well . . ."

"Dead? Takes more than that." Ku'Adsila touched her bloodstained side. "A graze, nothing more."

Lugh smiled, but part of him wanted to grimace. Ku'Adsila had saved his life, but that didn't change how things had to be . . . and that gnawed at him. Why should he care now? Why did it matter? He'd lied to so many, cheated so many, all for greed, and he'd never felt a thing. Yet now that he was doing it for Sabia, it made him sick and angry with himself. Hell of a time to develop a conscience for people other than his family. Or were those just splinters of Mother's goodness, somehow passed down to him? Either way, it wasn't him.

He studied Ku'Adsila, who was staring at the stone

in a trance again, her eyes glazed and dilating. There were weapons on the ground. He could take her hostage right now thanks to whatever the stone was doing to her. But what would Sabia think of that? Ku'Adsila had saved his life . . .

A high-pitched sound erupted from Kal's body, joined by a rush of sulfuric reek as dozens of familiar glyphs lit up on her corpse.

Lugh grabbed Ku'Adsila's arm and pulled them both down the slope. A fiery blast engulfed everything behind them. The gust of hot wind pushed them faster. When Lugh's world stopped spinning, he found himself on his back, Ku'Adsila on top of him, her lips almost touching his, her eyes still glazed.

Shit. Oh, shit. Lugh swallowed hard. "That was . . . too close."

Ku'Adsila blinked, then jumped back, her ashen face going red. "*That* was too close. What . . ." She wiped her mouth, eyes darting. "What happened?"

"Her corpse blew up. Magical dead man's switch. Flameshots can do that."

"Oh . . ." Ku'Adsila lowered her hand.

Lugh felt his own blush and a sudden urge to laugh. Instead, he took a deep breath and looked into the gloom, the sun almost gone in the hazy wasteland. "So, we're even?"

"You're keeping score?"

"I . . ." Lugh winced as the wind bombarded his face with sand. "Maybe we should get out of here." He tried to get up, and gasped when pain lanced up his thigh. A large splinter was embedded just above his right knee.

Why hadn't he felt it? Adrenaline? He sank down—and Ku'Adsila caught him.

"I got you, useful idiot. Use your other leg."

Together they climbed up the slope. Her face close to his. Her gaze as intense as ever. Again he stared. Again he felt doubt's gnawing. Again he pushed it aside.

"Thank you," he said at last. "You're the patron saint of human crutches."

"Just because I kill people doesn't mean I'm an asshole. You saved me in the barn. Again just now. I don't know about your kind, but the Uluru respect their debts." Ku'Adsila paused, huffing, her weariness showing at last. "And besides, it'd be a waste to let you die. You want to save your sister. I want to save my people. With the Godstone, maybe we can do both, right?"

Ice spread through Lugh's chest. "You . . . trust me?"

"I trust you about as well as you fire a gun."

Ruthless. "Then why are you doing this?"

"Like I said, debts." Ku'Adsila paused. They were halfway up the slope, sand rustling around them. Her face scrunched up. "My father always said there's a great big valley between trust and distrust. You're in there somewhere."

"So we're associates? Lugh and Ku'Adsila, limited liability partnership?"

Ku'Adsila snorted a laugh. "Don't flatter yourself." She took another step, then winced. "Dammit, for a stick you're heavy. Give me a minute."

They sat side by side on the sand, the Clysm a churning shadow in the distance. Lugh's pain deepened like a rising tide. The remnants of aversion's backlash pounded like a sinus infection from hell, in unison with the throb of his perforated leg. Still better than dead. A single star winked in the sky, the rest lost behind the haze. The wind rose and fell in somber moans. Cold, yet beside Ku'Adsila, warm enough. She was smearing more bullets with her blood.

"Do you ever not do that?" Lugh asked.

"It's how I stay alive. The fresher the blood, the stronger the magic. Without El-Suru . . . I wouldn't have made it this far." Ku'Adsila reloaded her revolver and tipped her battered hat down to block some of the wind. "And thanks, for saving me back there."

Lugh nodded slowly. "You seemed out of it."

"It was speaking to me."

"Really?"

Ku'Adsila gave him a sharp look. "Yes. I'm not insane. I don't understand it, but my people's sorcerers have always been intermediators for Ehekahl. I think . . . I think she's calling to me. From out there." She gazed towards the Clysm. "Your sister. What's she like?"

A question far from left field and a bloody obvious sign that Ku'Adsila didn't want to elaborate. Nonetheless, the question hit Lugh right in the gut.

"Sabia . . ." Lugh smiled despite himself. His headache suddenly felt miles away. "She's like the sun. Warm. Bright. Everywhere she goes she brings life, even though she's sick. She's innocent . . . pretty, like my mother was. If it weren't for the rusted lung, she'd be running around beating the boys at their own games and getting into all sorts of trouble." He laughed, eyes burning. "Still does, actually. Last place we were, she gave away half our food to stray cats."

Ku'Adsila made an amused sound at the back of her throat.

Lugh glanced at her. She still had the marigold tied to her necklace. "She keeps flowers, too. Tells me it's fun to help things grow up and be pretty. That's the kind of person she is, leaving things better than they were."

Would that he could say the same for himself.

"She sounds like a good person," Ku'Adsila whispered. "The kind worth fighting for."

"She is." Lugh winced at the pain in his leg. Worth more. Worth that wound. Worth lying for, too . . . and yet he doubted she'd agree.

"While we're speaking truths . . ." Ku'Adsila's rotated her revolver's chambers, the clicks rhythmic and precise. "This belonged to my father. He was an outsider from the east, like you." She touched the side of her face. "These are his, too."

"The freckles?"

"No pureblooded Uluru has them." Ku'Adsila smirked and dropped her hand. "Earned me a lot of jibes as a kid. Not that I gave a shit. My father was a good man, and that matters more than looks."

Lugh bit the inside of his mouth. His old man had only been charming in appearance, enough to lure Mother in, while inside he'd been a monster. "Sounds like someone worth fighting for, too."

"He was." Ku'Adsila's face tightened. She thumbed her revolver's grip. "My grandfather didn't like him much, especially after my mother died. Said he was poisoning our ways. But I never agreed. He was a lawman, but unlike most of the ones out here, he actually tried to make things better wherever he went. But not just that." She motioned at the wasteland. "Our home. He wanted to save it."

Lugh's stomach knotted. He knew trust, how it looked when people started giving it. Ku'Adsila could deny it all she wanted, but he'd gained a foothold, and she was more empathetic than she probably cared to admit. Normally he'd feel a rush of pleasure at knowing his target was opening up to him. Instead, he felt like he'd eaten something rotten. "Why are you telling me this?"

"Do I need a reason?" Ku'Adsila lowered her revolver, rubbing pensively at its trigger guard. "He left when I was ten to search for Kata-Uluru, the heart of Ehekahl's power. We lost it centuries ago, after your people destroyed our civilization. Most don't think it exists anymore, but he believed. He said it was the key to healing our land. The key to *everything*." A sad smile tugged at her lips as she touched the rim of her hat. "He gave me his hat before he left, told me to choose my way. To live free. Not bound by anything." Her hand fell to her lap. "I never saw him again."

Lugh looked at her bruised hand, then her somber face. "You think he's out there?"

"It's been nine years. I know he's gone. The wastes are unkind."

"I'm . . . sorry."

Ku'Adsila nodded. "I need to finish what he started. Whatever it takes."

Lugh frowned. "How does the stone factor into that?"

"No one knows for certain, but if I can find Kata-Uluru and get Ehekahl's Tear there . . . that's the best shot I can think of. Following in my father's footsteps. Your grandfather said you should return the stone. That must be what he meant. Return it to its origin and nothing less."

What would Grandfather have given to be here in my place? Lugh envisioned the hawkish old man. Thoughtful, intense, vanishing on his expeditions for years at a time. He'd only visited on occasion, but he'd always brought gifts for Mother and Sabia, and had taken Lugh on hikes and fishing when he was little. What would he think, knowing his grandson was in a position to influence the mysteries that he'd devoted his life to? How would he feel knowing Lugh was going to sell them out to the likes of Vyzeryn? Finding the Godstone had cost Grandfather everything, even his life . . . but he was gone, and it didn't matter anymore.

The ache in Lugh's stomach worked its way into his chest. He exhaled slowly. Mother was right. He was too much like his old man, dancing along the line between right and wrong, crossing it whenever it suited him. Would it be worth it? Lugh banished that train of thought and touched Ku'Adsila's elbow.

She pulled away. "Don't think I don't know what you're doing."

"Trying to show some sympathy?"

"Or trying to *pretend*, earn points because I have something you need."

"I . . . I'm sorry."

"Don't. It's not like I blame you. We're both here for our own reasons. Good reasons. I get it." Ku'Adsila grimaced and averted her gaze. "But that doesn't make us friends."

Lugh silently cursed himself. He'd miscalculated, shattered the mood . . . yet it wasn't the professional screwup that bothered him the most. It was the casual manipulation. It came so naturally, it blurred the lines between honest and sly. Where did his truth end and the lies begin? Gods, Mother would hate what he'd become. He leaned forward and rested his forearms on his knees, hands clasped together against the growing chill.

"I know I'm not good at this," he said. "But we can help each other. Like you said."

Ku'Adsila sniffed. "It's been a long time since an outlander did anything but hurt us."

And I'm the next one in line, aren't I? Lugh set his jaw. Damn conscience indeed. Feelings were just that, feelings, vanishing the moment life got tough. What remained? The painful facts. Wounded and out of sorts, now was not the right moment, but he would steal the stone. He would betray Ku'Adsila.

And then I'll sneak away again, like I always do.

The best way to bring Ku'Adsila to Vyzeryn alive was to simply take the stone. She'd chase him into hell itself to get it back—that's the kind of person she was. Damnation. The calculations came so easily, lurking in that corrupted corner of his mind.

It never changes, he thought. *I'm always . . . the same.*

Drawing blades scraped behind them.

Lugh and Ku'Adsila almost bumped heads as they whirled around.

Five figures on lean, white-speckled horses towered at the summit of the hill, their sand-colored cloaks hiding their faces but not their glowing emerald eyes. One barked something in lilting Uluru, gesturing with a rusted flintlock. Lugh showed his hands, chancing a glance at Ku'Adsila, who looked sour enough to curdle all the milk in Auklenn.

"Shit," she muttered.

"Those are your people, aren't they?" Lugh asked.

"Unfortunately."

Lugh swallowed as he heard more behind them. "They're friendly, right?"

"About that." Ku'Adsila raised her hands, slowly, as armed men and women boxed them in. "My grandfather said if I showed my face here again, he'd kill me."

Chapter Seven

Lugh squinted as a horse-drawn carriage swerved out of his way and splashed him with mucky water. The coachman twisted around in his seat and spat chewing tobacco onto the residential street's rain-soaked cobbles.

"Oi! Watch where you're walking, idiot."

"I'm trying," Lugh muttered.

"Seems like trying ain't your strong suit."

"At least I don't sit on my ass all day, ferrying ungrateful knobs around."

The coachman snorted and carried on.

Lugh muttered a curse after the wagon and kept walking, using his jacket's sleeve to clear a smelly glob of muck from his cheek. Perhaps someone else would see the muddy water as an improvement, since it washed some of the blood from his bruised face. Not him. At least the blood was his own, rather than the untold number of contributors to whatever the hell was in this street sludge. His cuts stung, and the bruises throbbed to the drumbeat of his heart.

Wait, what am I doing here? Wasn't I . . . somewhere else?

He paused in the middle of the tenement-packed street and noted the faded signs. Beckett Avenue, Athlone Burrow. His old stomping grounds. Right. Of course. He was walking home after a botched job. The Mulberry Street Barbers hadn't taken kindly to him running a fraud ring on their turf, and it had taken all the money in his pockets to have them use their fists instead of straight razors. Such gentlemen.

Dazed, hurting all over, Lugh pressed on through Auklenn's cocktail of coal smoke, putrid alleys, and spitting evening rain. The sewers were overflowing from the rainfall, like usual. The fancy uptown never flooded, but down here in the projects it was a regular occurrence, folk paying about as much mind to it as they did the flakes of ash raining from the smokestacks that lined the horizon. People hurried along, wrapped tight in coats and shawls and caps, the odd top hat here and there. Everyone ignored Lugh. Athlone Burrow knew Lugh the Liar, and it wasn't the kind of fame to be envied. Not that he cared.

Winter was coming, and the dark fell early. With the gas lamps switching on, it had to be around five, and that meant the nearby schoolhouses would be emptying.

Sabia couldn't see him like this. He had to get home before she did, and . . . and . . .

What? Clean himself up? Look like he hadn't been tenderized by four men?

Lugh gritted his teeth and checked his pocket, where three of those men's purses provided reassurance. Enough funds to make up for his mistakes. Enough to feed Mother and Sabia, keep the gas running, and pay for her classes. Maybe enough to afford a doctor's visit. Sabia was coughing a lot lately, and the medicine he'd bought last month hadn't helped. He also needed to refill Mother's painkillers. The aversion sickness was eating her alive, the agony from her disintegrating nerves getting worse by the day. The doctors might have given up on her, but he sure as hell wouldn't.

The rain fell harder, fat droplets slapping Lugh's face. It didn't keep him from noting shadows in one of the alleyways—men in dark coats and bowler hats, harsh faces outlined by the wink of their cigarettes. Father's hired men, likely tasked with keeping an eye on Lugh. It wouldn't do for him to change sides or go to the police.

Not that I would. You've left me no option. Lugh spat on the pavement as he passed his watchers. Father ran the majority of Auklenn's criminal underground, with a monopoly on trafficking, opium, and a dozen other markets. A man obsessed with money and power and prone to alcoholic benders, but so cunning on the outside, so false. He'd courted Mother because she was a sorcerer, in hopes of having many talented children to staff his ranks. To Lugh's morbid satisfaction, Father had only gotten Sabia and him: one without magic, and the other with a knack limited by aversion.

But Mother had always been his prized investment.

Father's most lucrative legitimate front had been a healing clinic that offered free services. There, Mother had used her knack to help the downtrodden. She'd loved the work—and Father had loved how it secured charity funding from the state's coffers, which he promptly funneled into his pockets. Mother hadn't known it at the time, and even though she'd known about her aversion and the risk of triggering full-on sickness, she'd never withheld her services. Her own kindness wore her down until aversion sickness manifested, ruining her body, her magic, her life . . . but to Father she was just a tool, and when she fell ill, he cast her out along with Sabia. He'd only kept Lugh around because he was *useful.*

Lugh hated that man more than anyone else in the world.

Yet he also couldn't get out from under his shadow.

Every man has a price. Gods know I know mine.

Father's rackets earned Lugh money at the cost of what little pride he had left. Money kept Mother and Sabia fed. Money paid their rent. Money was everything. And crime was the only work Lugh knew. If he could do things over again, he wouldn't let Father lure him into the trade with his honeyed lies and false approval. But like so many things, that ship had set sail over the stormy horizon. Everything he was, even his magic, bore that devil's fingerprints. Maybe one day Father would face justice, but he would drag Lugh down with him. Besides, the current police chief had just hung himself, half the force was bribed, and the new chief they were bringing up from the southlands, some woman by the surname Vyzeryn, wouldn't fare any better.

Even though part of Lugh wanted things to change, he knew they wouldn't.

Auklenn was, above all else, addicted to status quo.

Home waited on a narrow street of townhouses, squashed together with little front yards and rusted fences. Lugh limped as quickly as he could, but when he reached the gate, his hand froze on the latch. Light flickered in

Mother's window. Despite her illness, she was awake, probably reading, not that she could do much else with her body eating away at its own nerves. He leaned on the gate, wet metal chilling his hands, and took in a few long breaths. The rain could fall all it wanted, he'd never feel clean.

"I didn't want things to be this way," he whispered. "I wanted to get out. I really did. But I'm stuck, and this . . . this is all I can do to help." Words he wished he could say to Mother's face. Words he swallowed every time he entered her room. Despite everything, she still smiled at him. Even while their little slice of the world wilted like the dead marigolds in the townhome's front garden.

A sharp pain twisted in Lugh's chest like a knife. He'd already made up a story for the illegitimate money in his pockets, but he knew Mother would see right through it. She always did. Yet for all the disappointment that showed on her face, she'd never once refused it, and still told him, every night when he helped her to bed, that she loved him.

Was there anyone as forgiving as a mother?

A gasp behind him jolted Lugh out of his stupor, and the knife twisted harder.

Oh no.

Sabia stood a few paces away. At six, she had Mother's eyes, and those eyes widened as they took him in. Standing beneath a streetlamp's warm glow, dressed in her school's pretty blue dress and cap with a matching umbrella, she looked like everything Lugh knew he wasn't. He stepped back, away from the light, groping for words, hoping she didn't notice the blood.

"Lugh?" Sabia asked, her voice soft with fright.

"It's fine. It's nothing. Just a little accident—" Lugh's foot slipped, and before he knew it he was on his back, blinking away a taunting array of stars. He sat up quickly and threw on a quivering smile. "Oh, look at me. Caught a case of the clumsy."

Sabia blinked, eyes still owl wide. "You're hurt."

Dammit. Lugh got to his knees. "Go on inside, I'll . . . go clean myself up—"

Sabia slammed into him, little arms squeezing around his back, head resting beneath his chin. She smelled of books and flowers and toffee.

"What are you doing?" Lugh stammered. "Your dress. You'll get it dirty!"

Sabia squeezed him tighter instead.

Lugh thought of prying himself free, then froze, feeling Sabia's intertwined hands between his shoulder blades. Gods, it felt like mere moments ago she'd been too small to wrap them all the way around. Growing up so fast, while he was growing worse. Now he was getting blood and muck all over her uniform. "Sabia, I . . ."

"It's okay," Sabia whispered. "Everything will be okay."

No it wasn't. No it wouldn't. Yet the words caught in Lugh's throat. She didn't know about his work. Perhaps that was his biggest lie of all: the kind of brother she thought he was. He wanted nothing more than to crawl under a rock . . . but Sabia still needed that brother.

He wrapped his arms around her and hoped he sounded less broken than he felt. "Really, I'm fine. Just an accident at work."

Sabia let go and scowled at him. "Promise?"

A lump formed in Lugh's throat. "How was school?"

Sabia's face lit up. "Oh! We read stories and did numbers and played hunt the thimble and I helped Miss Pollock with the chalkboard and she even let me recite to the whole class for the first time!"

Lugh laughed and ruffled Sabia's hair. His pain suddenly felt worlds away. "You're the star of the class. You must work very hard."

"M-hm!" Sabia grinned.

"You should go tell Mom all about it."

"Oh, wait. Crafts!" Sabia ruffled through her bag. "I made this."

Lugh stared at a simple bracelet of painted wooden beads. She'd chosen blue, green, and red. Her favorite colors. "For Mom . . . right?"

"No, silly. For you." Sabia smiled, sapphire eyes glittering by the streetlamp's soft light. Despite the dirty smudges he'd left on her face, it was the most beautiful thing he'd ever seen. He took the bracelet and carefully slipped it over his wrist.

"It's . . . beautiful."

"Miss Pollock said to give it to someone I love."

Oh Sabia. Lugh blinked rapidly, glad for the rain. "Thank you."

Sabia toyed at the ground with her boot's toe, eyes flicking up at him occasionally. "So you . . . like it?"

"It's the best gift I've been given," Lugh said. "I feel all better already. I love you."

Sabia giggled and tackled him with another hug, speaking muffled *I love you*s against his chest. When she pulled back, she took out a white handkerchief and wiped

Lugh's face, pouting with concentration. Lugh didn't have the heart to stop her. She looked paler than yesterday, and as much as she tried to hide it, she was suppressing coughs. Yes, he would definitely get her to a doctor. Even if it meant he had to skip a few meals. Even if he had to lift more purses and piss off more thugs.

But that was tomorrow's worry. Right now, only this mattered.

Lugh opened the gate. "Come on. Now we *both* need to get cleaned up."

Sabia skipped past him and up the steps, flashing smiles back at him.

What did I ever do to deserve a sister like her? Lugh paused at the gate, in the growing dark, as Sabia opened the front door. No, it wasn't about deserving. It never was.

He stepped forward . . .

. . . and slammed flat on his face.

Auklenn's squalor disintegrated, becoming the Frontier's dry heat and biting wind, but the pain remained, throbbing in every joint and most certainly his face. Lugh coughed, blinking away sand and tears, head spinning as he tried to push himself up. His arms quivered at the effort, and the best he could do was get onto his elbows. Gods, where was he? Why did his skin feel like he'd been wearing sandpaper? And why were his wrists bound? He looked up, following the trail of the rope. Ten Uluru horsemen scowled back at him.

Oh. Right. His waking nightmare.

Three days of hell squashed back into his head. After his capture, the Uluru had forced him to walk behind their horses. His feet had more blisters than toes, and his throat burned with dryness, his saliva turned to smelly glue. He coughed again, but the sand kept getting in. His knees ached, and his thigh—albeit with the splinter removed and the injury bandaged—still burned like the devil's poker. He shouldn't be here. It wasn't supposed to be like this!

He swallowed an urge to scream.

"Oi, outlander," the largest Uluru growled, looming on horseback.

"Sorry," Lugh rasped, still leaning on his elbows. "Just . . . taking a break."

The man snorted. He was a grizzled, middle-aged warrior with tree trunk arms and more tattoos than skin, with a gruff, bearded face about as friendly as a firing squad, though Lugh didn't miss the laughter wrinkles by his eyes. Tahk, his captor, and the man whose horse he was tethered to. A real chap.

"You already had your break," Tahk said. "You were asleep on your feet again."

"And I was having the best dream."

Tahk pulled hard on the rope. "Get up, outlander."

Lugh's head spun, and his stomach twisted with cramps. "I . . . I can't."

"Get up or we leave you to the buzzards."

I can't! Lugh gritted his teeth, focus drifting to his wrist. He'd lost Sabia's bracelet during his time in prison. He still hadn't been able to apologize. What if he never got the chance? The thought scalded him worse than his sunburns. He struggled to his knees, only to fall again, this time to a chorus of impatient mutters from his captors.

Tahk shook his head. "Buzzards it is. Sorry, lad."

"Tahk, are you daft?"

Lugh's heart leapt at the sound of Ku'Adsila's voice. For the last few days, she'd been all silence and scowls.

Tahk looked past Lugh. "You speak as if you're not in our custody, Ku'Adsila."

"I speak as if I have common sense." Ku'Adsila trotted into view, at the reins of her own horse. "He's dehydrated. You've been walking him for days on almost nothing!"

The other Uluru shrank back. Prisoner or not, Ku'Adsila had sway with these people. Even disarmed and surrounded, she rode up to Tahk, eye to eye, as if she had all the guns and lead in the world. Tahk's brow furrowed. At last, he shrugged. "Typical outlander. Can't hold his water."

"He's no use to you dead."

"Not much use alive, either. He's an enemy. Why do you favor him?"

Ku'Adsila's face twitched. She glanced at the others, huffed, then slid off her saddle. "I don't. But we live by a code, don't we? He saved my life. That's a debt owed."

Tahk sighed and made no further argument.

Ku'Adsila pulled Lugh to his feet and passed him her flask. The warm water burned down his parched throat, but it may as well have been chilled nectar. Lugh closed his eyes and savored each gulp—until Ku'Adsila elbowed him.

"Not all of it, knobhead."

Lugh nodded and handed it back. "Thank you."

"Don't thank me. I'm not doing this for you."

"For your code. Right. No such thing as a personal kindness—"

Ku'Adsila dropped Lugh back into the sand.

He groaned. "All right, I take that back. I'm sorry."

Ku'Adsila snorted and helped him up again, then into the saddle of her lithe, speckled horse. She sat in front of him and took a swig from a metal flask she kept under her duster, then hunched over the reins. "Hands to yourself."

Lugh gripped the saddle. Ever since their capture, Ku'Adsila's mood had been lethal. This was the most she'd spoken in days. It was also the first time Lugh didn't have to focus on dragging his feet one in front of the other. As his mind caught up and put the last few days together, the relief quickly turned into a disconcerting knot. He'd missed out on two chances to take the Godstone. Would he even get another? They'd tied his bonds properly, but with his palms facing inwards. He could have Doppeled something when he'd fallen against the stony ground, but then what? He was outnumbered and outgunned. Even if his power was changing, even if the aversion was somehow less than before, he couldn't see a way out.

The procession continued through the windswept barrens, a faint suggestion of the midday sun glowing through the sky's anemic haze. Dead trees and tumbleweeds were their only company, besides squat, vertical formations of rust-red stone. Ku'Adsila's belt and weapons were missing, and with ten Uluru riders boxing them in, they may as well have been behind bars. There was no escape in the open. The Clysm loomed in the distance, closer than before, delayed rumbles trailing its lightning. The landscape carried nothing but bad omens.

Lugh studied his captors. Most wore a ramshackle assortment of clothes, from rough coats and dusters to stolen Auklenn uniforms, and headwraps to protect from the grimy wind. Aside from their gray skin and hair, their amethyst charms unified them. Bracelets, necklaces, piercings, or woven into their saddles and leather holsters, each stone etched with Uluru glyphs. Their swirling tattoos bore similar motifs, as did the carvings in the stocks of their rifles. Most people in Auklenn knew nothing about the Uluru besides their savagery. Yet like anyone else, they had a culture, artforms, a way of life. Grandfather had been enthralled by it. A good man who'd wanted to understand every mystery in the world. What would Grandfather have done in Lugh's shoes?

He wouldn't ever be in my shoes. He wasn't that kind of person.

"Where are they taking us?" Lugh whispered at last.

Ku'Adsila gave a noncommittal grunt.

Lugh frowned and noted the riders again. While walking, he hadn't had the luxury, but now he saw it: the nervous glances, hunched postures, the bandages worn by more than half, and the three empty horses tethered to other riders. Lugh lowered his voice.

"There was a battle, wasn't there?"

"A skirmish," Ku'Adsila murmured. "Lost four to an outlander patrol. So don't push them."

A chill crept over Lugh. No wonder Tahk and the others were so hostile. They'd lost friends to people like him . . . and Colonel Vyzeryn hadn't even joined the fray. What sort of hell was following him into this place? What role did Vyzeryn intend for him to play besides bringing Ku'Adsila and the Godstone to her? How long did Sabia have? The last thought hollowed Lugh out, and he resisted the urge to rest against Ku'Adsila's back. "Tahk took the Godstone, didn't he?"

Ku'Adsila tensed, then nodded. Her amethyst braids clattered.

"I'm sorry."

"Don't be," she muttered, coiling the reins around her wrists. "Wasn't you."

Lugh stomach knotted up. Good luck getting it back now without Tahk turning his face into a very deep bowl. Sabia didn't have time for this . . . and yet an odd relief eased the tension at the same time. Why? Because he hadn't had to steal the Godstone from Ku'Adsila? Because he hadn't had to lure her into Vyzeryn's iron grip? He looked at the back of her head, recalling the gruff kindness she'd shown despite whatever inner turmoil she was going through. To steal from her, to slink away . . . the idea seemed even worse than before, and it ratcheted up Lugh's nerves yet again. Now more than ever, he couldn't afford to be divided, yet the feeling persisted no matter how far he pushed it down.

Damnation. His magic. His doubts. Mysteries both, like the legends that had brought him out here in the first place.

Nightfall brought a chill as bad as the heat. They sheltered between two rock formations, beneath a jutting overhang. The Uluru dug campfires in the ground. Two deep holes connected by a tunnel—the empty hole for upwind, the other set to flame with scraps of deadwood and grass. Ku'Adsila made another fire for Lugh.

"So no one sees the flames," she said. "Been making these since I was little."

Lugh hovered his hands near the hole, wincing from the heat. With wind breathing through the connected hole, the fire burned hellish hot, and the warmth radiated beneath the overhang. "Thank you."

"No need."

"Debts. Right."

Ku'Adsila frowned, tugging at one of her braids.

What little food they gave Lugh tasted bland, but it offset his clawing hunger, and it was a blessed break from his bonds. The wound in his thigh throbbed worse than ever, but at least he could rest it. Ku'Adsila tended to her horse, then sat next to him, expression hard as she stared into the pit. Her eyes glittered. The Uluru set watch and otherwise ignored them.

"You talked to her," Ku'Adsila said at last.

"Who?"

"Your sister. While you were dozing on your feet."

"Oh . . ." Lugh swallowed hard. "I dreamed about her. Well, more like a memory."

Ku'Adsila sighed. "Was it a good one?"

Lugh nodded, massaging his wrists.

"We should be there tomorrow," Ku'Adsila said. "Tahk's a careful man. He's been taking the long way, to throw off pursuit."

"And what happens then?"

Ku'Adsila worked her jaw and fiddled with her empty holster, as if yearning for a revolver's cold reassurance. She looked afraid. Terribly afraid.

"Why don't you run?" Lugh asked.

"Running won't fix this. Not anymore."

"You think they'll help?"

"I think you should stop *suggesting* things." Ku'Adsila ceased fiddling and folded her hands on her lap. Pale scars crisscrossed both hands. "My people are quick to forgive but also quick to judge. If I run away, it'll make me no different than what they claim I was. A coward. A traitor to my kin. The first time was different. Now . . ." She glanced towards Tahk, who was studying the Godstone by firelight. "I have to face this. It's been a long time coming. And you're getting dragged into it."

Lugh glanced at Tahk. He had no shortage of pebbles at hand. Perhaps he could stumble closer to him on a pretext of having to take a piss and being night blinded by the fires. He could swap the Godstone for a pebble and make a break for it. Doable, but even if it worked, he was in the middle of nowhere with a bum leg. Success only meant wandering off to die in the desert somewhere. And with Ku'Adsila so close, face bright by the flames, he realized he didn't want to try it. Not yet.

But I'll have to, won't I? I can't keep putting this off forever.

He picked up a pebble and a piece of kindling. He hadn't used his sorcery in days, and it came sluggishly, the click in the back of his mind duller. Hunger and sleep deprivation would do that. He Doppeled the wood into a pebble. Ku'Adsila eyed it warily.

"So that's how you duped me back in Capstone."

Lugh flinched. Damnation, now she knew. No putting that cat back in the bag. He was too tired for his own good. He sighed and nodded. Ku'Adsila clicked her tongue.

"Huh. Never thought you'd be a sorcerer."

"Not much of one." Lugh compared the pebbles. "I'd take detecting truths and guiding bullets over making fleeting facsimiles. Besides . . . all it does is remind me of my old man."

Ku'Adsila frowned. "Why?"

"I wasn't lying back in the bar when we met. He's like rotten mold. I can never get his stink off of me." Lugh clenched his teeth, knowing he should hold his tongue, but part of him yearned to put into words what he'd always felt. "My power is as much a joke as that man calling himself a father."

"All gifts are given for a reason."

"A gift?" Thinking back on his life, and how he'd chosen to use his power, Lugh couldn't help but smirk. "I'm not so sure about that."

"Well, I am." Ku'Adsila took a stone from Lugh's hand and rolled it between her fingers. "My mother taught me that Ehekahl works in unfathomable ways. That everything has a purpose, and every happening, even misfortune, carries a promise."

"You really believe that?"

"I didn't for the longest time." Ku'Adsila tossed the pebble into the fire. "I want to."

Looking at her now, Lugh sensed vulnerability, the conman inside him sitting up and taking notice. He hated that part of himself—the one always looking for an edge or opening, the part he'd needed to survive in Auklenn's unforgiving streets, the part Father had encouraged. Yet what was he out here for, but for another con job? He wasn't here to help the Uluru. He wasn't here to help Ku'Adsila, no matter what small, remaining, decent part of him yearned to. Colonel Vyzeryn held Sabia's life by a thread. Eirlys could end Lugh's with a snap of his fingers. The cards in his hands were few, the game rigged. Lugh hefted his little pebble, then tossed it into the pit, reversing the Doppeling so the stick would burn.

"Everything I'm doing is for my sister," he said. "If there's a reason I have this power, a reason why I'm *here*, it's her."

"Then it's not a joke."

"No . . ." Lugh trailed off, the idea sending tingles down his spine. "For her, it isn't."

Ku'Adsila nodded. "She's worth very much to you?"

"She's worth it all. Even this." Lugh rolled his bloody wrists. He wished there was another way to play this game. "I realize I'm out of my depth here. I know I don't believe in the same things you do. But we can still find a way out of this. If my grandfather knew your grandfather—"

"Don't."

"What?"

Ku'Adsila grimaced. "That's a thin rope to cling to."

"It's something." Lugh slowly, carefully, touched Ku'Adsila's elbow. This time she didn't pull away. "You saved my life several times. I may be an outlander windbag who doesn't understand shit about what's going on out here, but I do know a thing or two about debts."

Ku'Adsila's expression changed, her emerald eyes lambent in the dark, her lips slightly parted. She blinked, as if shaking a thought. "We're in this together, I suppose, whether we like it or not. Histories be damned." She nudged him with her elbow. "What a weird duo. A city-rat magician and a down-and-out gunslinger."

"Could be worse."

"Could be better." Ku'Adsila stood and brushed her trousers off. "For what it's worth, Lugh, whatever your father did, don't start thinking you're cut from the same cloth. No one is cut from the same cloth as anyone else. Good night."

Lugh opened his mouth to retort and caught a rolled blanket to the face. Ku'Adsila smirked at him and trudged into the dark, the amethysts in her hair winking in the dwindling firelight. He stared after her until only darkness remained. Sabia would get a kick out of someone like her . . . but he doubted they'd ever meet.

In another life, Lugh thought as he lay on cold stone. *In a better life.*

Chapter Eight

An Auklenn patrol found them at sunrise.

Lugh woke to shouts and gunfire and howling bullets. He scrambled to his feet, only for Ku'Adsila to tackle him from behind.

"Idiot! Do you have a death wish?!"

A bullet screamed over their heads and cracked against the overhang, showering them with stone fragments. Lugh squinted through the chaos, heart pounding. Dust whirled across the campsite, turning dawn to gloomy shadows, veiling darting silhouettes. Gunshots flashed. Hoofbeats thumped. Horses nickered. Saddles rattled. The Uluru warriors, hunkered behind rocks, returned fire, their blood sorcery tingeing the air with the same metallic, citrusy odor, though weaker than Ku'Adsila's.

"What do we do?" Lugh asked, flinching at every gunshot.

Ku'Adsila's face was a twisted mask of rage, her dominant hand white-knuckling a sharp rock. "We wait. Stay small."

The gunfire soon dissipated, as did the dust storm. Several bodies lay on the barren ground beyond the overhang, along with riderless horses bearing Auklenn saddlebags. Three more riders sped off, retreating in the far distance. Tahk fired three shots with his repeater rifle, then muttered a string of Uluru curses when none hit. He waved to the others, who had sustained only minor injuries.

"To horse! We can't let those outlanders bring their friends out here!"

The Uluru raced into action, but their spooked horses were difficult to mount.

Ku'Adsila sighed and stood up. "Stay down, Lugh."

"What are you doing?"

Ku'Adsila ignored him and approached one of the Uluru warriors, a woman with short-cropped hair and amethysts braided along her scalp. "Gun. Now."

The warrior blinked at Ku'Adsila, then glanced at Tahk. The man nodded.

Ku'Adsila took the antiquated musket that had probably seen a century of use. She used the blood from where a bullet fragment had cut her forearm to smear a musket ball, then plopped the ball down the barrel along with two powder charges and wadding. She muttered under her breath and worked the ramrod as if she were stabbing someone she hated. The Uluru riders stood by, tense, while Tahk scowled at the distant riders.

"That's at least a thousand yards—" Tahk started.

Ku'Adsila shouldered and fired without hesitation. Powder flashed, and the flintlock let out a deep *clap* and a cloud of pale smoke. The metallic-citrus odor that followed outstripped the others of the Uluru by far. Crimson sorcery zipped with the bullet trail, but the gun smoke marred the view. Ku'Adsila huffed and shoved the weapon back into the woman's hands. "Let's get going. I don't have all day."

Tahk and the others kept staring as the smoke dissipated.

Sure enough, three riderless horses ran in the distance, bodies in the sands behind.

The Uluru muttered oaths and touched their amethyst charms. Needless to say, they gave Ku'Adsila plenty of extra space after that.

Lugh stole a glance at the closer bodies as they rode out from the campsite. His stomach turned, so he focused on Ku'Adsila's dusty back. Yet again, she'd done him the kindness of sharing her horse. Tahk took them deeper into the rock formations, through small canyons and valleys, then out over windswept barrens, ever closer to the towering Clysm. Judging by the hunch of her shoulders, Ku'Adsila's tension ratcheted up with every mile.

Lugh couldn't help but feel the paradox of the situation. Here she was, many times stronger than all of her captors combined, yet both she and they went through the motions, keeping up the appearance of her being under their power. It reminded Lugh of prison, where the high-profile prisoners virtually owned their captors with bribe money and threats, yet cordially went to their cells and wore their manacles as mere formalities. Unlike them, however, Ku'Adsila wasn't behind bars. Her chickens had come home to roost, and she was facing them head-on—something he'd avoided doing his whole life.

Just who was Ku'Adsila anyway? Who was her grandfather? He dared not ask, but given how the other Uluru treated her, she was important. The light had begun to fade when they reached another string of crumbling rock formations. They passed over glimpses of an old railroad, its rusted metal and cracked crossties poking through the sand like bones. An overturned steam engine, rusted to hell, lay against a sand drift, its side bearing the flaking yellow name, *Frontier Diamond Co. Ltd.*

"Lesson to you, outlander," Tahk called back. "No matter how many times you people try to tame this land, you will fail."

Lugh craned his neck, staring at the train, until Ku'Adsila pulled their horse to an abrupt halt.

A series of shallow holes had been cut into the rock face's rust-red stone. Each had metal bars bolted across, like prison cells. Tahk motioned to Lugh.

"This is where you get off, lad."

Lugh blinked. "What? Here? Where are we?"

"What does it look like?" Tahk clicked his tongue, and two warriors dragged Lugh off Ku'Adsila's horse and pushed him towards the rocks.

"H-Hey!" Lugh stammered. "What are you doing?"

"What it looks like, outlander." Tahk spat on the sand. "Putting you somewhere you can't cause any trouble. A fitting spot don't you think?"

Lugh's blood ran cold as he eyed the shallow cave. It wasn't fair. To be left here to rot? He'd lose his chance at everything! He dragged his feet and tried to break free, but the Uluru were far stronger. With muttered curses, they threw him into the cave so hard he slammed against its wall, scraping his hands on rough-hewn stone and reopening the laceration on his palm. The steel bars squealed and flaked rust when the door slammed shut, but Lugh knew sturdy metal when he saw it, and the heavy chain and lock they added looked brand new. He threw himself against the bars.

"You're just going to leave me here?"

Tahk ignored him, instead nodding to Ku'Adsila. "Come. It's not much further."

Ku'Adsila grimaced. "He's part of this, too."

"He's an outsider."

"So am I at this point."

"You know what I mean."

Ku'Adsila's eyebrows knitted together. She gave Lugh an apologetic look, then let her captors guide her away. He grappled for something to say, but all he came up with were pleas he knew they'd ignore. Soon he was alone, trapped in a few square meters, wind lashing him with grit. Someone had carved dashes against the rock wall. He stopped counting at thirty rows and sank against the wall adjacent to the bars. Blood slicked his scraped hands. Lugh rubbed them off on his battered tweed jacket, then shook his left arm until a wax paper packet slid out. He'd blindly filched it from one of the Uluru warriors during the struggle. He unwrapped it eagerly, only to behold a hunk of stale, half-eaten bread. He'd been hoping for a knife or maybe the Godstone itself.

So much for that.

Lugh chewed on the stale bread as if it were the manifestation of all his worldly problems. Once finished, he took a deep breath, then forced a chuckle. "Well, this is a right and proper mess."

A few seconds of listening to wind and skittering sand passed.

"Shit!" Lugh kicked the steel bars as hard as he could, only for a blinding lance of pain to remind him of the unhealed wound in his leg. He rocked back, tasting bile, sputtering every curse he'd garnered from Auklenn's worst and even adding a few new ones of his own. By the time the pain receded into its low throb, he was sweating. The deep pain in his thigh had spread, and last night's sleep had been hot and restless, feverishly sweating out more water than he'd taken in. If the Uluru didn't come back and kill him, infection or dehydration would.

Lugh gritted his teeth, shivering. He knew he could just Doppel the bars into something smaller, but what would that accomplish? He couldn't leave without the Godstone. Besides, with an injured leg and no water, he had about as much hope in that desert as a canary had in an illegal coal mine. So, here he was again, just like in Auklenn—in those smelly, damp prison cells, pestered by rats, lice, and bedbugs—knowing he could escape, knowing that would only make things worse for him and Sabia. Sometimes a man had to square himself up and endure.

What could he do now?

Lugh found himself eyeing a head-sized rock near the cave wall. He had no energy to waste, but his curiosity got the better of him. Ever since his run-in with Kal he'd been wondering why his aversion hadn't hit him as hard as it should have. Taking up a small pebble, he rested his other palm against the big rock—and tried condensing it to the smaller one, normally a one-way ticket to a blackout. *Click!* It happened with a subtle flash, and with only a brief flutter of palpitations. Lugh thumbed the new pebble, too stunned for words. So it wasn't just a one-time fluke. His knack had changed, and the aversion with it. How? Was it the Godstone? Lugh had only kept it on his person since fleeing Auklenn a few months ago. Correlation did not mean causation, but what else was there?

The wind blew into the cave, peppering Lugh with sand. He groaned and tossed the condensed pebble against the far wall, where it reverted to the rock and promptly cracked in two. Changed or not, a dishonest knack couldn't help him out of this mess.

Nothing could.

Night fell. Cold crept in. No one came. His chills and sweats worsened. Had they left him here to die?

Lugh forced his mind to Sabia. Her smile, her laughter, her kindness.

That only made him feel worse, and with exhaustion catching up, he swung between dozing into heartsick dreams and waking to heartsick reality. A dead end. Was this how Grandfather had felt on his deathbed? Powerless yet so filled with yearning? Drowning in it?

"Unite them. Return them. Open the eyes that bloodshed closed. Prove . . ."

Lugh stared into the impenetrable darkness. What would Grandfather do?

A lighter flashed in the dark.

"Wish I could say it gets easier, kid," said a familiar, drawling voice. "But what you need are true words, not honeyed ones."

Lugh gasped. "You?"

"Aye." The Drunk lit a cigarette, flame outlining his unkempt face as he sat against the rocky wall just outside the rusty bars. He still wore his old military jacket and boots. Still reeked of alcohol, too. He blew a jet of smoke and watched it curl into the night. "You're in a real pickle now. A shiny quandary."

Am I dreaming again? Lugh rubbed his eyes. "What are you doing here? How—?"

"Came back for my purse." The Drunk waggled his coin purse, then flashed his decayed smile. "Nah, that ain't it. Sometimes a man doesn't need a reason to visit a poor lad stuck in a dusty hole in the middle of nowhere. I did warn you, didn't I?"

"Great. Just the company I needed." Lugh sank against the wall and leaned against the cold bars. His mind went back to the train ride into Capstone. "You're not real."

"Now that stings, lad. Good thing a certain concentration of alcohol in the veins keeps one free of existential crises." The Drunk tapped on the bars, and the vibrations shivered through Lugh's shoulder. "The line between real and unreal is rather thin out here, city boy. Thought you might have learned that by now."

"I've learned that a snowflake has better chances up a Flameshot's arse than you have stumbling all the way out here."

"That so? I must be a very lucky man."

Lugh groaned. "I'm exhausted. Sleep deprived. Dehydrated. That's all."

"I used to tell myself that, too." The Drunk took another drag, eyes glinting in the cigarette's flare. "What are you going to do now?"

Lugh sighed. What was the point of arguing with a hallucination? Yet he found himself muttering anyway. "No matter how I look at it, I can't see things ending well. I'm . . . out of my depth, here."

"Life hits you in the face on the best of days."

"And the worst of days?"

"Kills you. But you're not dead yet, are you?"

Lugh sniffed. "*Yet*. Key word."

"True. Death's been all the rage in this land the last hundred years." The Drunk patted the bars, flaking off rust. "These cages are good old Auklenn steel, put in during the cleansing campaigns. Twentieth Engineer's Regiment to be exact. You see, mobile armies don't have much space or means for prisoners. So they beat out some rock and left the Uluru to starve and thirst in the open air. Men. Women. Families. Didn't matter who." He took another drag. This time his eyes were clear, staring intently into the dark. "The tabloids back home made a big clean show of things. Victory. Heroism. Good versus evil. All parades and banners and patriotic drivel. But war's a coward's game, in the end. Heroes? They end up buried, while the coward figures out how to survive at any cost."

"Are you saying I should choose the coward's path?" *Like I always do.*

"I think you're in a different kind of prison, one without bars. One where you need to find out what kind of man you want to be." The Drunk flicked his cigarette into the night. "There's a lot of different men in all of us. The tyrant, the saint, the fool . . . there's a soldier in me, a father, a son, gambler, thief." He took out his metal flask and tapped it against the bars. "And a drunk."

Lugh snorted. "And you let the drunk win out of all of them."

"Because unlike all the others, the drunk didn't waste his time fighting it." The Drunk took a swig and breathed out a weary sigh. "But this show ain't about me. It's about you. Question is, kid, which man inside *you* is gonna win? Because only one can."

As tempted as Lugh was to ignore the Drunk, he couldn't help but wonder. There *were* many men within him, each beholden to someone else, each burning with a different set of desires. Was it even possible to be a unified whole? Or was life just making do with ramshackle diplomacy in a fractured being? He opened his mouth to speak, but boots scraped in the dark, and a blinding light exploded through the bars. Lugh shielded his eyes.

The Drunk was gone. Instead, three Uluru warriors loomed with horses in tow, Tahk at the forefront with a shielded lantern.

"It's time," Tahk grunted.

Finally. Lugh squinted against the light. "Time for what?"

Tahk frowned and lowered his lantern. "Ku'Adsila won't cooperate without you, and I'm tired of dealing with stubborn prodigies." He shoved a blindfold between the bars. "She cares about you. Outlander or not, that carries some weight around here."

Lugh stared at the blindfold, for a moment seeing nothing but Ku'Adsila's emerald eyes and ashen freckles. An ache swelled in his chest and throat. Gods, she cared, and all this time he'd been looking for ways to go behind her back. Was that the man within him he wanted to win?

"Hurry now, lad. Her grandfather wishes to speak to you." Tahk shoved the blindfold closer. "Fate's a cruel thing, but there's no sense in delaying what must be. That, and making a chieftain wait is unwise."

Lugh's stomach dropped. Ku'Adsila's grandfather was an Uluru chieftain? Gods, the hole just kept getting deeper and deeper.

The grim expression on Tahk's face was exactly like the prison guards he'd seen taking men to the gallows. Were they going to discard him once his usefulness expired? After what his ancestors had done to the Uluru, to expect them not to want blood for blood was naïve. The Drunk's words echoed in his mind, and cold stone pressed around him, the whispering sand so much like the voices of the dead . . . but that fear paled in comparison to what came when he pictured Ku'Adsila's face, and in that moment, he knew why.

I'll have to choose.

As divided as Lugh was, he would soon have to choose. Was he ready?

A rusty memory rekindled as if in answer—from years ago, when his grandfather had taken him hiking in the foothills north of Auklenn. Rain had muddied every path and turned the promising retreat into a nightmare, yet Grandfather had never once complained, nor suggested they turn back. When Lugh mustered the courage to ask why they should keep going, Grandfather paused beneath a gnarled oak tree. Fallen against a boulder, its trunk had bent upwards, compensating for its precarious lean.

"What do you think happened to this tree, Lugh?"

"A storm uprooted it?"

"Many years ago. Before my time. Yet did it die?"

Lugh remembered gazing up at its canopy, which had sheltered them from the rain.

"The Uluru have a saying from the days of old," Grandfather said. "Trees don't lie down. It means that a tree might be cut or broken or plagued, yet it utters no complaint, makes no quarrel, and keeps growing the best it can. There isn't a single tree in this world that grew half as tall as it could. A tree only perishes when it has no other option. And even in death, the tree becomes the soil that will bring new life."

As windswept rain battered the two of them, Grandfather clasped Lugh's shoulder, his intense face softening into a gentle smile.

"You ask me why I keep going? Because it's a lesson you must learn, one your father never understood. That no matter what happens, you can choose to face it with courage, dignity, and grace."

They'd finished the hike to the summit, and there the wind and rain had ebbed, breaking to a golden sun. A beautiful view over rolling farmland and brook.

"And here's another lesson," Grandfather said. "Despite all the trouble it took to go this far, can you say it wasn't worth it in the end?"

Lugh, stunned by the view, could only shake his head.

Grandfather turned to the west, a wistful look on his wrinkled face. "There's a mountain in the far west. One the Uluru held dear."

"Did you climb it?" Lugh asked.

"It hasn't been found for over a hundred years." Grandfather smiled sadly. "But not all mountains are literal, Lugh. We each have one to climb in this life. You will find yours."

Lugh had forgotten all about that day until now, amidst so many terrible memories of toil and loss. Staring at the blindfold in Tahk's hand, he wished he could be even a tenth the man Grandfather had been, that maybe that man was in him, somewhere, behind all the rust and cobwebs, that maybe the Drunk was right.

Regardless, he hadn't played all his cards yet.

Lugh took the blindfold. "Let's get this over with."

Chapter Nine

Five summers ago in Auklenn, Lugh had experienced the unpleasant sensation of being dragged to a ready grave. The gangsters, swarthy rivals from the docklands, had picked him up in hopes that he'd serve as leverage against his father. Idiots. His father had outright ignored them. For that, they'd thought to take it out on Lugh by shooting him in the back of the head before a shallow grave on the riverbank. Lugh still remembered the damp, the stink of cigarettes and mud, the flutter of crows gathering in the stunted marsh trees, and the crushing presence of the wet earth beneath his knees that would soon be piled upon his corpse.

He'd survived that day only because Mother had changed his father's mind. How she'd broken through to that calloused man, Lugh still didn't know, but he'd never forget the grim atmosphere of the place that should have been his end.

This new predicament reminded him of that night all too well.

Despite the tent's rich carpets, glyphic designs, and intricate decorations of amethyst and crystal beads, Lugh's first thought was whether they'd make a mess of the carpet by killing him inside, or if they'd do it on the sands outside. He closed his eyes, trying to block out even a fraction of doomed thinking. At least he was out of the biting wind.

He doubted he'd ever get all the sand out of his mouth, or the smell of horse from his nose. The citrus-scented candles helped only a little. His throat ached with a rising urge to beg, but the steady glares of the Uluru warriors towering over him made silence wiser. Funny, how quickly courage could flee. Grandfather's words on the mountain seemed leagues away, while a thousand little doubts squabbled for his attention. After being taken through their camp blindfolded, catching only glimpses of massive wagons, tents, bonfires, and shadows, he now knelt on a carpeted floor at the mercy of a people he knew he deserved no mercy from. To his surprise, the Clysm's rumble seemed muted here, wherever here was.

A copper bowl a meter in diameter sat before him, and in the flickering candlelight he thought he saw old blood crusting its grooves.

Great. More blood magic. Just bloody great.

Ku'Adsila knelt beside him, but instead of matching the other Uluru glare for glare, she stared at the bowl, a sadness to her face that made Lugh wonder how true her grandfather's death threat was.

"Ku'Adsila?" he whispered.

One of the Uluru warriors jabbed Lugh in the shoulder with the butt of his rifle, knocking him over and blinding him with pain. No one helped him up, and with his hands bound and his leg throbbing, it took him five tries and a wave of nausea to get up. His wound kept getting worse by the hour. Images of rot and amputation crowded Lugh's mind, and it took several deep breaths to push them back.

"Don't provoke them," Ku'Adsila whispered. "They'll kill you."

Lugh rolled his eyes. *Preaching to the choir.*

The tent's curtain whispered, and in limped an elderly Uluru man, his ashen face more wrinkled than tree bark and his body all angles and blotchy pewter skin. His robes, however, were bright with glyphs and beaded tassels, and his long white hair had at least thirty braids, each beaded with amethyst. His eyes, rheumy yet sharp, swept across the room, ignoring Lugh, settling on Ku'Adsila for what felt like an hour. She didn't flinch, but her hands clenched until the knuckles turned white. With a rattling sigh and clicking of arthritic joints, the elder sat on the pillows opposite them. One of his guards placed a curved dagger on his right and the Godstone on his left.

"Ku'Tiaman," Ku'Adsila breathed.

"Adsila," the old man, Ku'Tiaman, said in a leathery voice. Deep yet brittle, like a canyon made of glass.

They held each other's gazes, saying nothing more. Lugh knew that what was going between them went far beyond what words could convey. Like his arguments with his mother—the looks she'd given him when he'd brought money they both knew was illegitimate, the volumes of hurt they'd spoken. A lump formed in his throat. He looked down at the bowl, his mind drifting to Sabia.

I can't let it end like this.

What could he do here? What cards could he play? He forced Grandfather's image into his head, groping for courage.

Beads clattered, and Lugh found Ku'Tiaman studying him, his gaze even more dissecting than Colonel Vyzeryn's. Lugh's mouth went drier. "Um . . . I . . ."

"I speak your tongue well enough," Ku'Tiaman said. "And you will be silent."

Ku'Adsila tensed. "Grandfather—"

"Silence, Adsila. I will not hear it from you."

"You can't command my silence."

Ku'Tiaman tensed. "After you abandoned our ways and followed in that fool's footsteps?"

"He was my *father*."

"And he let your mother die."

Ku'Adsila flinched, mouth hanging open.

"And now you return with this . . ." Ku'Tiaman wrinkled his nose, "Stringy little accessory. He ought to be left in the cages his ilk built for us."

"He saved my life!" Ku'Adsila shot to her feet, teeth bared. The guards stepped back. Even Tahk, looming by the exit, looked unnerved. "He had the other half. Ehekahl's Tear is complete thanks to him."

"I've seen." Ku'Tiaman eyed the Godstone. "You still believe what your father believed? That you can undo that which cannot be undone?"

Ku'Adsila crossed her arms. "I do."

"Then you're just as foolish as he was," Ku'Tiaman murmured. "Ehekahl abandoned us after we failed to protect Kata-Uluru. The age of gods is dead. We live in the age of blood and steel, where strength is the only way."

"Is that why you're gathering the tribes?" Ku'Adsila asked. When Ku'Tiaman's face tightened, Ku'Adsila's paled. "Grandfather, what are you doing?"

"The only thing we can do. Auklenn has left us no choice."

Lugh remembered the Drunk's omen. "War."

"No!" Ku'Adsila said. "You can't!"

Ku'Tiaman lifted his chin. "What else do we have? We are dying. For two centuries we searched for a better way. For two-hundred years we tried to show the mercy and forgiveness Ehekahl stood for. What did that do but give the outlanders room to build their mines and march in their armies?" He gripped the knife at his side, polished blade gleaming. "Violence begets violence. Hate begets hate. But that is the way of this godless world. The Clysm will grow, consuming the lands. There is little for us here, and soon there will be nothing. We must outpace it. So we must go to war and take from the outlanders what they took from us."

"But—!"

"You're a hypocrite to talk, child. You tell me to not fight, yet what have you been doing, but waging your own little war against the outlanders?"

"I did it to find the stone," Ku'Adsila said. "I had no other choice!"

"You had a choice. I don't. You talk as if I haven't exhausted every bloodless avenue." Ku'Tiaman snorted and tapped the blade with a long, yellowed fingernail. "Excuses will not wash the blood from your hands any more than justifications will wash it from mine. No more than it absolved your father of his sins. I have the grace to admit it. You are a hypocrite, Adsila. I am ashamed of you."

Ku'Adsila sank to her knees. Tears ran down her face.

Unite them. Return them. Open the eyes that bloodshed closed. Lugh grated his teeth. It was risky to say anything, but Ku'Adsila had taken risks for his sake, too. "You're wrong."

Ku'Tiaman glared. "What did you say?"

"You're wrong." Lugh looked him in the eye. A gamble, but it wasn't just what Grandfather would have said, it was what he wanted to say, too. "There's another way—" A hand gripped Lugh's throat and pulled him over the bowl, so sudden that it took him a moment to realize it was Ku'Tiaman's grip crushing his windpipe, bony fingers digging like claws. Ku'Adsila shouted something, but the guards drew their weapons on her. Ku'Tiaman's breath blew hot into Lugh's ear, reeking of tobacco.

"You would lie to me again, as so many did before you? As you lied to my wayward granddaughter?"

"I'm not—" Lugh coughed. "Lying!"

Ku'Tiaman pricked Lugh's neck with the blade. "Your blood will tell after I fill this bowl."

"You knew my grandfather. Amon. Amon Ahearn!"

The blade paused. "Yes . . . I did, once."

"He gave me the stone. He wanted me to help! Please—"

"And you consider that adequate? He was an honorable man, but he is dead. You are nothing like him, and your lineage doesn't change that. You reek of lies and broken promises."

The blade pressed in again, drawing blood—and

then someone tackled Lugh aside. He fell on his back and found Ku'Adsila crouching over him with one of the guards' revolvers in hand.

"He's not lying!" she shouted. "I tested his blood. Or will you defy the old ways like you claim I do?"

Everyone froze. Ku'Tiaman grimaced, then stared into the bowl as if it held all of his memories, the best and the worst. His wrinkled face changed. From anger, to hurt, and at last to sadness. He whispered something under his breath.

"It's true," Ku'Adsila said. "Please believe me. Give us a chance. I'm not as lost to the old ways as you think. Neither am I stupid enough to trust an outlander on his word, but the blood rites are sacred. Ehekahl does not lie!"

"Then his blood will speak the truth again," Ku'Tiaman said.

"He saved my life!"

"So you said already."

"Am I worth so little to you?" When Ku'Tiaman didn't answer, Ku'Adsila blinked, as if she'd expected him to object. Lugh couldn't take it anymore.

"She's the only family you have left, and this is how you treat her?" Lugh braved the fiery glares of the Uluru. "I've lost everyone but my sister, and I'd sure as hell do anything to keep her. Me, a filthy outlander. What does that say about *you*? My grandfather said you were the kindest people he'd ever met. Where is that kindness now?"

"Be careful what you say, boy," Ku'Tiaman said.

"And you be careful who you're throwing away."

Ku'Tiaman's grip on the ritual knife tightened until his knuckles popped.

Ku'Adsila looked to Lugh, eyes wide. Her lips parted, then pressed into a firm, resolute line. She gave Lugh a subtle nod and faced her grandfather anew. "Please, give us a chance. If not for me, for my mother."

The wrinkles on Ku'Tiaman's face deepened, as if another decade had passed, and his bony shoulders slouched. He chuckled wearily, shaking his head. When he looked up at last, his watery eyes studied Lugh as if for the first time. "You may not have his face, but you have his eyes, and his reckless guts. You're indeed an Ahearn."

"Then let me try." Lugh's stomach twisted worse than ever, but he ignored it. Now was not the time for doubt. "When my grandfather died, he entrusted me with the stone . . . and words. He was feverish. I thought it was nonsense at the time but—"

"The words, boy," Ku'Tiaman said. He was shaking, as if he feared what he'd hear.

Lugh took a deep breath, closed his eyes, and forced out the words that had been trapped rattling in his mind ever since his grandfather had passed. "'Unite them. Return them. Open the eyes that bloodshed closed. Prove . . .' But he died before he could finish."

Ku'Tiaman became very still, but he remained silent, his watery gaze staring at nothing.

Lugh licked his lips, as tense as piano wire. "I don't know who Amon was to you, but all I'm asking for is a chance. Hold off on your war. Give us time to fix this. We can. I swear it."

"So you believe the legends?" Ku'Tiaman sounded tired. "You, an outlander."

"My grandfather did. That's enough for me."

Ku'Adsila knelt at Ku'Tiaman's side. "This world isn't godless, Grandfather. Why else would we still have our El-Suru? The blood sorcery has always been our connection to the divine." She gently took his left hand. "If Ehekahl's gifts to us remain, she must not be totally lost to this world, or to us."

Ku'Tiaman closed his eyes. For a few minutes, the only sounds were the muffled wind and the old man's unsteady breaths. When he spoke at last, it was in a whisper nearly lost in the breeze. "Seven days. No more."

Seven days to find Kata-Uluru. Seven days to return the Godstone. Seven days to fix whatever had been broken. How would Lugh make it work? How would he keep Colonel Vyzeryn out of it? How—? Lugh flinched, the implications of those thoughts striking him like bullets. He'd just changed sides. Just like that, he'd set his heart on betraying Vyzeryn, the woman who held almost all of the cards. Madness . . . and yet he felt a little less sick, a little stronger. He'd made his choice. The fear that had plagued him was still there, but something else rode over it, like a ship dancing over treacherous waves. It reminded him of something his mother had once said.

"True strength is found in the hearts of the good, Lugh. Evil may look strong, but it is brittle at best. Stand for what's right, and you'll outlast what's wrong."

Lugh swallowed hard. He pushed the thoughts aside for later and looked at Ku'Adsila, who was staring at him with surprise. "Is seven days enough?"

She blinked, then nodded.

"Two conditions," Ku'Tiaman said. "Firstly, if you fail, Lugh Ahearn, you will die."

Lugh shuddered at the thought, but he forced himself to nod. No different than his other deal.

"The other. Ku'Adsila."

Ku'Adsila stiffened but kept holding her grandfather's hand. "Yes?"

Ku'Tiaman's brow furrowed. "I still haven't forgiven you for abandoning your duty. You are our strongest sorceress. Your place was here, at my side, to take the reins when I pass on. You abandoned that. I won't pretend I can make you do it now . . . but tomorrow is the new moon. Do you remember what that means?"

Ku'Adsila nodded slowly. "The Solstice of Fire."

"And at its heart, a priestess to bring Ehekahl's favor upon us."

"I thought you said Ehekahl had abandoned us."

Ku'Tiaman's face wrinkled with bitterness. He placed his other hand over Ku'Adsila's, a tremor to his bony fingers. "I spoke wrongly. It has been years since I honored Ehekahl, years spent furious at her for letting my daughter die. I called you a hypocrite, yet what am I? Denouncing you for abandoning our ways while I myself had let my faith fall along the wayside. Please, Adsila. Just for tomorrow night, be the granddaughter I wanted you to be. Give us a chance for the one we are giving you . . . and give me a chance to rekindle the faith I so foolishly lost."

Lugh saw the trembling of Ku'Adsila's face, the tears in her eyes. The hurt. The yearning.

"I will," she whispered at last. "I swear it on my blood."

Ku'Tiaman nodded. "Then as they say in Auklenn, we have a deal."

Chapter Ten

Deal or not, the blindfold went back on.

"Really?" Lugh muttered as Tahk guided him outside.

"Think of it as probation." Tahk pulled Lugh's elbow, steering him around something. The sandy ground gave beneath every step. "That, and what's the fun in spoiling a surprise?"

Lugh tried not to scowl. "Last time I was blindfolded, I found myself *surprised* by an open grave and men eager to put me in it."

"If that was our intention, you never would have left that tent alive."

Oh, I feel so much better. Part of Lugh refused to err on the positive side, but he knew he ought to. He'd made a commitment. There was a chance to set things right, and he had to take it. One step at a time. After three deep breaths, he focused on the present. Firelight glowed through the blindfold, as did a campground's aroma of woodsmoke, roasting meat, tobacco, horse, and leather. The wind was gentle here, somehow, barely any grit in the air, even the distant thunder of the Clysm muffled.

Hushed voices spoke in his passing, all in lilting Uluru. Blindfold or not, he felt many eyes boring into him. They'd probably never seen tweed before—or a filthy, half-dead outlander. His leg throbbed worse with every step, tingling below the thigh, and sweat had soaked through his undershirt. The infection was getting worse. How long until it went gangrenous? His optimism fragmented with memories of Auklenn slums, where a simple cut could easily fester. Had he come all this way, survived gunfights, even a Flameshot, just to die by a splinter? It was so ridiculous he scoffed.

"Something wrong?" Tahk grunted.

Lugh sucked at his teeth. "My leg . . ."

"Don't worry so much, lad."

"Don't worry?" Lugh flushed. "It's festering like mad! What if I lose it—?"

Tahk yanked his blindfold off. They were inside another tent, sparsely furnished with woven blankets and dusty pillows, warmed by a brazier whose smoke curled through a hole in the ceiling. Citrusy incense permeated the air, and thank the gods, the floor was carpeted too. Tahk nudged Lugh forward, dusting his hands off as if ridding himself of an annoying responsibility. "Stay here. Maya will take care of the rest."

"Maya?" Lugh turned. "Who's—?"

Tahk was already gone, and a middle-aged Uluru woman ducked through the tent's heavy curtain instead. She wore a simple ribbon-adorned skirt, with an animal skin yoke decorated with beads and hawk feathers, and several necklaces laden with gold and copper charms in the shape of moon phases. Her hair was done in a single long braid woven with amethysts. Yet, all that may as well have disappeared when she smiled.

It looked exactly like Mother's smile, right up to the dancing wrinkles by her eyes.

Lugh stared.

"Sit," Maya said. Gentle yet firm, barring any argument. Motherly indeed.

In a daze, Lugh sat on the pillows.

"I'm Maya," she said, sitting next to him. "Don't fear. I'm a healer. Now let me see."

What could he do but nod?

Maya hummed to herself as she unwrapped his leg. Her thin eyebrows raised when she bared the wound, but her humming didn't falter, and she got to work with dizzying efficiency, cleaning the gash with a flask that had a sharp, alcohol-like smell. Burned like hell, yet the pain seemed distant now, and something far closer . . . memories, yes, old memories of when Mother would do the same, cleaning him up after he got into fights or worrying over him whenever he caught a chill. The best mother he could have asked for . . . and yet he'd ended up hurting her so much, in the end. A painful lump formed in his throat. Maya paused, her gentle brown eyes inquiring.

"Does it hurt too much?"

"No, it's . . ." Lugh averted his gaze, pretending to be interested in the patterns in the woven carpet. "It's fine."

"You see someone else in me, don't you?"

Lugh winced. "What gave you that idea?"

"Your face speaks of longing."

Longing. Lugh swallowed hard. Yes, that's what it

was, the deep heaviness in his chest, the void where something good used to be. "My mother. You . . . have her smile."

Maya sighed and went back to work. "There are special people in our lives who never leave us, even after they are gone. It was the same for my parents. And my sons." A sad smile wrinkled her face as she dabbed the wound dry. "She is with you. No matter where you go."

The idea of Mother seeing him now swung Lugh between comfort and terror. He covered his mouth and nodded, not trusting his voice. Sabia had that smile, too.

Maya took out a needle and thread. "This will hurt."

"Not nearly as much as this." Lugh touched his chest.

Again with her sad smile, Maya nodded and went to work.

A short time and plenty of pain later, the wound was clean and sutured. Maya smeared a dark paste like wet ashes overtop, then wrapped it in fresh bandages. She finished off by handing Lugh a small glass bottle with a cork lid. "Drink this and go to sleep."

Lugh took the medicine, but it slipped from his trembling hands. Gods, he felt like his heart would drop into his feet. He played it off with a chuckle and tried to pick the bottle up. A teardrop rolled off his chin and splattered on his forearm. He stopped, watching the teardrop snake along his pale skin. He'd shed many such tears for Mother, but no amount would ever feel like enough. "Does it ever get easier?"

Maya picked up the medicine and placed it in his hands, then gently wrapped hers around his. "To have lived, and to have given someone a piece of yourself, a piece that is lost in their absence, is a beautiful gift. You must learn to hold it in your heart."

Lugh nodded and wiped his eyes. "Thank you."

"You are welcome." Maya stood with a clatter of beads and charms, then paused at the exit. "The pain will go away. The leg, I mean. The other . . . it is a different kind of pain. Like the wind, it chooses its comings and goings. I'm sure you understand."

"I do." Lugh rubbed at his shoulder, faint tingles needling where Eirlys' curse lurked. He winced. He hadn't even looked at himself to see whether there was a mark or just skin. Even with his wounds tended, he still shared his saddle with death.

"Are you hurt there, too?" Maya asked.

"N-No, it's nothing. I . . ." Lugh let go, ashamed. "Just another memory."

Maya dipped her head, and then left him alone.

Would they be so kind if they knew what he was hiding?

The sour medicine, whatever it was, knocked Lugh out like too much opium. He didn't even dream, and when he woke, the pain was gone. Lugh tested his leg, then stood, then dared to jump up and down. No weakness, and only a faint, dull ache. He muttered an oath and couldn't help but laugh. He jumped again—and heard a scratch at the tent flap. Four heads poked through, each on top of the other. Uluru children, around Sabia's age, each with their own little amethyst charms and skin like unblemished clay. Lugh slowly raised a hand and waved.

"H-Hello there," he said.

The children blinked in unison. One, a girl with dazzling green eyes, chanced a smile.

Outside, Tahk bellowed something in Uluru. The children vanished with a chorus of laughter. A few seconds later, Tahk ducked inside, smiling to himself and shaking his head. He wore trousers and a simple vest, and with the daylight blazing through the flap, he looked ever more a sea of tribal tattoos and muscle. Leather bracers, woven with amethysts, clung around his massive forearms.

"Good morning," he said. "How's the leg?"

"Better." Lugh bounced on it again, still in disbelief. "It's . . . *incredible*."

"Maya is our best. And as much as you outlanders love your flashy sciences, the old wisdom is called *wise* for reason." Tahk plopped down a wooden bowl. A porridge of some kind. "Eat up. Before it gets cold."

As boring as it looked, the porridge tasted divine, spiced with something akin to nutmeg. He finished it in seconds and gave Tahk a thankful nod. The man crossed his arms.

"Good. Because I made that, and you were eating it one way or another."

"Didn't take you for a chef," Lugh said.

"A man must wear many hats. A father more so." Tahk nodded at the flap. "Daughters are a handful on the best of days."

"Captor. Soldier. Guide. Chef. I've never been so spoiled."

"Our way dictates that I guide you through whatever happens here. First as the man who took you captive, now as the man who makes sure you don't do anything stupid."

Lugh smirked. "Much obliged."

"Don't get used to it." Tahk grinned.

It felt odd, seeing the big man smile. Lugh set aside the bowl. "You were ready to leave me for dead before. What changed?"

Something flickered across Tahk's face. He sighed and took a seat, resting his thick forearms on his knees. "A good night's sleep surrounded by family will do that to a man. That, and I've decided to revise my initial impression of you."

"Which was?"

"A wiry whiner who couldn't fight his way out of a paper tent."

"Charming. And now?"

"A wiry outlander with a surprising amount of guts." Tahk took out a bone pipe and lit it with a match. "Looks are deceiving. It's been a long while since I've met an outlander on terms other than violence. You and Ku'Adsila have brought a lot of change on your trail. Ehekahl willing, it'll be change for the better."

For the better. Lugh's shoulders tensed, and he rubbed his cursed shoulder again. His mirth over his healed leg evaporated like water in a coal oven.

"Nervous?" Tahk offered his pipe.

"Thanks." Lugh took a puff, then coughed. Only then did he notice the amethysts seated in the pipe's stem. They bore the same glyphs as the ones woven into Tahk's bracers. "What's with all the amethysts?"

"Ah, Ku'Adsila didn't tell?" Tahk took the pipe and savored a long pull. When he breathed out, smoke danced around his distant expression. "It is said that the great shrines of Kata-Uluru were made entirely out of amethyst. Imagine that. I wish I could have seen it." His face hardened. "They were shattered in the war. The survivors took what pieces they could and carried them on their bodies. Over their hearts. In their hair. Their way of keeping Ehekahl with them, no matter where the troubled world forced them to go. These stones . . ." He gently thumbed his left bracer. "They are passed down from father to son. Mother to daughter. And they always will be, as long as we survive."

Lugh wished he had something of his mother to hold. But after Father's arrest and hanging, their home had been raided, possessions taken by the police, probably locked away in some dusty evidence locker or filched by greedy constables. All he had now were memories. He rubbed his wrist, picturing Sabia's bracelet and how invincible he'd felt when he'd worn it. Is that how the Uluru felt when they carried those stones? "Do you . . . believe in the legends, too?"

"My father raised me to be pragmatic. To believe in what is seen and heard and touched. But my mother balanced that out with a sprinkle of the divine." Tahk savored his pipe, embers winking in his eyes. "Yes, lad, I do believe. Life has been hard out here for all of us. One has to believe in something." He smiled. "I'm glad you brought Ku'Tiaman around. It's been a long time since I've seen him dare to hope."

Lugh shrugged and looked at the carpet. "I didn't do much."

"You brought his granddaughter back to him."

"That was you."

"She could have fled at any point. The Godstone changes everything."

The mention of that stone, and everything it had taken him through, stabbed Lugh with painful doubt. Just last night he'd felt determined to help these people, to find a way to abate Colonel Vyzeryn and the others. But was that even possible? It was like trying to win a rigged game of Stacks. He wasn't doing this alone anymore . . . but he was still keeping so many secrets about his original motivations, ones he knew he couldn't reveal even if his heart had changed. Part of him ached to tell Tahk anyway. The Uluru deserved to know. Most of all, Ku'Adsila deserved to know.

"Where is Ku'Adsila?" he asked at last, filing away that festering itch.

"In her grandfather's tent, making the necessary rites and preparations."

"The Solstice of Fire. What's that about?"

Tahk stood up and rolled his shoulders. "It's a secret."

Lugh huffed. "Let me guess, more blindfolds?"

"This tent is your blindfold now, lad. I'll come for you at nightfall. Get some rest." Tahk paused at the flap and winked. "You'll need it."

Chapter Eleven

That night, Lugh stepped out of the tent—and his eyes got clobbered with such an overwhelming display that he almost ducked back inside. Instead of a gloomy, dust-encrusted camp, he stared at a bright, colorful ocean of festivity.

Countless Uluru crowded around bonfires and cooking pots, while others danced or played wooden flutes or drank competitively from red-painted flasks. Multi-colored streamers dangled from posts driven into the dry earth, their playful flutter accented with hanging chimes of amethyst and crystal. Enormous wagon houses and tents had been arranged to form corridors and walls, and ropes suspended oiled tarps overhead, all enclosing a vast space away from the elements. Laughter and shouts drowned out the muffled wind and thunder. Lugh stared, dumbfounded, wondering how a people so lost and oppressed could look happier than all the prosperous folk back in Auklenn. *Is this how they always were, before my people came?*

Lugh found himself gripping at a twinge in his shoulder. He was noticing it more frequently, but he was also *worrying* about it more. Was it just in his head? It had acted up the most during his encounter with Kal. Had the Flameshot's proximity made it react as it did then? Or was it something else? He knew little about their power, what it meant, what it could do . . . but he couldn't hide the curse forever, no more than he could hide his deal with Vyzeryn. He'd promised to help these people. He *wanted* to, but it wouldn't take much to shake their trust. Changing sides while playing the other, saving Sabia, helping Ku'Adsila and her people, beating Vyzeryn somehow, surviving the curse, the Clysm . . . his head hurt just thinking about it.

What the hell was he even thinking? He wasn't his grandfather. He was just one person and a shitty one at that. Who was he to act like he could change everything? Especially after everything he had failed to change . . .

His thoughts trailed off when he realized the entire gathering had stopped to stare at him.

"Don't worry, outlander," grunted Tahk, standing beside Lugh with his arms crossed. "They're just surprised. You're the first outlander in years to step out of Ku'Tiaman's tent alive. *I* sure didn't expect you to."

Lugh winced. "Thanks."

Tahk sucked on his pipe. "My pleasure."

"I wasn't expecting something like . . . this."

"With the world as it is, all the more reason to celebrate life while you still have it."

"But there's nothing out here. No food. No water. How do you do it?"

"There are ways, if you look hard enough. We Uluru have had much time to discover them."

"I suppose." Lugh frowned. "Are you here to hold my hand or something?"

"Hardly. Just to smooth things over." Tahk took a deep breath and bellowed for all of the gathered Uluru to hear, speaking in a lilting tongue Lugh had no hope of understanding. Whatever was said, it sent ripples of curiosity through the Uluru, followed by chuckles. Lugh blinked as people crowded towards them.

"What did you just tell them?"

Tahk put a giant hand on Lugh's shoulder. "To show you *hospitality*."

Before Lugh knew it, he was shoved into the masses, instantly overwhelmed by fragrant spices and smiling faces. The flow of humanity tugged him toward the largest bonfire, and for a second, he thought they'd throw him in it, but to his greater amazement they sat him on cushions and bombarded him with sizzling food in painted bowls. At first he considered declining it, but when Maya offered him a cup, her laughter wrinkles tugging at his heart, he folded. Silence reigned. Everyone was watching. Maya said something in Uluru this time, then gave that warm smile that reminded him so much of his mother. Lugh frowned at the cup's frothy contents.

"She says drink," Tahk said, suddenly beside Lugh again. "Unless you Auklenn folk can only handle watered-down milk."

"I can handle my drink well enough."

"Then prove it. It's a deadly mistake for a guest to refuse a drink from an elder."

I'll show you. Lugh drank it all back in one go—and felt as if someone had poured molten lead down his throat. He coughed violently and started sneezing.

"And almost as deadly a mistake to drink it!" Tahk guffawed and slapped Lugh hard on the back. Everyone cheered, raising their own cups, and the chaos of laughter and music and dance slammed back into a full, dizzying gallop.

Lugh rubbed his throat, but quickly found himself overwhelmed with attention: the smiles, the well-meaning but uninterpretable words. And the food—damn, the food, spicy as hell but delicious. Lugh couldn't recall the last time he'd eaten so well. Even when he'd occasionally had money, he'd always saved the best for Sabia.

Sabia. Remembering slapped Lugh back into grim focus, and he found himself taking in the sights for what felt like the first time. He watched as a group of children danced in a circle, arms linked, stone-braided hair glinting in the firelight. Sabia would have loved this. Lugh's throat tightened. What was he even doing? Did he really think he could redeem himself? That he had anything more than a losing hand? He stared at his empty plate, at the pale, scarred hands gripping it, each scar a memory . . .

A cluster of little feet poked into his vision, and he looked up to see a group of Uluru children ogling him. The same ones as before, led by the girl with the brilliant green eyes. He tried a smile. "Hello again?"

They kept staring.

Never seen an outlander before today, I bet. Lugh got an idea. He soon had the empty bowl in one hand and a pebble in the other. With a flash of his knack, the pebble

Doppeled into a second bowl. The children jumped back, eyes owl wide. Lugh laughed despite himself, made a show of changing the bowl back, and then did so again with a painted ceramic cup. The Doppeling came easier than ever, and he felt no strain.

"That's interesting," said Tahk, ever his shadow.

"I call it Doppeling."

"Didn't know you were a sorcerer."

"Not a very useful one."

"I know the feeling. I can only steer a bullet to a single target, and I can't prove truths like the elders or Ku'Adsila can."

"Still better than mine," Lugh said.

Yet when the children took greater interest, and Lugh began working sleight of hand into his tricks, an idea shot into his mind, a vision of him and Sabia in a small Auklenn village, putting on magic shows. He smiled despite himself. A traveling performer? That . . . might have worked, and would have been honest, too. A lump formed in his throat as the children cheered for another trick. Too late. Always too late—finding an honest use for his knack now, at the end of everything. Lugh smiled ruefully and surprised the children with tricks he'd learned in gambling dens. Funny, how he could use them for good. Maybe . . . maybe it *could* still happen, despite what his cyclical habit of self-doubt wanted him to believe. But damn did it feel good to know that he might have done something authentic, that there was a place for him beyond the cage his old man had forced him into.

As the minutes blurred on, and the Uluru people showed him kindness after kindness, he saw their smiles and realized it didn't matter that he couldn't understand them. Mother had called smiles the universal language of the heart.

A smile was a smile no matter where you came from.

The children soon returned with more of their friends, bobbing excitedly on their toes. *My infamy precedes me.* Lugh prepared to show off his tricks again, but with the suddenness of lightning, the entire gathering went silent. Lugh looked around, then followed everyone's eyes, and saw the drapes of Ku'Tiaman's tent fly aside, between them stepping the most beautiful young woman he had ever seen. A segmented warrior's dress of crimson and gold and sapphire, skirts like licking flames, glossy gray hair tied into a complex mesh of braids aglitter with amethysts, her ashen face seemingly aglow, etched with crimson paint in patterns that brought out the brilliance of her emerald irises.

Ku'Adsila? Lugh blinked, wondering if it was the drink, realizing it wasn't.

Barefooted, she walked between a divided sea of Uluru. She still had the marigold flower bound to her necklace. Someone began beating a drum, each thump matching her step. Every head bowed. Lugh did likewise, but glanced up, his chest tight with something he couldn't quite name. He realized he had no words. Not even thoughts. Only that nameless feeling, as Ku'Adsila walked barefooted towards the largest bonfire. An ocean of glowing coals surrounded it, but Ku'Adsila padded onto them unharmed—and the bonfire itself moved, fanning outwards like the petals of a blooming flower, allowing Ku'Adsila to step right into the heart of the inferno, the crimson marks on her skin glowing red, the hum of her blood sorcery riveting the air alongside prickling static.

In the flames, she began to dance.

Lugh realized he'd halfway stood up out of fear. He sank back down, mouth agape. The drum gained pace, and flutes joined, then strings and clacking stones. Ku'Adsila spun faster, faster, the fiery petals of her dress fanning, the flames whirling with her. The red markings on her skin glowed brighter, but her eyes remained closed, her face tense with concentration.

The static in the air grew, and so did the flames, climbing high through a gap in the overhead tarps yet never burning anything. The night sky beyond glowed red, and the clouds, when Lugh glimpsed them between the tarps, began to churn to the same tempo. In that moment, any doubts he had about the Uluru's legends evaporated, and he understood, a little more, what wonders had made Grandfather gaze so wistfully to the west.

Faster. Louder. Thumping drums. Lilting woodwinds. Chanting pipes. The Uluru people began to sing, a flowing, heedless song that made no apology. People stomped their feet, thumped their weapons, and one by one the Uluru joined the dance around the fire's edge. Thunder rolled. Lightning clapped. Fire grew. And Ku'Adsila went faster still, her grim frown blooming into a smile, her eyes suddenly open and blazing hotter than the flames. Her gaze snared his for a fleeting moment. It lasted an eternity. Lugh couldn't tear his eyes away.

She's beautiful . . .

"In the fire we are reborn," said a leathery voice.

Lugh blinked and found Ku'Tiaman seated on the

cushions next to him, a bone pipe in hand. A tender smile graced his face as he watched his granddaughter. "Ehekahl first spoke to us through the fires," Ku'Tiaman said softly. "Fire has always lit the way through the dark, guiding us. The dance of our priestesses, our sorcerers, was to light that fire every year, to strengthen our connection to Ehekahl." A tear ran down his face. "It's been ten years since her mother taught her that dance. She hasn't missed a single step."

Lugh watched Ku'Adsila, trying to reconcile her with the gunslinging outlaw he'd met in the saloon. Something about what he saw now felt more authentic compared to the other. Was this who Ku'Adsila really was? So many people, be it in Auklenn or the Frontier, took on masks out of necessity, smothering their truest selves. Lugh had, too, first because Father had demanded it, and then because he'd felt there was no better option. He'd been wearing it for so long he didn't know if he could take it off—that, and part of him feared it wasn't a mask at all, but simply who he was. Yet the doubts over the last days, and his reckless choice to change sides, challenged that idea. So did seeing Ku'Adsila now, free of the bloodstained outlaw she'd been. In the dance she became a different person. It made him wonder. Who was he really? Who did he truly want to be? He'd thought the boy Mother loved had suffocated under the weight of poverty, crime, and greed . . . but maybe that wasn't true. Maybe he could change. Maybe Sabia could have a brother she could be proud of. Lugh rubbed his forehead. The drink muddled his thoughts. His head buzzed like a beehive.

"You see something in her," Ku'Tiaman said.

"I . . ." Lugh frowned. "Yes."

"As do I." Ku'Tiaman sighed, his pipe forgotten. "The magic still flows. Ehekahl, at least a part of her, is still in this world. Even I had stopped believing. I was wrong." He took a deep breath. "Thank you, Lugh, for saving my granddaughter. I owe you an apology."

"It's all right," Lugh said. "She saved me, too. And I—"

"An apology is a gift you've earned, not a choice. Please, accept it."

"I . . ." Lugh ignored the tension in his chest. "I accept."

"Good." Ku'Tiaman dipped his head, pipe flaring as he brought it to his lips. "I was angry with her, and I had the reasons, but it was foolish to threaten her. We say things in anger, but we do not always mean them."

The dance had grown into a boisterous chaos. Lugh felt an urge to join. To make a fool of himself and not give a damn. Maybe it was the drink. Maybe it wasn't. Instead, he glanced at Ku'Tiaman. "My grandfather. Who was he to you?"

"Ah . . ." Ku'Tiaman lowered his pipe. "Do you really want to know?"

"He once told me that ignorance is a noose, not a shield."

"Wise words," Ku'Tiaman said as he watched the dance. "He came with the colonials during their third cleansing campaign. They had hired him to liaison with us—their fancy term for negotiating our demise. But unlike all of your people who wanted to force us to understand them, he sought to understand *us*. He was against the war, but he was smart. His superiors didn't know until it was too late." Ku'Tiaman smiled reminiscently. "He saved my life after I was wounded in battle. Carried me back to my people, that reckless fool. The only reason my people spared him was because I was conscious enough to vouch for him."

Lugh frowned. "He joined you?"

"He kept us alive." Ku'Tiaman folded his hand, arthritic joints popping. "We were scattered, our best sorcerers lost. Your armies were too vast. But your grandfather knew their movements, played both sides, fed them with false victories while helping my people stay two steps ahead of them. Eventually your government realized it wasn't profitable to destroy us. They never knew that they'd lost because of the very man they hired to deceive us. To our people, he was a hero. To me . . . he was a friend."

It took Lugh a moment to gather his thoughts. Grandfather had spoken openly of the Uluru, but had been tightlipped about his dealings with them. There was so much Lugh hadn't known, yet now it all clicked together. Now what memories he had made sense. The way Grandfather, in his sickness, had gazed longingly out the window to the west. The Uluru artifacts he had cherished like life itself. The intensity in his eyes when he'd given Lugh the Godstone. A mere archeologist wouldn't have felt that way. A friend would.

"He didn't tell me," Lugh whispered at last.

Ku'Tiaman nodded. "The matter of Ehekahl's Tear, the Godstone, was one he kept secret. He told me he would find the half that was taken back to Auklenn. I will admit, I lost hope. But . . ." He puffed on his pipe and pointed a crooked finger at Lugh. "Here you are."

"He said something about the world ending," Lugh said. "Is that true?"

"The Clysm grows," Ku'Tiaman said. "When the Ravaging happened, and Ehekahl withdrew from this world, it left a void that only destruction could fill. Its wrath is patient, but it will continue to grow as long as only echoes of Ehekahl remain. I think, just like me, she needs to be shown that this world still deserves her faith."

Is that what must be proven? The knot returned to Lugh's stomach. Was he doomed to choose between Sabia and these people in the end? Even though he yearned to follow Grandfather's path, if came down to it . . .

"Adsila trusts you," Ku'Tiaman said. "More than trust, I think."

Lugh didn't know what to say.

"Do not betray that." Ku'Tiaman took Lugh's hands, his own shaking. "I pray to Ehekahl that she is right about you, and that what your grandfather prophesized is true. Don't make me a fool. Promise me, as your grandfather once did."

The music reached a peak, and when Lugh glanced into the fires, he saw that Ku'Adsila was laughing, burdenless and free. Was this another promise he couldn't keep? Gods, he wanted to, but Eirlys's curse itched as if to remind him of the odds. It hurt to look into the Ku'Tiaman's rheumy eyes. Burned like hell.

"I promise."

Chapter Twelve

Hours later, Lugh stumbled into the tent they'd prepared for him, tripping over pillows and carpet and wondering if his liver was shot. His nerves certainly were. A normal person would have felt good after such a celebration, but he couldn't take his mind off the promise he'd made and the curse that would turn him to ash if he didn't *break* that promise. Collapsing onto the pillows, Lugh put his head in his hands, only to hear the tent's flap open with a clattering of amethyst beads.

Ku'Adsila swept inside with a flare of her red dress and a self-satisfied laugh.

Lugh blinked. "What are you—?"

"It worked!" Ku'Adsila did a twirl, teetered, then regained her balance, grinning wide.

"I suppose it did."

"Oh, come on." Ku'Adsila took his hand and pulled him to his feet. "We made it work. We actually did it! I was scared my grandfather would never come around."

"That makes two of us."

"And thanks to two of us, we bought ourselves a ticket out of this mess." Ku'Adsila did another twirl, steadier this time, eyes bright as she looked down at her dress. Her father's hat dangled against her back, its leather cord secured around her neck. "And the dance . . . that scared me too. I never did that for real before, only practiced it . . ." She trailed off and rested her hand over her heart. "With my mother."

Lugh forced a smile. "That was . . . beautiful, what you did out there."

Ku'Adsila frowned. She unceremoniously pushed him back onto the cushions. "Damn better have been— that was bloody hot. Sorcery only keeps the burns away, not the heat." She flopped down next to him, hands behind her head. The marigold was still on her necklace, unburned but dried out and retaining most of its color. "You were pretty amazing too. That took guts, standing up to my grandfather like that. I didn't think you had it in you."

"Me neither," Lugh said.

She chuckled, then sprang up to a seated position, fists clenched. "We can do this. My grandfather will help. We have Ehekahl's Tear. With the Godstone and my sorcery, we can find it. What your grandfather said makes sense. Unite them. Return them. That must mean returning it to Ehekahl's throne."

"She has a throne?"

"Kata-Uluru, where Ehekahl's Tear fell from the heavens. If there's one place where we can undo all of this, it's there. Just as your grandfather's words imply. If we are to make her see again, to prove ourselves, we need to be in the place where her connection is most alive."

"Makes sense," Lugh said.

"Of course it does." Ku'Adsila spoke faster, the excitement in her voice mounting. "No one's found Kata-Uluru since the Ravaging. The Clysm must be hiding it, but when I held that stone . . . I *felt* it, Lugh. It called to me. We can be the ones to finally make it. We can find Kata-Uluru. I can finish what my father started." Ku'Adsila gripped Lugh by the shoulders. Tears glittered in her eyes. "I waited for this for so long. I almost gave up."

Lugh swallowed hard. "I'm glad you didn't."

"Are you?" Ku'Adsila cocked her head, face suddenly stern. "There's nothing you've been keeping from me, is there? If I tested your blood right now?"

A lance of ice shot through Lugh's stomach—and Ku'Adsila broke into laughter.

"Just screwing with you. The look on your face!" Ku'Adsila shoved Lugh back, pinning him down. Suddenly they were nose to nose, eye to eye. Lugh blinked, heat rushing to his face as Ku'Adsila studied him from her vantage point, her beaded braids dangling. "You know, no one's going to disturb us in here."

Oh crap. Lugh glanced around, face burning even hotter. "What are you suggesting?"

"I think you know exactly what I'm suggesting." Ku'Adsila leaned closer, breath hot and tangy, her grip far too strong to escape. "You saved my life. You stood up for me. Your grandfather, my grandfather, it's all full circle." She smiled. "Ehekahl works in funny ways. I think she brought us together for a reason. I'm seeing it now."

"You're drunk."

"Oh?" Ku'Adsila's smile turned into a wicked grin. "So what if I am?"

"You're not thinking straight."

"Really? I drank much more at that saloon and still downed thirty men with one shot. I think I can take one wisecracking outlander."

Lugh bit his tongue and averted his gaze. Ku'Adsila pouted, then rolled so she lay beside him.

"Damn, I'm sorry. What's bothering you? Worried about your sister?"

"It's . . . more than that."

"You can tell me."

Lugh bit his tongue. Tell her what? That he was cursed? That he'd made a deal with the enemy? That he'd been a criminal most of his life and that only recently had he resolved not to betray her? The right thing to do would be to tell her, but gods, it terrified him. "I don't want to dump it on you. I only met you, what, a few days ago?"

"And we've been through enough to count for far more than that."

"Ku'Adsila . . ."

"Call me Adsila. You've earned it. The *Ku* is just an honorific." Adsila nudged him with her elbow. "Come on. We survived two gunfights together, took out that Flameshot bitch, and earned the help of my people. I don't know what you Auklenn folk say about closeness, but out here, warriors who fight side by side share a bond as strong as blood."

Lugh snorted. "I'm hardly a warrior."

"There's more than one way to fight." Adsila waited, and when Lugh kept stewing, she sighed and sat up, a small needle winking in her left hand. She poked her finger and touched Lugh's forehead, putting her other hand to his lips. "Stay still."

She's smearing blood on me. Lugh felt the slick warmth on his forehead and stifled an urge to pull away. When Adsila leaned back with that little smile of hers, he tried to look more curious than grossed out. "What was that about?"

"I marked you," she said matter-of-factly.

"You *what?*"

"It's like the opposite of a curse. Because you're worrying yourself to death." Adsila clasped his shoulder. "It will help protect you if I'm not around. I'm scared, too. I don't know what to expect tomorrow. Hell, I don't even know if this plan of ours will work. We might end up dead, or worse. But I go forward anyway, because I choose to." She paused, looking to the side, a blush showing on her ashen skin. "I've been working alone for so long I forgot how it felt to have someone else to rely on. I know we started off a little rough, but . . . I appreciate it, Lugh. I feel like you're one of the few people who understands."

"Understands what?"

"How it feels to be lost." Adsila sighed. Her hand sought out the delicate marigold. "We might be from different worlds, but we both come from the same place. You're afraid of the past, the things you think you did or didn't do. The mistakes." She grimaced, lines furrowing her pewter skin. "So am I. I'm an outlaw for a reason, Lugh. Not everyone I've hurt was like those goons at the saloon. I've . . . screwed up, out of anger. Did things because I felt I had no other option. But I was lost. Like walking blind in a sandstorm, and sand was all the anger and hate and grief I carried for years."

Lugh's throat tightened. Such vulnerable honesty from someone so strong . . . it tore at him like honeyed claws.

"I really was close to giving up," Adsila whispered. "I took over that saloon in Capstone so I could drink it all away with only wilting flowers for company. Hell, I didn't even care if people came gunning for me. But then you show up and . . . everything changed."

"Because of the stone."

"Stones don't have legs, idiot. Who carried it all the way out here at the risk of getting sand in his pants? Who saved my life?" Adsila flicked him on the arm, a beautiful quirk to her lips despite the pain in her eyes. "You did. Think what you want about yourself, city rat, I'll veto it every time. You're not a bad person. You just rolled some bad dice, like I did. And we'll set it all right together."

I can't do this anymore. Lugh felt his fears crumble like thawing ice. He was done. He would tell her about his deal with Vyzeryn, about Eirlys's curse, and about Sabia's captivity. If anyone would understand, it was her. Lugh looked into her big eyes, the words forming in his mind.

He was done with being a liar.

"Lugh?" Adsila cocked her head. "You okay?"

"More than okay."

Adsila arched an eyebrow. "Why do you look like you're about to take your turn at pouring your heart out?"

"Because I am." Lugh took a deep breath, wagering everything on the truth. Adsila had told him that he wasn't cut from the same cloth as his father. In that moment, more than anything else, he wanted to prove her right. "I—"

A muffled thump sounded in the distance, followed by a chorus of others like rolling thunder. Lugh stood up with a gasp and dropped to his knees when pain lanced through his shoulder. It felt as if someone had slid a hot pin right into the nerves. Adsila grabbed hold of him.

"Lugh? What's wrong? Lugh!"

A deafening blast slapped the tent with enough force to snap half of its supports, snuffing the candles and leaving Lugh and Adsila groping in the dark. More blasts shook the ground, punctuated by screams and gunfire, and this time the hot, acrid wind ripped the tent away. Lugh squinted through the spray of sand and fumes, unable to do anything but cough. Adsila crouched beside him, her eyes wide as she stared at his shoulder.

Eirlys's curse glowed bright gold, visible through every layer of his clothes. A palm-shaped blaze etched from innumerable jagged glyphs.

"Lugh, what is this?" When Lugh couldn't find his voice, Adsila hissed a string of curses and stood, yanking a revolver out of the folds of her dress. "Shit! Stay right there. Don't you bloody move!" She sprinted into the fiery night without waiting for a response.

Lugh stared after Adsila, but he couldn't see her through all the chaos. Burning tents, shattered wagons, the burst of artillery shells, the madness of scattering people and bodies in the sand. Lugh gripped at his shoulder. It burned like when Kal had found them, but far stronger.

Eirlys was here.

That bastard!

Lugh gasped against the pain and stood, stumbling in Adsila's direction. Every step made it worse, until he could barely walk. He walked anyway, closer to the man who could turn him to cinders with a mere flick of a finger. It didn't matter. He now knew why this was happening, just as he now knew how Eirlys's subordinates had found them before.

They can track me with the curse. There's no other explanation.

Another blast shook him to the core. Embers stung his face.

They used me.

The thought sent Lugh's stomach charging into his throat. He keeled over and retched violently. All of this was his fault—everything, coming apart in fire, because of him. How could he have been so blind? So naïve? Hadn't he been through enough of Auklenn's dregs to know better?

In Father's syndicate, they'd used the same brand of trick.

A useful idiot to sniff out the prime targets.

Lugh threw himself into the carnage, not knowing what else to do. He pulled wounded out of wreckage and tied off wounds with whatever scraps he could find. He helped people delirious from smoke inhalation get to the helping hands of Uluru warriors who ran back and forth, doing the same. Apologies would have poured from his lips had breathing not been so difficult. Everything blurred together—the fire, the smoke, the gunshots, the screams, the stench of death and burning, the pain in his shoulder—until he saw a flash in the haze, followed by a column of fire that rammed through a row of wagons like butter.

Lugh snarled. *There you are, Eirlys Fawkes!*

He gripped something smooth, and realized he'd picked up a bone-handled knife. Suicide, taking on a Flameshot with a blade, yet his legs moved forward anyway.

A cluster of figures materialized in front of him. Men and women in dusters, armed to the teeth. Eirlys's desperados. Gasmasks covered their faces, tubes running from their mouths to small packs on their chests. Firelight shone in their circular goggles, and when they spotted Lugh, they shouldered their rifles—only for a barrage of gunshots to rake them from the side, leaving them dead in the sand. Lugh squinted through the smoke, recognizing Tahk and three other Uluru warriors. Another desperado leapt through the smoke and rushed them from behind, brandishing a hatchet, but Tahk whirled and clotheslined the man with a thick arm, the amethysts in his bracers winking in the firelight. While his colleagues finished the attacker off, Tahk faced Lugh, grunting as he loaded blood-smeared bullets into his lever-action rifle.

"There you are. Hurt?"

Lugh shook his head, numb all over.

"Good. Come." Tahk gripped his shoulder. "We're retreating. We don't know what the hell we're up against."

I do. Lugh felt sicker than ever. He opened his mouth to speak, but then saw the civilian Uluru tagging along behind the warriors. Maya worked amongst them, going from person to person to check wounds she'd bound, her face calm yet firm. Blood stained her shirt and dress. Lugh pulled free of Tahk's grasp. "Get your people out of here. I'm going after them."

Tahk scowled. "You're not a warrior."

"No, I'm not. But there are other ways to fight." Lugh stepped away, even though his knees wobbled. "Don't worry about me."

For a moment Tahk looked ready to grab Lugh and carry him like a small dog. Instead, he sighed and pulled a spare revolver from his belt. "You'll need this, then. Once I get our people free, I'm coming for you, dead or alive."

Lugh stared at the battered gun. "Why?"

"Adsila's fond of you. I'd prefer not to piss her off."

Tahk waved to his men, sparing Lugh one last glance, and then escorted the others away from the fighting. Lugh went the opposite direction, toward the flashes of Eirlys's fire. His racing heart drummed in his ears. A scrawny youth with a six-shooter against a psychotic Flameshot? He'd have laughed had he not been too busy coughing. Another burst of fire lit the haze ahead. Lugh advanced, revolver aimed, and tripped over something that crunched and stank like burnt bacon. A body. He rolled, bumping into another immolated corpse. Bile charged up his throat. He retched again.

Eirlys stood twenty paces away, arms spread wide and spewing columns of fire into the camp. The air shimmered with heat and reeked of the sulfuric aura of his sorcery. Corpses littered the area, burnt black, and Eirlys stomped over them with his riding boots, crunching bones like eggshells, his black duster billowing like the vestments of death itself. He laughed as he raked fire through more wagons.

You monster. Lugh got to his knees and fired. The recoil twisted his wrist, but the bullet took Eirlys's hat off. Eirlys sidestepped and ducked, face twisted with anger, but when he saw Lugh, he showed a wide grin of tobacco-yellowed teeth.

"Look who it is. You've got some nerve, shooting at me."

Dammit! Lugh fired again, missing.

Eirlys summoned a coiling flame around his right arm, but instead of unleashing it, he cocked his head like a cat studying a mouse.

"Nah, too easy."

Eirlys drew his revolver in the blink of an eye and shot Lugh's gun right out of his hand. Lugh found himself on the ground, shrapnel wounds all along his forearm, pain throbbing like hell. He bit his tongue, trying not to scream as he pressed on the ragged wound.

"You're a brave idiot," Eirlys said, looming over him. "I didn't think you had it in you. But then again, I didn't think you'd go over to the savage's side either. Traitor." He spat a mouthful of tobacco juice at him, then drove his boot onto Lugh's sternum. "Funny story, Kal and her boys turned up dead outside of Capstone. Found your stupid derringer there, too. Know anything about that?"

Lugh could hardly breathe. "Fuck . . . you . . ."

"Choice words." Eirlys laughed, as did the dozen desperados who'd appeared behind him. He stepped back and lifted a finger. "I'll make it slow, for Kal's sake. Best way to roast a pig."

The curse on Lugh's shoulder jolted with an electric rush of magic. He stifled a cry, jaw set against his terror.

Nothing further happened.

Eirlys blinked. "What the hell?"

Something burned on Lugh's forehead. Adsila's mark. Crimson light webbed down his neck and competed with the curse's golden blaze, and then overwhelmed it, swallowing the latter whole and ripping it clean off his skin. Lugh gawked.

"Blood magic," Eirlys hissed. He channeled flames. "Still, won't be enough—"

A gunshot barked through the haze, and an ensemble of high-pitched whistles zipped overhead. Eirlys's men dropped one after another, blood spattering, and the enchanted bullet then rammed into Eirlys's chest with a loud *clang*. Eirlys reeled backwards, air escaping his lungs with a wet gasp, and slammed face-first into one of the burnt corpses. Lugh turned in time to see a flash of emerald eyes, and then Adsila was amidst the remainder of Eirlys's men, still in her segmented dress but now with her hat on, gun barking like a hellhound. Five more shots. More corpses in the sand. Adsila's machete flashed from its sheath. She cut through the last two desperados and then leapt at a recovering Eirlys, machete coming down in an overhanded swing.

Eirlys blocked the machete with his revolver. Sparks showered between them. Adsila attacked again, but her swings were wide, and her footing kept wavering. She overextended herself on a stab, and Eirlys grabbed her arm, yanked her forward, and then took her by the throat and choke-slammed her into the ground. She kicked and spat, but Eirlys ended that with two swift punches to her face, knocking her hat off and leaving her limp.

"Bloody witch." Eirlys spat a mouthful of blood and cinders, then felt at his chest, where the bullet had torn his shirt to reveal a steel plate beneath. He kicked Adsila in the ribs, then crouched down, fishing through her necklaces. "Now, where the hell are you . . ."

"No!" Lugh struggled to his feet—only for four blinding beams of light to lance through the smoke, followed by a rumbling groan of metal on metal. A towering shadow materialized. An armored machine with a wide maw that bled a constant shriek of gears, pistons, and metal. Intricate steel arms moved at its bow like an insect's mandibles. The machinery compacted the earth, laid gravel ballast, ties, and then projected steel rails from conveyors. Smaller mechanisms fastened the ties and drove iron spikes into place with hot flashes of sparks. Lugh stared, caught between awe and horror. The armored train made its own tracks and crept along at a walking pace.

That crazy drunk was right.

Lugh stumbled aside as a piece of track shot out and almost impaled him. The train was thrice as wide as any train he'd seen, bottom-heavy and supported by two rows of track. The six engines at the front were emblazoned with the blue insignia of the Auklenn Army: an eagle bearing saber and torch. Alongside the insignia was the train's name, *Andrasta*, scrawled in proud gold. Other cars carried materials for the track, and soot-stained workers swarmed about to keep the laying machine fed. The train lumbered past, the length behind it seemingly going on forever into the hellish night, car after car, thickly armored and bristling with artillery and machine guns.

With a great groan and a rumbling huff from its

engines, the train came to a halt. Eirlys muttered a curse and gave up searching Adsila. With a sour frown, he stepped aside and crossed his arms. The lead engine's side door opened, and Colonel Vyzeryn stepped calmly down the ramp, like a smug landlord come to collect overdue debts.

"Good evening, Lugh. You look confused."

Lugh glanced at Adsila, who was still unconscious, then at the burning camp. "P-Please . . ."

"Please what? Stop this?" Vyzeryn halted before him, right hand resting on her sword's hilt. "You seem to have forgotten whose side you're on. Just like your grandfather did. Yes, I know of his exploits. And I also know the look of a traitor. Still . . ." She nodded at the carnage. "You did well, leading me right to the heart of these elusive sand vipers."

Hearing it from her added another spike through Lugh's heart. "You used me."

"Of course I did. That is what people like you are for."

Fury burned up Lugh's throat, but motion to his left dashed it with frigid horror. Adsila was awake. Her swollen eyes drilled into him like glowing-hot rivets.

"L-Lugh . . . ? What is she . . . ?"

"Adsila, I—"

Vyzeryn interjected, waving dismissively. "This is exactly as it seems. Lugh was my rat, and he did exactly what rats do. Although it seems like he sought to exploit things to his carnal advantage as well." When Adsila stared in wide-eyed horror, Vyzeryn made an amused sound at the back of her throat. "Don't look so surprised. He lied to you. That's what he does. What he'll *always* do."

It wasn't true. Lugh wanted to scream that out, but Adsila shrieked before he could. She burst to her feet, machete in hand, eyes streaming tears as she swung for Lugh's neck. It all felt slow, timeless, as that blood-crusted metal flashed towards him. He didn't move. He knew he deserved it and far, far worse.

Sabia . . . I'm so sorry . . .

Steel sang. Vyzeryn slammed the flat of her fine sword into the back of Adsila's head. Adsila dropped like a ragdoll, machete stabbing the sand between Lugh's legs.

"Close call," Eirlys grunted.

"Predictable." Vyzeryn nudged Adsila over and used the tip of her sword to brush the hair from the other's bloodstained face. "Such a shame."

"Don't hurt her!" Lugh rasped.

"I don't intend to." Vyzeryn found the Godstone tied around Asila's neck and tore it free. Eirlys's expression deepened into a bitter scowl, but he quickly replaced it with his usual grim mask.

Lugh licked his lips. "Eirlys is going to stab you in the back."

Vyzeryn studied the Godstone. "And why would he do that?"

"He tried once already to take the Godstone for himself. He'll do it again."

"Boy's lying," Eirlys grunted.

"I'm not!" Lugh bared his teeth. "Kal, was it? That crazy bitch tried to cook me!"

Eirlys's expression cracked as he glanced at Vyzeryn. "Ma'am, he's trying to divide us."

"I know. Rest assured." Vyzeryn turned the Godstone

over a few more times before shaking her head at Lugh. "So that's the best ploy you have left? More lies? Eirlys is a bloodstained dog, to be sure, but he's not stupid enough to ruin our arrangement."

Lugh's weak hope evaporated as Eirlys's mouth curled into a satisfied grin.

Vyzeryn nodded to the soldiers streaming from the train. Two picked Adsila up, while another took a compass-like device from a hard case. Lugh hated that all he could do was watch, feeling his world, his *life*, crumble to ashes. The soldier sliced Adsila's palm and filled the device's flat, silver pan with her blood. Vyzeryn placed the Godstone at the center. The blood glowed crimson, and the stone migrated to the northeast corner of the device until it tapped against the pan's border. Vyzeryn smiled.

"Their goddess will not be able to hide in the Clysm anymore, not when we have the blood of one of her chosen. Lieutenant, take her aboard and get the compass to the navigators."

A grizzled lieutenant snapped a salute, and the soldiers carried Adsila's limp body towards the train. Lugh reached out to her, but Vyzeryn's sword blocked his path, its polished surface mirroring his bloodshot eyes.

"Know when to quit," Vyzeryn said. "I have not forgotten our deal. I am a woman of my word. I got the stone and the savage, and you are free to go. Your record is clean. Your sister is safe." When Lugh kept staring into the blade, she clicked her tongue. "Isn't this what you wanted? You have your victory. It's over."

It wasn't a victory. Not even close. Lugh felt like the train had run him over, splintering every rib and squeezing every drop of blood from his corrupted heart. He shook his head, eyes burning, stumbling over words, groping for anything other than the crushing anguish that made him want to die.

"There, there." Vyzeryn knelt and wiped his tears with a gloved hand. "You shouldn't cry when you get what you deserve. Did you think this could have ended any other way?"

Lugh glanced at the machete, still within reach. Vyzeryn's mouth quirked.

"Go on, try it. It's a good blade. Better yet, use that useless knack of yours." Vyzeryn gripped his chin and twisted his head upwards, forcing him to look into her icy blue eyes. "I hate liars. I hate traitors even more. And do you know what I hate more than both of them? Cowards."

Vyzeryn pushed Lugh into the sand, then wiped her hands on a blue handkerchief from her breast pocket. "Follow the tracks. They will take you back to Anchorshaw and your dear little sister." She pulled out a silver time-piece. "You have five minutes to get out of my sight."

Screams still echoed from the camp, but the shooting had ceased. Metal groaned as the *Andrasta's* armored artillery turrets lowered for close range. Lugh jumped to his feet, ignoring the rifles aimed at him as he found his voice. "Wait! Don't do this! You've already won. Let them go. You don't have to kill anyone else!"

Vyzeryn paused at the engine's ladder. "You seem to have mistaken my efficiency for mercy. Experience has taught me the folly of half measures."

A salvo roared from the artillery. The blast waves slammed Lugh onto his face, filling his mouth with sand

and ash. When he looked up again, Vyzeryn was leaning out the train engine's door, explosions flashing in her cold eyes.

"Well done, Lugh. You won Auklenn a war before it even began."

Chapter Thirteen

Dawn bled across the horizon by the time Lugh had another coherent thought. Sunlight warmed the hazy wasteland and banished the chills that had left him shivering with every step. Buzzards cried overhead. He blinked wearily, wondering where he was, how long he had been walking, how many dawns had passed. Not that it mattered. Adsila's hat was still clutched in his hands. He didn't remember picking it up, but he dared not let it go.

Keep walking, he told himself. *Just keep walking . . . away . . .*

Away from Adsila. From the man he could have been.

The thought made him sick, but he had nothing left to throw up. The hastily-laid tracks stretched out before him, two double bands of silver in an ocean of dirt and rocks and abandoned farmsteads. Sand and dried blood coated his tweed jacket, still reeking of death and burning. He looked at his feet and saw that his boots had fallen apart. His feet were cracked and bloody, and the wound in his forearm looked infected. He didn't feel any of it. Didn't care.

Sabia. Sabia. Sabia.

He thought it over and over. The only thing that kept him going. Yet every time he thought of that name, another echoed alongside it.

Adsila. Adsila. Adsila.

Lugh's throat tightened. What had he done?

Countless times he thought of falling down and not getting up, to let the buzzards eat his worthless corpse. He should have told Adsila the truth before it was too late. She could have taken the curse away and prevented Vyzeryn from finding them. There was no rationalizing his failure. Innocent people were dead. They'd welcomed him into their homes, shared their food with him, and now they were dead. Lugh couldn't get the images out of his mind. The heartbroken look on Adsila's face came every time he blinked, like sunlight burned into his retinas.

Colonel Vyzeryn was right. He was just a worthless liar.

And I always will be.

The thought stung deep in his chest . . . and he'd felt this way before. For a moment, with Adsila, he'd had hope. Like when he'd finished his prison sentence a few years ago, he had dared to hope that he could go straight. With Father hanged the year prior, and Vyzeryn gutting the remnants of the criminal underworld, there hadn't been anyone to pull him back into the business. He'd promised Mother that things would be different. But when he tried to find work, no one would take him. His criminal record. His father's blight. He might have served his sentence, but nothing could change that reputation. Lugh the Liar, son of the worst man in Auklenn. Cut from the same bloody cloth.

He still remembered the rainy day he'd sunk back into the criminal life.

And here he was again, sunk in that void.

Who was he to think he could be a hero? Stupid, foolish Lugh. A dressed-up pig was still a pig. A morally conflicted con artist was still a con artist.

What would Grandfather think? What would Mother think? Lugh felt their eyes on him from the heavens.

"I'm sorry," he said. "I'm—"

Something tripped him. He sprawled in the dirt and found himself staring down the length of a small train station. Anchorshaw? Already? How many days had passed? He didn't remember eating or drinking anything over that time. He ought to be dead from dehydration alone. His confused thoughts flaked away as he took in the view again. An unnatural quiet gripped what should have been a noisy supply depot. He got up, skin tingling as he squinted through the haze. This was definitely Anchorshaw, which was a small town, yet all Lugh saw was half the trainyard.

The rest was half buried in sand.

What happened? A sandstorm? Lugh walked faster— then yelped when a shriveled arm crunched beneath his feet.

Bodies.

There were bodies everywhere. Sticking out of the sand. Leaning against walls. Fallen in the streets. Tattered, worn, grit packing their mouths and eyes. Suffocated by relentless sand.

Sabia! Lugh whirled in the direction of the hotel. He stuffed Adsila's hat on his head and ran as fast as he could, tumbling over ruins, doing his best to avoid the bodies. His wounds numbed, their pain distant, but a new, crushing agony pressed on his chest. When he found the crumbling hotel amidst the haze, he burst inside, tripping over more bodies as he staggered for the stairs.

He shouldn't go up there. He knew what he'd find.

He went anyway, screaming as he threw his shoulder into the bedroom door. "Sabia!"

A cloud of dust greeted him. He waded through it, coughing, but the room was empty. Where was she? Lugh stumbled into the corridor, searched every room, every corpse, but found no signs of his sister—or Vyzeryn's people, for that matter. Just civilians. Strangers. Innocent people who had nothing to do with this war of gods and blood. The wind howled, and the hotel groaned, the air filling with a cascading crackle of snapping timbers. Lugh threw himself out the nearest window, landing hard on the sand and rolling until an overturned cart stopped him. The hotel collapsed behind him. Lugh remained on his back, staring at the rusty sky, heart swinging between relief and despair.

They took her.

Lugh grated his teeth.

Vyzeryn took Sabia with her. She must have.

And had left him to die on his own in the desert.

"That lying—!" Lugh screamed and drove his fist into the sand. The sound of his anguish echoed through the dead street and into the vast emptiness beyond. Vyzeryn had lied to him. Deceived him . . . Lugh sputtered a bitter laugh. *So this is how it feels.*

"Find enough trouble out here yet, lad? Nice hat by the way."

Lugh whirled to find the Drunk sitting on a sand mound, military coat covered with grit, his sunburned face split by a sardonic smirk. A whiskey bottle dangled from one hand.

"You again?" Lugh rubbed his eyes. "How are you—?"

"Alive? Don't know." The Drunk put the bottle to his lips, scowled, then overturned it. Sand poured from the bottle instead. "I suppose that's a curse we share. We keep surviving things we shouldn't. Even the wrath of outlaws and gods."

Lugh simmered. "Just leave me alone. You're not *alive*."

"Sticks and stones, city boy. I feel therefore I am." The Drunk tossed the bottle aside. "So, how's it going? The big question and all that. Did you find your answer?"

Lugh wasn't in the mood to speak to the Drunk, whoever or whatever the hell he was. Maybe it was all just in his head. More ghosts to keep the rest of his demons company. He stared at the sand as it whispered past his bloody feet.

"What's wrong, lad? Sand in your mouth?"

"Shut up."

"Ah, just bitterness, then. I understand." The Drunk fished through the sand and came up with another bottle, this one still sealed. He popped the cork and took a swig. "I came out here as a soldier thinking my enemy was a bunch of soulless barbarians. Imagine my surprise when I'm tasked with killing people who remind me of the good folk back home. That's war, I suppose."

"They didn't deserve this," Lugh whispered. "I brought so much suffering on them . . ."

"You wouldn't be the first to have that revelation." The Drunk stared off into the distance, twirling the bottle loosely by three fingers. "And I've had nothing but time to think about mine. It stews in your chest like a bog. Weighs you down, till all you want to do is go down with it." He took a long swig. "But see, that's a decision, lad. Not a verdict."

Sure as hell *felt* like a verdict rung into unavoidable fact by a judge's hammer. Lugh felt like death, but worse was all the death on his shoulders. The Drunk had asked him which man he'd let win, and the answer echoed along with every scream and corpse in his memories. "He won. The coward and the fool. Not the man Sabia needed. Not the man Adsila wanted. Just a terrible failure of a man. Gods . . . that's all I've ever been."

"But you're not satisfied with that man, are you?"

Lugh shook his head.

"Then why not give him the boot?"

"You think I haven't tried?" Lugh sputtered a laugh, and it hurt all the way into his aching heart. "I don't change. Try all I want, I always end up . . . *here.*"

The Drunk grunted and went to take another swig. He stopped short and, with a sigh, rested the bottle in the sand. "You can never try too many times. I wish someone was around to tell me that when I was your age. Before I ended up . . ." He gestured at nothing, everything. "Here."

Part of Lugh wanted to try again. *Burned* to try again. Yet what was left to try? The Drunk gave him a sad smile, and a gleam winked in his dark eyes.

"You're at a fork in the road, lad. Not the end of it. So, what will you do now?"

"What can I do?"

"You can make a choice. I was offered many. And every time I knew what my heart wanted. Problem was my orders were the opposite." The Drunk stood up, coat shedding a layer of sand. "Eventually your heart stops talking. Or your gut. Whatever the hell you want to call it. Opportunity only knocks for so long before moving to the next door."

Lugh swallowed hard. He knew what his heart wanted. But it was too late. He flinched when the Drunk flicked something in his direction, but he managed to catch it. A blue chip from the saloon he'd gambled in not too long ago.

"You're still in the game," the Drunk said. "Why not keep playing while rotten luck is still on your side?"

Lugh shuddered. "I don't know if I'm strong enough . . ."

"Strong enough?" The man turned away, seeming to meld with the wisps of blowing sand. "Lad, you don't know how strong you are until strong is the only option you got."

The blue chip felt heavier than it should have. Lugh turned it over, its smoothness stark against the gritty dust. When he looked up again, the Drunk was gone, only a bottle remaining upright in the whispering sand.

Still in the game? What cards did he even have left to play? The ache in his chest told him he wanted to try, odds be damned. Yet so much of him just wanted to keel over and be buried, grain by grain. It was the man he wanted to be versus all the shadows he'd been. And the choice . . . gods, if that's all he had left, the ability to choose, then so be it. He would choose the better man. That's what Grandfather would have done. That's what Mother would have wanted. That's what Adsila and Sabia needed.

Most of all, he realized it was what Lugh needed. More than anything.

To change.

Lugh forced himself to stand. The Drunk was right. For better or for worse, he couldn't die now.

He looked toward the Clysm. Suffocated bodies speckled the fields beyond Anchorshaw, having failed to escape. The wrecks of Auklenn airships lay on the outskirts, thin metal hulls reduced to tattered rings of steel ribs and armored plates. The Clysm towered above all. Mere days ago, it hadn't been visible from here. Now it dominated the horizon, firing off more tempests than before, great walls of wind and sand that blasted through the wastes far faster than any horse could gallop. If one of those offshoots had taken out Anchorshaw, what would the Clysm's full might do to Auklenn? Lugh shivered at the thought. How was he even alive? Surely the storm would have also hit him during his dazed walk here. Lugh touched his forehead. The faint warmth of Adsila's mark prickled his fingertips. It was still working, still protecting him.

Guilt flooded Lugh once again. Not only about Adsila, but for all the innocent people in the sands around him. Anchorshaw might have been a hard-bitten place, but most of the folk hadn't been bad. Lugh glanced at the ruined hotel. The owner had given them a reduced rate because of Sabia's condition, and he'd even provided meals free of charge. What was his name? How many of those bodies had been people just like that? Honest, hardworking folk with good hearts. Yet they were dead, bereft of second chances.

And here I am. Alive.

Lugh swallowed hard and whispered a silent apology to the dead. All he could do now was earn this second chance. He set his jaw and put the pieces together in his mind. Vyzeryn needed Adsila and the Godstone to navigate the Clysm. With that armored train of hers, she could do it. But why?

To kill a god, she'd said.

To kill Ehekahl.

Stopping the Clysm had to be one of Vyzeryn's goals. Yet she intended to do so by slaughtering the Uluru people and their goddess. A ruthless method while Lugh and Adsila had been on the verge of setting things right.

I can't let it happen like this. Lugh knew he'd likely die if he went back, but he didn't care. Something in him had already died, and what remained was different, maybe better than what he'd lost. Coward and fool, maybe, but during that moment with Adsila, he'd been so close to embracing courage and responsibility. As long as he still breathed, he could do so again.

You can never try too many times.

Lugh took off Adsila's hat and gently ran his thumb along the rim, flaking away a layer of grit. Perhaps people like him could change—at a steep price, but change nonetheless.

Lugh scavenged what he could from Anchorshaw, stuffing it into a leather rucksack. He also took the time to wash out his wounds with what alcohol he could find and wrap them with bandages. It burned like hell and probably wasn't enough for the wicked gash on his forearm, but it would have to suffice. Between that and the paltry amounts of water and canned food he dug up, Lugh felt a little less like a walking corpse being held together by protective sorcery. Halfway through the search, he came across the body of a lawman—the lower half that wasn't buried, at least. The man's stiff legs pointed at the sky, the spurs on his riding boots crusted with dirt.

Lugh stared at him for a long moment, then swallowed his nerves and started digging. First his belt, where a revolver was still holstered and more or less in working order. Then for his hat—he did his best not to stare at the corpse's sandblasted face, but the man's hat was gone. He whispered an apology as he donned Adsila's hat instead and stuffed his wild hair beneath it. The weight of the weapon on his belt made him queasy, as did the burden of a hat he had no right to wear, but he forced himself to feel both. It wasn't the power he'd feared. It was responsibility.

He was tired of running away from it.

Now how the hell did he catch up to Vyzeryn?

A pump trolley sat on one of the depot's tributary tracks, but when Lugh tried to work it, he found its mechanisms rusted solid. He checked the nearest airship for anything he could use but came up empty. The stables had no horses, either. Lugh tore through the stable's supplies, panic squeezing his chest. How long did he have? How much longer did Sabia and Adsila have? Was this it? Even after making the choice to follow, was he trapped here, unable to do anything?

The ground began to shake.

Lugh froze—and then heard a familiar sound echo through the dead town. Pumping steam pistons. Grating wheels on tracks. Voices shouting. Lugh ducked out of the stables and hid behind an overturned wagon, uncomfortably close to the lawman's corpse. A train surged through the haze and slowed to a halt on the tracks in the middle of the ruins. It was one of the regular supply runners, ten boxcars and an engine at each end, with ploughs to clear sand from the track. Not military, but the men and women who leapt out still sported lever-actions and revolvers. Judging by their curses and shouts, they were just as baffled by the destruction as he'd been.

A tingle crept down Lugh's spine as he eyed the front engine. He'd never stolen a train before. Damn, even the thought was ridiculous. But what better option did he have? And what was one more crime on his record?

"Hey, someone over there?" shouted one of the guards.

Shit! Lugh ducked behind the wagon. Too late. A trio of armed men were already approaching. He reached for his holster only to drop his hand. He wasn't a killer. These weren't bad people. The dead lawman's badge glinted within arm's reach, but Lugh knew he had no right to take it. Not the real one, anyway. Instead, he used a pebble and Doppeled a fake badge.

"Oi!" shouted the guard. "Come out! We won't hurt you. Just what the hell happened here?"

Lugh pulled Adsila's hat snug and took a deep breath. *Here goes.* He lurched out from behind the wagon, falling on his side and faking a ragged storm of coughs. The trio of men stopped ten paces away. He didn't give them time to speak. Bursting to his feet, he staggered up to them with the most desperate expression he could fake—and frankly, most of it was honest. "Thank the gods you're here! This . . . this place . . ."

The foremost guard, bald with thick muttonchops, slung his rifle and offered a hand. "Slow down, sir. You look like you've—"

"Been through hell," Lugh said. "Not over, either. I need your help!"

"What—?"

Lugh flashed the badge. "Please. I still have a job to do."

Muttonchop frowned. "You a lawman?"

"Of sorts. I bet I look rougher than a new-sheared sheep though."

"That's an understatement."

Lugh pocketed the badge before it could revert, then chanced his luck by pushing through the men and staggering towards the train. They didn't stop him, but they kept close behind, whispering to each other.

"So what the hell is going on here?" Muttonchop asked. "We got a telegram overnight, but it was bloody gibberish."

"Of course it was. Hard to send one when you're suffocating."

"The Clysm?" Muttonchop nodded towards the storm. "Couldn't see it last time I was here, but now it's bloody close. Do you think . . . ?"

"Yeah. It is. Must have been one of its offshoots. Blasted sand over everything, too fast for anyone to get out. And it's only getting worse." Lugh forced another ragged cough as he reached the engine's ladder and grabbed the lowest rung. "The towns beyond this point were hit worse. There are still people out there."

The guards muttered oaths. One made a sign to ward against evil.

"I need to speak with whoever is in charge of this train."

"That'll be Ester," Muttonchop said. "He's up top."

"Thank you."

Muttonchop grunted and barked orders for his men to search the town for survivors. Lugh sighed with relief and climbed up the ladder on the side of the train, wincing as his blistered feet touched the sun-heated metal. He'd need a new pair of boots. Should've taken the lawman's. Lugh heaved himself over the edge and ducked into the locomotive's engine room. Dials, pipes, and levers gleamed, the smell of burning coal and the hiss of steam a constant companion to the wind outside. A wiry youth missing half his teeth was busy shoveling coal into the burner. He barely paid Lugh a glance. The old man at the chief engineer's seat was even less alert. Bent over a map, spectacles perched on his long nose, Ester tugged at his gray beard as if it were a very persistent weed.

"Not possible," Ester muttered to himself. "It

shouldn't be possible. Not here. Not so fast. It was just a bloody myth . . ."

Lugh reached into his pocket and still felt the badge. It had definitely been five minutes. Not only had his knack changed in power, but it also lasted longer, and he still didn't know why. He took the badge out and tapped it on the wall, snapping the engineer out of his dazed muttering.

"What? Who . . . who are you? What are you—?"

"A lawman. Constable Pike. The guy with the muttonchops let me up."

"I . . . I see." Ester fixed his glasses and set the map aside. "You were here when it happened?"

Lugh didn't have to pretend to shiver. "I heard you muttering. You're right. The rumors were true. The Clysm isn't staying put. It's growing with a vengeance and ain't nothing standing in its way. We just didn't notice before because it was too far away and expanding too slowly. But now . . ." He nodded towards the window and the constant tinkling of sand. "Here it is, sped up like a racehorse on cocaine. Proof we were all fools."

Ester made a sign across his chest.

Someone shouted outside, but the details were lost on the wind. Tension coiled through Lugh's legs and chest. He didn't have time to waste.

"On that note, sir, I'd like to requisition this train engine. People are stranded further out, and I'll be damned if I let them die too."

Ester blinked. "Of course, officer. We'd be happy to help."

You'll die if you come. I'm doing this alone. Lugh

grappled for a convincing argument—only to hear boots and the click of weapons behind him. Muttonchop and his men loomed in the doorway, their scowls almost as intimidating as the barrels of their revolvers. Lugh reflexively backed against the wall, bumping into one of the crew's large water barrels. The youth kept shoveling coal as if nothing was happening.

Ester balked at the standoff. "What's the meaning of this?"

"Boy's a liar." Muttonchop showed a badge. "Found a lawman's corpse. Same badge and serial number. Must have had two and this rat stole one to pose as a dead man."

Lugh sputtered. "There must be some mistake."

"Yeah. Trying to dupe us. *That's* the mistake." Muttonchop took a step forward, only for the youth to bump into him as he shoveled coal from the tender to the firebox. "Oi, Mordecai, can you stop shoveling for just a few seconds?"

The youth kept going, humming a tune to himself.

"Lad's deaf and a simpleton," one of the other men grunted.

Muttonchop rolled his eyes. "Right, well. Anyway." He waited for Mordecai to pass again, then aimed his revolver at Lugh's head. "Keep your iron in its leather. This won't end well for you otherwise."

Great. Just great. Lugh felt the water barrel behind him with his left hand. Could he use this? He had more pebbles, but the barrel was large, and condensing was still dangerous . . . but his aversion had changed. He had to try. He waited until Mordecai bustled between them again, then Doppeled the barrel, turning it into a pebble that fell easily into his hand. He slumped against the wall with a gasp. The effort of the spell buzzed in his mind like an angry wasp, and his stomach clawed as if he'd not eaten in days. Yet just like with the machine gun and that large rock, the aversion didn't kill him, and this time the palpitations were minimal. *Damnation.* Condensing a whole water barrel to a fraction of its size? This was insane. Having guns aimed at his face undoubtedly helped. "I don't want any trouble."

"You found it," Muttonchop growled.

Ester showed his palms defensively. "How about everyone just calms down?"

"Man's right," Lugh said, gripping the pebble. "We can talk."

Muttonchop waited for Mordecai to pass, then advanced. He cocked his revolver. "I don't talk with lying cheats like—"

Lugh threw the pebble and reversed the Doppeling. With a flash of light, the pebble morphed into a full water barrel in midair, slamming into Muttonchop and throwing him back against his men and out over the low railing. He fired as he fell, the bullet screaming past Lugh's ear and cracking through the opposite window. Ester cried out and covered his head. Mordecai kept shoveling.

Damn, that actually worked. Lugh stifled a laugh and drew his revolver. "Ester, kindly start the train."

"But—"

"Don't make me ask unkindly!"

"Y-Yes sir." Ester worked the levers. The train lurched and moved forward.

Lugh kept the weapon aimed in Ester's general

direction. Shouts echoed outside, and a glance revealed Muttonchop and his men jogging alongside the train. Lugh aimed over the side and fired a few shots well over their heads, sending most of them scrambling for cover. Muttonchop kept running, face twisted with a furious snarl. A good man with a sense of duty. Lugh whispered an apology as he grabbed a second shovel, filled it with coal, and lobbed it off, hammering the man hard enough to make him lose his footing. Lugh waved, but a gunshot from further down the train sent him scrambling for cover.

Right. There were still people on the other cars. He ducked back into the engine room, tripping over Mordecai and his shovel full of coal in the process.

"I did what you asked," Ester said.

"Yes you did. Two more things. First, your boots."

Ester kicked them off without hesitation. "And?"

Lugh winced as he juggled shoving his blistered feet into the boots and keeping his revolver menacingly handy. "And I just need you to uncouple the cars for me."

"But they're shooting at us!"

"They're shooting at me, not you."

"I-I suppose you're right." Ester stood up, glanced at the door, then bolted. He grabbed Mordecai and leapt out into a passing sand drift.

Well, shit. Lugh glanced down the train again. A cluster of armed men and women were working their way along the rooftop.

A walkway ran along the outside of the coal tender, leading to the coupling, but the moment Lugh stepped onto it, he attracted a hail of bullets. He crawled over the rockslide of coal in the tender instead, then fired overtop, startling the gunmen and forcing them to flatten themselves against the roof. Praying it bought him enough time, Lugh pulled himself over the lip and climbed down the ladder rungs on the opposite side, descending between the tender and the first supply car.

Wind and sand buffeted him as he got closer to the ground. The coupling shifted and groaned, the oval couplers secured by a large cast-iron pin. He tapped into his knack. Once more it clicked in his mind. The magical strain from the water barrel still ached behind his forehead like a sinus infection. Hefting a hunk of coal in his other hand, Lugh touched the pin and Doppeled, turning it into coal—which instantly shattered under the tension and confines of the pin. The coupling failed, and the gap between the cars lengthened.

Just in time for one of the gunmen to peer over the roof and aim.

"Bugger off!" Lugh threw the real lump of coal, pegging the man in the face. Then he drew his revolver and fired the last shot, sparking it off the roof of the lagging car.

By the time the gunmen exposed themselves again, the gap was too great, and Lugh had slinked his way back to the engine room. The pop of distant gunshots and the useless pings of bullets against the train's hull brought an exhausted smile to Lugh's face.

He'd stolen a train, and for some masochistic reason, he'd enjoyed it.

Lugh looked through the window into the impending Clysm. "Hold on. I'm coming."

And then what? Take on Vyzeryn and her army?

I'll figure something out. Lugh touched his pocket and blinked. The badge was still there. Even though it had been well over five minutes, and even though he'd Doppeled twice afterwards, the fake badge was still there. He took it out and marveled. Could he Doppel more than one thing at a time now, then? How much of his knack did he not yet understand? Knacks weren't supposed to change. Neither was aversion. Yet so much had changed for the better. If only . . . Lugh's throat tightened. If only Mother had been given this chance. It was so unfair, but he couldn't wallow in it now.

Lugh took a deep breath, and then noticed the sheer multitude of dials, levers, pipes, and switches in the room. How did he control this thing? The train kept gathering speed. Lugh picked up a shovel and looked between the firebox and the coal bunker. *When in doubt . . .*

He shoveled coal, wincing against the hellish heat of the firebox.

Hopefully the locomotive didn't explode.

Chapter Fourteen

The locomotive didn't explode.

Instead, he couldn't figure out how to slow it down. Lugh held on for dear life as the train rattled like mad. Sand was creeping over the tracks, and the train's plough could only handle so much. Every impact felt like it would cause a derailing. It reminded Lugh of the time he'd stuffed himself into a barrel as a kid and had his friends roll him down a hill. Except *this* barrel weighed five-hundred tons and was going over a hundred miles per hour on hastily laid track. Too much coal? Had one of the bullets hit something important? Half of the gauges were in the red, and an ominous, high-pitched sound kept shrieking from deep in the locomotive's guts. Maybe it *would* blow up and scatter him across the wasteland in the goriest disappearing act in history. *Poof!*

Stop thinking like that! Lugh stumbled his way to the window. The world beyond was nothing but reddish haze. The Clysm had engulfed everything, its wind buffeting the train. Besides extra ammunition, Lugh had taken goggles and a breathing mask from the locomotive's equipment, but looking out at that devastating force, he doubted he'd make it on foot.

All the more reason to ensure the train didn't crash.

Lugh climbed into the driver's seat and scowled at the levers and switches. How the hell did anyone learn all these without putting labels on them? Everything had red handles, meaning everything was important, meaning he was in deep, deep shit.

"Come on," he muttered to himself. "Think of something!"

Think he did, and he arrived at the conclusion that he'd best start pulling levers. He started with the biggest one, whispering a prayer as he yanked it down. It snapped off. A great start. Lugh studied the remaining levers—and then noticed a shadow looming through the front window.

A mountainous sand drift covered the tracks.

Lugh blinked. "Oh—"

The impact blew his world to pieces. His forehead hit something, hard, but in the chaos of dust, shrieking metal, and howling wind, he couldn't tell what. Glass shattered. One moment he was looking at that imposing sand, the next he was flying through open air, followed by an impact that knocked the breath from his lungs. He lay on his back, gasping, staring into the rusty glow of the sandstorm sky. His body ached all over, and his forehead burned where Adsila's mark had once been—of its presence, only a painful absence remained. The traces of its power must have protected him during the crash—while it had ignored his lesser wounds, it seemed to have kept him from dying, just like during his trance-like walk to Anchorshaw. Lugh looked to the side. The train burned nearby, derailed and overturned halfway up the mound. A Lugh-sized hole gaped in one of its windows. He rolled onto his side, testing his limbs and sucking air through the sour, itchy mask. Cracks webbed his goggles. Probably webbed half his bones, too.

Get up.

The wind hammered Lugh like an angry mob.

Get up! You did not come this far to die now!

Screaming with the effort, Lugh stood at last. His head spun for a moment, but besides the dull throb of the still-healing wound in his thigh, his legs didn't hurt. Adsila's mark had granted him another undeserved mercy. Her hat lay nearby, caught on a twisted piece of metal debris. He donned it again, holding it down against the gusts as he trudged forward. The wind came from the same direction as the tracks went, and after the giant sand drift, the tracks appeared again, faint shadows of hope winking through oblivion.

How far did he have left to go? Every step against the wind strained his muscles, and with all the grit in the air, his mask's filter wouldn't last long.

Doesn't matter. There's only one way now. Forward. Play your hand, Lugh. If nothing else, you're good at that.

The trek seemed endless. Every laborious step was the same, the world a uniform chaos of sand and wind. No boulders or dead trees. Not even hills. Just a flat wasteland that refused to let him see more than ten feet. He glimpsed silhouettes in the swirls of sand, but they always vanished. Just his imagination. And yet, the longer he walked and the more he pushed against the Clysm's might, the more he felt like an immense *something* was watching him. Like he was swimming in an ocean with a monster just below him. Lugh knew he'd have felt tingles down his spine had the wind and sand not been biting through his coat at every moment. It wasn't all in his head. Something was there.

Keep walking, he told himself. *Don't stop. Just keep—*

Something caught his foot. He fell on his face, nearly breaking his mask. A slate-gray hand protruded from the sand. Charred and stiff, and joined by dozens of other mounds.

The Uluru camp.

A lump formed in Lugh's throat. Sand had pounded over the ruins, hiding the bodies, the burnt carriages and tents, but not the memories. He closed his eyes, tugging at his hair, but he couldn't block out their faces. Tahk. The children. Maya, who'd reminded him of Mother. The dance. The laughter. The kindness.

And he'd brought it all crashing down.

Lugh knew no one other than himself who had survived so many things while so many others deserving better didn't. Lugh, the lucky goddamned liar.

Mother had been honest to a fault and had died in squalor. He could never forget that moment, in that wretched-smelling room, holding Sabia's hand as they said their final goodbyes. All the regret he'd swallowed. All the times he'd looked in the mirror and wished Mother had been the one who'd lived, because surely she was the person Sabia needed.

Lugh tore his gaze from the corpse and glowered down the tracks. Sand tinkled against his cracked goggles like dirt landing on a coffin six feet below. He knew he was spiraling into self-loathing, but he couldn't just ignore it. With her final breaths, Mother had told him and Sabia three things: to take care of each other, to be strong, and that she loved them with all her heart. She'd loved *him*, despite everything. She'd always seen in him the man he could be, not the man he was.

Yes, he'd lived when many better folk had died. Yes, he'd been given so many mercies. Yes, he felt like he didn't deserve it. But there was only one thing he could do about it now.

I will earn it.

Or die trying.

The invisible presence grew like changing air pressure. His ears popped, and for a moment he caught more glimpses of something in the sands. Was it Ehekahl? Or the spirits of all the lives that had been lost in this troubled land? He pressed on, but his knees gave out. His mouth burned. Water. How long had it been since he'd had water? Again he rose. Again he felt his weakness press on him like a giant thumb. He collapsed by the tracks—and bumped into something else sticking from the sand.

The handle of a blade. Its amethyst-woven lanyard swayed in the wind.

Adsila's machete.

Lugh remembered the look on her face. The hurt. The rage. The sorrow. How she'd tried to kill him. How he'd almost wished she'd succeeded. Was this it? Was this the furthest he could go? A half-baked act of heroism? Lugh snarled and grabbed the handle of the blade, yanking it from the sand.

The presence grew. His ears popped again.

"I made a promise," Lugh hissed. "To Mother. To Grandfather. To Sabia. To Adsila . . ."

He stood, tensing the burning muscles in his thighs.

"I will return the stone. I will open your eyes, Ehekahl. I will prove . . ."

Prove what?

Looking at Adsila's blade, watching sand dance off its bloodstained edge, he knew.

"That my life is worth something . . . that *we* are still worth something . . . that we can change. I promise."

The wind eased a little, and through the reddish haze Lugh saw the silhouette again, there one moment, gone the next. A voice, whispered from all directions, gentle yet filled with a yearning that tore at his heart.

"Keep it."

His promise. Lugh set his jaw against every excuse and fear that bubbled from the back of his mind. He wouldn't let who he had been stop him from becoming who he had to be. As unfair as his hand had been in life, he could play it—and unlike in a game of Stacks, you could change your hand if you truly wished. He lacked a sheath for Adsila's blade, so he wrapped it in a piece of his tattered coat and tucked it into his belt.

Onwards through the Clysm. Time and time again, the train tracks disappeared beneath the drifts, but when they did, he touched the last visible stretch of track and tapped into his knack, bringing it just shy of Doppeling. The power always gave him a sense of the object he was touching, and when he touched the track, he sensed the length of metal and predicted the direction he'd have to go. After some trial and error, it worked. And the more he used his knack, the more he realized he could sense things more clearly than before. It was like using glasses after a lifetime of myopia.

However this change was happening, be it the Godstone's influence or something else, he'd use it as best he could.

Lugh pressed on through the chaos. He kept Sabia's face in his mind's eye, her smile, her laughter, and her innocence pulling him through every painful step. Adsila's face stormed his mind as well. Her reckless courage, strength, and perseverance pulled him up every time he stumbled. It could have been in his head, but it also felt like the wind kept at his back, pushing him forward with every gust like a multitude of encouraging hands.

And suddenly, after what felt like a lifetime, he heard the familiar groan of metal.

The outline of the *Andrasta* loomed in the haze, the lights along its hull glowing like streetlamps along a foggy quay. It crept along steadily, but far slower than before thanks to the intensifying storm.

I made it. Lugh stared in exhausted relief until he realized the armored train was disappearing again. Stifling a laugh, he trudged after it. He felt the presence out in the storm still, but behind him now, as if it couldn't follow him into this outlandish machine of blood and iron. Four massive engines composed the rearmost cars of the *Andrasta*. Sheltered walkways ran along the periphery of each, and the last one had an observation deck with machine gun emplacements—and a ladder two feet from the ground. Lugh ghosted toward the ladder. A rifle clicked on the deck, and a fog lantern blazed from the railing.

"Who goes there?" shouted a deep male voice.

Lugh jumped forward, rolling beneath the rear of the train and almost getting caught in a wheel. He grabbed hold of the frame and held on as the train inched forward, letting it drag him. The light shone behind him, outlining the track—and then a pair of booted feet slammed down a foot from his head. The soldier stepped a few meters out on the ground, aiming into the haze but always backpedaling in pace with the train.

"Don't go too far," a higher female voice called from above. "That wind out there will eat you alive."

"I swear I saw someone," the soldier growled. "That spindly little midge who could bathe in a shotgun barrel."

Gee, thanks. Lugh held his breath.

"That boy from before?" The other soldier scoffed. "He's dead. Colonel said as much. Bones on the track by now."

"Could be those savages."

"After we bloodied them? Unlikely. Besides, the sand is covering the tracks. They won't find us in this storm."

"I'm afraid *nobody* will find us out here. I keep seeing things. Shapes. This place is hell." The soldier swept his barrel left and right one last time, then lowered it, de-cocking the lever action. He snorted and hawked phlegm on the sand. "Cursed place. Can't wait till we're done with this bloody business."

"I second that," the other said. "But until it's over, we'd best keep our wits and not do anything stupid like jumping off a moving train in a sandstorm."

"All right, I get it. Bull's balls, you worry too much."

"Someone has to look out for your sorry ass."

"Thanks, Helga. Didn't feel sorry enough already."

The soldier trudged back to the ladder and grabbed hold. Lugh eyed his long army overcoat, and before it disappeared from view, he tapped it with his free hand. Just as fast, he channeled his knack into the pebble that had once been the badge, Doppeling an overcoat that would fit in much better amongst these soldiers. His tweed had given up its ghost, riddled with holes and filthier than a slum's gutters, and the overcoat would hide Adsila's machete far better. Lugh clambered to the side of the train, using the frame to reach the right side of the balcony. The two soldiers were both looking down the track, weapons cradled.

"So, you think it's true?" the woman asked. "What the Colonel said?"

"Course it is," the man growled. "She's taken us through hell and back before. You saw the destruction along the way. It's not natural. Sure as hell isn't staying put either. I don't know about you, but I'm not letting some vengeful deity eat my family. If the Colonel thinks we can kill it and stop the Clysm, we sure as hell can."

Lugh winced as he juggled hanging on to the railing while taking off his own tattered coat and keeping the Doppeled one pinched between his knees. The wind was blowing hard.

The woman pulled her hood tighter. "I just can't wait to get away from all this sand. I feel like I've got the crotch rot."

"Then cinch up your pants better," the man said.

"I'm using two belts and I've tucked the bottoms into my boots, in case you didn't notice. What else can I do?"

"Wear two pants?"

"Screw off."

All right. Lugh let his tweed jacket go. It fluttered down the tracks, twirling into the guards' view, drawing their eyes away from the door into the train.

"The hell?" The woman fumbled her rifle. "Someone up front lose their bloody coat?"

Lugh was already up, ducking through the well-oiled door and into the covered walkways. Deserted and dimly lit with electric lamps, the hall was all he could ask for. After dusting himself off, he threw on the military coat and carefully tucked Adsila's hat underneath. Then he briskly strode forward, head down to make himself look like a man hunched after a long, boring watch duty.

Voices spoke from the doorways leading into each engine. Engineers. But they were far too busy keeping the engines running or playing cards. Soon Lugh reached the first of the supply cars. Doors and lamps lined its corridor. How long was the train? How much time did he have before his disguise disappeared? He should have timed how long it took that badge to revert.

At least it was a train and not an airship. Everything was connected by a single corridor, car after car. Easy enough—as long as he didn't get caught.

Lugh battled an urge to run. Even harder to fight was the urge to glance around at everything. *Keep your head down. You're not curious. You're bored. You belong here.* Lugh traversed three cars without incident. Most were storage warehouses on wheels, packed with rivets, spare track, and crates upon crates of provisions and all manner of military hardware. Massive railway guns and artillery magazines came and went, the weaponry housed in armored casemates on the rooftops while the ordnance lay below, ranked and orderly. Lugh shuddered as he passed through, noting the empty spots on the shell racks—each for a shell that had been fired into the Uluru camp. He forced himself to keep track of his progress. *This should be car sixty.*

Next came bunking rooms crammed with snoring Auklenn soldiers, a forest of arms and legs dangling from berths. Lugh slipped through, thankful for how terribly thin he was. On his way, he swapped his Doppeled overcoat for a real one, just in case it reverted. Then he snagged leather gloves and a military cap, tucking Adsila's hat under his armpit as he donned the latter, then making sure her blade was still secure in his belt. The beginnings of a smirk tugged at his mouth.

He could do this all day.

And then he tripped.

Lugh hit the floor, hard.

The nearest soldier stopped snoring, muttering a curse as he stirred. A few seconds later, the snoring resumed. Lugh breathed out slowly and went to get up, only to find himself eyeing the nearest rifle. They were lined up against each bunk, paired with a soldier's boots. He hadn't kept track of how long the Doppeled badge had lasted, and the rules were probably all different now . . . He touched the rifle and a boot, Doppeling the boot into the former, then Doppeled the rifle into the other boot.

He couldn't help but smirk. *How many more can I*

Doppel? Is there a limit anymore?

Lugh licked his lips and did another, then three more. By the time he started feeling faint palpitations, he had Doppeled every rifle in the car, about a hundred. He went on to the next car and ghosted through, swapping hats for rifles, boots for hats, stifling giggles all the while. It was wholly inappropriate, but as he reached two-hundred spells, he could barely contain his excitement. The aversion ought to be turning his heart into a squirming eel. Whatever was changing him was still working, pushing the aversion so far back it barely bothered him. He would have laughed had he not been surrounded by sleeping enemies. Instead, he pushed his wonder to the back of his mind and carried on—Doppeling every rifle he found along the way. Depending on how long it lasted, these soldiers were in for a bit of fun.

Too bad Eirlys's goons didn't share the same area. He needed every advantage he could get.

After several more berths and another string of supply cars, Lugh found the prison. Heavy steel doors ran along one side of the corridor while windows went along the other side, sand tinkling against glass. Only one of the cells had guards: four heavily armed men geared with armored chest plates, full-face helmets, and state-of-the-art auto-loading rifles. They looked his way when he entered the car. Hesitation meant suicide. He walked straight toward them in a deflated manner, cap pulled down to veil his eyes as he contemplated the floor, like a man thoroughly fed up with his job. Hopefully these soldiers hadn't seen his face before.

"You're up early," one of the guards said. "Or were you

the night watch?"

"Night watch," Lugh said in a rasp. "I'll be shitting sand for a month."

The guards nodded as if the complaint were an expected password.

"Still," another guard said, "I'd take shitting sand over guarding the blood witch. Killed thirty of our guys back in that savage camp."

"Monster," the first muttered. "Should kill her before she tries something. But orders are orders."

The other three grunted in agreement.

Lugh kept his head down and paid them a curt nod in passing.

"Hey, bunks are back the other way," one of the guards said.

Lugh froze, then slapped his head and played it off with a tired laugh. "Sand's gotten into my brain, too. I swear this place will be the death of me."

The guards all grunted unanimously.

That was close. Tense as a spring, Lugh went back the way he came. He counted ten cell doors after the guarded one, then stepped into the gap between the two cars, which was rife with wind and sand despite its sheltering.

Adsila was in that cell. But how would he get in? A distraction? He looked at the edge of the junction. No ladder, but there was a ledge along the side due to differences in the layers of armor plating. Lugh took off the stolen cap and put Adsila's hat back on, making sure it was snug.

This will either work or get me killed.

His hands were still cracked and bloody, so he pulled

on the stolen gloves, bit his tongue against the pain as the fabric chafed his wounds, and edged onto the ledge, fingertips digging into the tiny grooves in the armor plating. Ten doors. Ten windows. He started forward.

Wind and sand ripped at him fiercely, but he held on, grating his teeth with every inch. It took him until halfway before he realized a flaw in his plan. When Adsila saw him, there was a high likelihood that she'd kill him on the spot.

And I'd deserve it, Lugh thought. *Whatever happens, I can't back down on account of myself. This isn't for me anymore. Risk and reward. Risk it. I have to play the hand.*

With that, Lugh took another deep breath and edged beneath the next square window. He caught a whiff of fragrance. Lavender. The same perfume he'd bought Sabia as a gift last month.

Sweat broke out all over his body. Sand glued to his exposed skin, but the howling wind ebbed into a steady but gentler rhythm, giving him a respite. He pulled himself up, slowly, craning his neck to see into the room. The window had no bars, unlike the others, and had a fine mesh screen that kept out the sand while letting in fresh air. Even in the wind and rumbling thunder, Lugh recognized the dull hum of a misting machine. The light of a small electric lamp beside the bed was just enough to recognize Sabia's golden curls. Tucked beneath a blue duvet, with two big pillows and her stuffed teddy bear, his sister looked at peace.

Seeing her there lifted a weight off Lugh's chest, letting loose a rush of emotions. Tears stung his eyes, and a sob tore up his throat, but he forced them back. He could climb in there, but then what? Take Sabia into the polluted air? Into danger? She was so close, yet impossibly far.

"I'm sorry about all this, Sabia," said a familiar voice.

Steel gleamed in the room's shadows. Lugh flinched and almost fell. Vyzeryn was seated on a metal stool by the far wall. Her elegant sword lay across her lap as she oiled it. As impeccable as ever, uniform perfect, face regal and calm. Yet Vyzeryn's voice sounded weary.

"I have always done what I thought was for the best," Vyzeryn murmured. "That does not mean it is right. Necessity is a burden, and the fate of nations is borne on the shoulders of those who are willing to sacrifice themselves for what must be done."

Sabia stirred. "What . . . ?"

Vyzeryn laughed, sounding almost like a normal person. "Oh, did I wake you? I'm sorry. I talk to myself sometimes. I was keeping an eye on you, making sure the misting machine does the trick. Did you sleep well? Is your breathing okay?"

"Yes." Sabia rubbed her eyes. "Is Lugh back yet?"

"He's still out working. But he'll be back."

Liar. You stole my sister and left me for dead. Lugh reached for the revolver in his pocket, but he stopped shy of drawing it. His other hand burned as it kept him balanced on the ledge. The wind picked up. He eased his head closer to the window, straining to hear.

"Are you lying?" Sabia asked.

"Lying?" Vyzeryn sighed as she wiped the blade with a white cloth. "What would an innocent girl like you know about liars?"

Sabia sat up, her pale face scrunched with

determination. "Not much. My brother never lies. He's nice."

Lugh grimaced.

"I see." Vyzeryn arched an eyebrow. "You love your brother very much."

"Of course I do! He's the best brother in the whole wide world!" Sabia made a show of ruffling her teddy. "He got me Tabby. See? And the perfume. And the dress. He was going to get me a mister just like that one, too!"

"A very good brother." Vyzeryn turned her blade over, brow furrowed. "You're lucky to have one. Mine . . . his name was Leo. Five years my senior, but a stick of a lad, more into books than sports. I always beat him at wrestling and ballgames, but he always knew how to help me pull up my grades. He had a talent for making me laugh. I . . . was never good at that."

Sabia flopped back into the pillows, hugging her teddy. "Where's he now?"

"Dead." Vyzeryn remained impassive as she wiped the blade again. "Died on the Frontier. The savages ambushed his caravan, killed him and everyone else. Just an accountant, a glorified bookkeeper, and they killed him." Her face twisted ever so slightly. "Didn't even leave a body. Just . . . dirt."

You think that excuses what you've done? What you're planning to do? Lugh drew the revolver and pulled himself up, slowly. Vyzeryn was right there, an easy shot, and as he gently pressed the revolver against the screen, his finger itched to do it. He was not a killer, sure, but all things had exceptions. He set his jaw against a flutter of dread and tried to keep Mother out of his mind.

"I'm sorry," Sabia whispered timidly. "Is that why you're so sad? Because he's gone?"

"It was a long time ago."

Lugh trembled. One shot. That's all it would take.

Sabia shifted towards Vyzeryn, putting her golden curls just shy of Lugh's aim. "You're trying to hide it, but you're sad."

"How do you know?"

"Because Lugh does it all the time. He always smiles for me, but he's sad. Did you know smiles can be happy or sad?"

"All too well."

"You're sad, too. But you're nice. Like Lugh."

Dammit. Lugh's aim wavered.

Vyzeryn laughed and shook her head. "You're right. But if anything, I'm angry, not sad." She inspected her blade, eyes shining in reflected lamplight. "Leo taught me to always be prepared. How you do one thing is how you do everything. I did not get this far by luck, and certainly not by a broken heart. Attention to detail. One detail can save your life. Wars are won in the minutiae."

"That's confusing," Sabia murmured.

"I digress." Vyzeryn stood up with a creak of her stool. She sheathed her blade with a flash of perfect steel. "I will leave you be. You need sleep, not the bitter ramblings of an old soldier. I'll be sure to have your breakfast brought soon. Ham and eggs and toast with jam. Sound good?"

Sabia nodded and burrowed back into her sheets.

Now! The thought boomed in Lugh's mind, yet instead of pulling the trigger, he lowered the gun and breathed a strangled sigh.

"Everything will be okay. I promise." Vyzeryn closed the door and locked it behind her.

Move on. You need to help Adsila first. Yet Lugh took a minute to watch Sabia until he was certain she would fall into an easy slumber despite the wind. Then he tore his gaze away and began to move.

"Is someone there?" Sabia whispered.

Lugh froze. Had she glimpsed his shadow? He ached to respond, to hold her in his arms, to be the brother she needed.

Instead, he kept going, through the biting sand, through layers of shame and loathing. He almost didn't have the strength to reach Adsila's cell, and when he gripped the corroded metal bars, he wondered again if this was a bad idea. Nonetheless, it was all he had left. He pulled himself up and looked into the darkness. He cleared his throat.

"Adsila?"

Only the wind responded. Wind, and the pulse drumming in his ears.

"Adsila?" he said, louder. "It's . . . It's me. Lugh."

Someone stirred in the darkness. A rattling breath. A sniff. Clinking chains. Lugh eyed the bars. Solid iron, each bar a separate fixture and bolted fast. But he had a pocket full of rocks. He thumbed one in his free hand. Touching the first bar, he tapped into his knack and welcomed the rush of tingles, Doppeling the section of steel. The bar flashed out of existence, leaving a pebble in his hand and the bolts behind. Lugh threw the Doppeled pebble away and reverted it, moving to the next bar, all while teetering on the ledge. Soon the window was clear. Narrow, but enough to squeeze through. Breathing out as much air as he could, he pulled himself in headfirst.

The stench of vomit hit him like a fist.

Lugh froze, only halfway through. Darkness gripped the chamber. He couldn't even see the floor, and the only sounds were the steady rhythm of the train and the howling wind. Was he too late? Panic squeezed his chest, but he breathed through it, trying not to gag from the eye-watering smell, and wiggled enough of his body through to twist around and grab the windowsill. He lowered himself down until his toes met the floor.

"Adsila?" As his vision adjusted, Lugh almost wished he hadn't found her. Shackled against the wall by her wrists, ankles, and neck, she looked like a corpse, limp and only upright thanks to her chains. Lugh shuffled closer. Her breaths were so shallow she seemed dead, but they were there. "Hold on, I'll get you out."

Adsila remained silent and still, her eyes closed. Her ashen hair hung over her face, tangled and matted with blood, half of her amethyst braids cut off. What remained of her dress was tattered and bloodstained. Most of her necklaces were missing, but a few remained. The dried marigold, bloody and holed with cigarette burns, remained as some kind of sick joke. She'd looked like beauty itself when she'd danced. Now she looked like the squalor and death Lugh had seen in Auklenn's worst slums. A lump formed in his throat.

I did this.

Lugh Doppeled her chains, breaking the links. He saved the arms for last, breaking one then supporting her shoulder and ready to catch her as he Doppeled the last—

Adsila's right hand grabbed his throat, and her full weight slammed down on top of him, pinning him against the floor and knocking his head so hard he saw a maddening chaos of stars. Fingernails bit his skin like daggers, but Adsila's eyes were far worse—wide and bloodshot, with a bruised, tear-streaked face that warred violently between emotions.

"You liar." Adsila added a second hand around his throat. Her breath reeked of vomit. "You. Fucking. *Liar!*"

Lugh gagged and sputtered. He kicked, tried to pry her hands away, but her crushing grip doubled, compressing his airway and carotid arteries. Pressure mounted behind his eyes, and darkness tugged at the corners of his vision. Adsila's bloodied face showed no hints of mercy.

She really was going to kill him.

Chapter Fifteen

I'm going to die.

Panic ripped through Lugh's chest. Die here? Now? After everything he'd made it through? To hell with that! Not while Sabia lived. Lugh desperately groped for ways to reason with Adsila, but his thoughts quickly muddled, and darkness crept further over his vision. Gods, he couldn't even speak. Using the last of his guttering strength, he drew the revolver and jammed it in Adsila's face, grip toward her.

Adsila's eyes flicked to the weapon. Her grip eased a fraction.

Lugh sucked in precious air. "Listen! I know I don't deserve your forgiveness. There's not a damn thing I can do to make up any of it. But if you're going to kill me, at least do me the courtesy of a bullet. I didn't come all this way to be strangled by someone like you!"

"Someone like me?" Adsila whispered, almost inaudible.

"Someone I want to save." Lugh's voice came out like sandpaper. Gods, his throat burned. "I know you hate me. I know what I did was stupid and wrong. I can't make things right, but I want to at least try to keep them from getting worse. Please . . . let me at least *try*."

Adsila's mouth twisted, but the fury in her eyes ebbed. A tear ran down her face, and her grip loosened completely. "I trusted you. Hell, I even *liked* you."

"I know."

"Then why should I trust you this time?"

"Because I'm giving you a bloody gun?"

"Is it even real, or just a fake? I should just kill you, take the gun, and finish this myself."

"Go ahead." Lugh held her fiery gaze. "But two is better odds than one."

Adsila's lips curled. She took the gun and jammed its barrel under his jaw. "Lugh the good for nothing Liar. You earned that name well. Is that all this is? Another lie for your own gain? Do you even *have* a sister? Or are people's hearts just strings for you to pull?"

"I wasn't lying about her!"

Click! Adsila cocked the revolver. "How the hell am I supposed to know that?!"

Lugh glanced at the door, hoping the thick metal was insulating their argument from the guards. He tapped the machete sticking from his belt. "Test my blood. Just like before."

Adsila winced. "I did that. And it was wrong."

"You just asked the wrong questions."

"How about I empty all but one bullet and see how lucky you really are?"

"Playing roulette won't get you the truth. My luck is shit." Lugh slowly drew the machete an inch, then slashed the side of his left hand. Blood slicked his palm.

Cursing under his breath, he shoved his bleeding hand towards Adsila. She shrank back, but kept the revolver aimed. "Take it. Prove me a liar, and I will gladly eat a bullet."

"You're asking me to believe in something after you shattered my faith in it?"

"Was your faith so weak that a city rat could destroy it?"

Adsila grimaced, then grabbed his palm, letting the blood pool in her free hand. With a shaky voice, she whispered incantations. The blood became like glass, mirroring her eyes. She took a long, slow breath. "All right, pisshead, lie to me first. You're a good person with no criminal record and parents who both loved you."

Damnation. Lugh sighed. "Yes."

The blood rippled, patterning around the edges like frost.

"Figures," Adsila muttered. "You came here to unite the stones. You said it was to save your sister. Is that true?"

"Yes."

This time, the blood shifted inwards, condensing on itself with small, curling patterns. Truth. Adsila pursed her lips.

"Did you know you'd lead those outlanders to us?"

"No. They put a curse on me. I thought it was just a kill switch. I didn't think it could track me . . . but I was also afraid to tell you about it."

Truth. Adsila glared. "Why?"

"Because they have my sister as collateral. She's here, on this train. Five doors down."

Truth again. A fraction of the malice drained from

Adsila's face, but the revolver never wavered. "And so you found me at that saloon, pretending to want to help me, when in truth you were working to please that imperious bitch."

Lugh sighed. "Yes. I had no choice."

"We always have a choice. Just not good ones." Adsila leaned closer. "And what about now? What do you want? To save your sister?"

"Yes. And . . ." Lugh paused, minding his words. "You, your people—"

"What does a pasty cheat like you even know about me and my people?!"

"I know that you're on the right side of things."

"Anyone can see that."

"I want to be on that side, too. Like my grandfather was." Lugh leaned forward, pressing his forehead against the barrel, never taking his eyes from Adsila's. "Yeah, I'm a con artist. And you're an outlaw. But no one's just a single label. We both have something to protect."

Adsila's face twitched. Her finger rubbed against the gun's trigger guard. Sand, carried through the window on the moaning breeze, danced between them like curious insects. The blood resonated truth. She clenched her teeth as if she wished it hadn't.

"I want to help you," Lugh said. "I hate myself for what I did. I want to make it right."

The truth in the blood added another crack in Adsila's hateful mask.

"Vyzeryn has the stone," Lugh said. "She's out for revenge against your people and your goddess. And the Clysm is spreading faster than ever."

"You think you can stop all of that?" Adsila's voice sounded hollow.

"Yes." Lugh leaned closer, slowly lifting his unwounded hand in a promise. "I made your grandfather a promise, and I broke it in a heartbeat. I should have told you about the curse. It was my fault. I'm not asking for your forgiveness. But if I have one more chance, I will keep my promise to him."

Truth.

"I've lost everything," Adsila said. "What the hell can you promise me now?"

Lugh slowly put his hand on the gun, then her hand. "That all isn't lost. And that I'll see this through with you to the end."

A tear dripped from Adsila's chin and rippled the enchanted blood as it resonated truth. Her raw voice cracked with desperation. "Will you betray me again?"

"Adsila . . ." Lugh slowly took off his hat with his other hand and placed it on her head. "I will never betray you again."

A final truth swirled through the blood. Adsila's face warred between emotions, but at last, she let him lower her hand and the gun. She touched the rim of her hat and tugged it down over her eyes. "Stupid city rat."

"I know."

"I should have left your ass tied up in that barn."

"I should have done a lot of things, too." Lugh offered the machete. "So how about we do things right from this point onward?"

Something crossed Adsila's face, there and gone like a ripple of lightning on the horizon. She wiped her eyes with her forearm and brushed her hand off with her filthy rags. In an instant, her stricken expression solidified into vicious sternness. She opened the revolver's cylinder and dumped out the bullets, then smeared each with blood from her many wounds.

"Keep the blade," she said. "And get in the corner before I lose my patience."

"Why—?"

Adsila grabbed Lugh by the left side of his neck and strongarmed him into the corner. She loaded the bullets and flipped her revolver shut, spun its cylinder, cocked and de-cocked the weapon, and nodded grimly. Then she grabbed a length of chain hanging from the wall and wrapped it around her throat, putting enough weight into it to begin choking. She hid her gun behind her back and started kicking the door.

Lugh gasped. That was her plan?

Adsila kicked harder.

The door flew open. Three guards aimed their rifles in.

"Shit!" one said. "She's trying to strangle herself!"

"Stop her!" another screamed. "The Colonel needs her alive!"

They lowered their weapons—and Adsila whipped out hers. The gunshot was deafening in the small space, and with a zigzag of red, the bullet pinged around the walls, killing the guards. Adsila leapt, tackling the fourth guard as he stepped in. She shot him point-blank in the neck and used his falling corpse as a springboard into the corridor. More gunshots and screams followed, and then the droning of the train's raid sirens. Lugh huddled in the corner, hugging the machete to his chest.

So much for doing things quietly.

Lugh forced himself to get up, but he shivered at the sight of the corpses. These were his countrymen, people who had mothers and fathers and sisters and brothers. It sickened him. This war. This madness. It had to end. He had to help make that happen. Using the last stone he had in his pocket, he Doppeled one of the automatic rifles, turning it into a pebble. Easy, compared to condensing that water barrel. He hid it up his sleeve and went for the exit, machete gripped tight.

Get to Sabia's cell. Get the stone, and then . . . Lugh didn't know, but they would figure it out.

The corridor was a bloodbath. Adsila stood midway down, bloodstained and surrounded by corpses, a revolver in each hand. She aimed at him, eyes wild. It took her visible effort to lower the guns.

"Are you hurt?" Lugh asked.

"Nothing I didn't have already." Adsila wiped blood spatter off her face with her forearm. Then she wrestled the coat off one of the smaller corpses to cover herself up. "So, what happens next? You have a plan?"

Of sorts. Lugh opened his mouth—only for a column of fire to erupt from the far end of the train car. Adsila ducked beneath. Lugh fell and knocked his chin against a door handle. Heat and sulfuric stench throttled him, turning every breath into hell. Windows and electric lamps exploded. Glass and embers rained amidst a blinding gust of acrid smoke. Lugh tried to roll into the prison cell, but a boot stomped on his arm and twisted until he let go of the machete. Cold steel pricked his throat.

"Color me impressed," Vyzeryn said.

The smoke thinned via the shattered windows. Moaning wind and whispering sand took its place. Vyzeryn towered over Lugh, and Eirlys lurked at the other side, sorcerous flames coiled around his arms, an army of desperados at his back. Adsila was on her knees, coughing from the smoke, one gun aimed in each direction. Vyzeryn clicked her tongue.

"Go on, blood witch. Pull the trigger and he dies."

Adsila bared her teeth. "You think I care?"

Lugh had expected her to say that, yet it still hurt.

Vyzeryn chuckled. "No honor amongst thieves. Still . . ." She grabbed Lugh by the collar and pulled him to his feet, using him as a shield. "I think you're lying."

Adsila's eyes darted one way and the next. "Do you have any idea what you're doing to this world?"

"Ridding it of a vengeful deity and her backward people."

"My people don't deserve this!"

"Oh yes they do." Vyzeryn's mouth quirked. "I'm doing the world a favor."

Adsila screamed and aimed both revolvers at Vyzeryn, but Eirlys and his men aimed just as fast. Adsila leapt out the window instead, disappearing into the blowing sand as she fired her last bullet. The shot ricocheted off the walls, screamed past Lugh's ear, and pinged off the flat of Vyzeryn's blade, ending up in the ceiling. Meanwhile, the desperados, shouting in rage and frustration, unleashed a storm of lead out the window.

"Hold your fire!" Vyzeryn shouted. By now her own troops were pouring in from the berths, armed to the teeth.

Eirlys lit a cigarette with his knack. "Shouldn't we go after her?"

"There's no surviving out there." Vyzeryn touched the side of Lugh's neck, as if feeling for something, then let go. She studied him, her pale face lined with a mixture of curiosity and disdain. "Only the savages seem to survive in the Clysm. Makes me wonder. How did you get this far?"

Lugh's mind reeled from what had just happened. Between catching his breath and keeping his legs from wobbling, he almost didn't hear Vyzeryn's question, but he forced himself to face her. She'd damn-well not have the satisfaction of his silence. "How am I still alive? Maybe because I'm not trying to destroy everything."

"Their mad goddess is the one who is trying to do that."

"Fighting fire with fire isn't going to stop this."

"Oh? And what way have *you*, a conman and a coward, discovered?"

Lugh held back a few choice words. "Make peace. Return the Godstone. Show Ehekahl that there's still hope in this world. In us."

Vyzeryn blinked—and then barked out a laugh so hard she almost dropped her blade. She wiped her eyes and shook her head, then grabbed Lugh by the collar and slammed him against the wall, nose to nose. Her breath reeked of garlic. "So she's wormed her way into that porous brain of yours. Spouting such sappy drivel. You think I'm a fool? There is no negotiating with mad gods. The only way is to put them down. And I will. I know how to shatter her connection with this world once and for all. As for you . . . you should have died in the desert. Your sister would be better off. You know why I tricked you? Because you don't deserve her. All you've ever done is drag her along on your multitude of failures. I'll give her everything. A vetted foster family that will love her. An education. A future. With me, she has a chance. With you she has *nothing*." She drew back a little and softened her tone. "I promised she would be safe. That includes keeping her safe from *you*."

The words slid between Lugh's ribs like a stiletto. He choked out his reply. "You know how it feels to lose a brother, yet you'd do the same to her?"

"Ah . . ." Vyzeryn pressed her blade under Lugh's chin. "So you eavesdropped on that. I had a feeling. But she doesn't know you're here, and she never—"

A door creaked, and a little voice whispered. "Lugh?"

Vyzeryn flinched. Lugh did, too. The door five down from Adsila's was open, its heavy lock on the floor, smoldering from Eirlys's earlier attack. Sabia peeked through, blue eyes owl wide, expression caught between hope and terror. She didn't even seem to notice the bodies or the bad air moaning through the shattered windows.

"Sabia." Vyzeryn softened her tone and hid her sword behind her back. "You should be asleep, it's—"

"Let my brother go," Sabia said.

"We were just having a chat."

"I saw your sword. I'm not stupid."

Vyzeryn faked a laugh. "That was just—"

"Let him go!" Sabia threw the door open harder than seemed possible. "Now!"

Vyzeryn's grip weakened. Lugh yanked free and put

himself between her and Sabia. The moment he felt Sabia's hand grip his, everything became crystal clear, the gunfire in his mind settling into a peaceful focus. "I won't let you take her."

"Unfortunate . . ." Vyzeryn regained her composure. Calmly, she sheathed her blade and lifted her chin. "You don't have the power to make such claims, boy."

Lugh knew it painfully well. He glanced at the machete on the floor but abandoned the idea. Even with the Doppeled rifle hidden in his pocket, it would be suicide to fight. Why then did he feel so confident? So strong? Gods, it was Sabia. With her hand in his, he felt invincible, and while that couldn't be further from the truth, he silently thanked her. Suddenly all the hell he'd been through seemed a pittance. And compared to the hell of losing her, it was. He squeezed her little hand, resolving to play this right.

A reckless idea had festered at the back of his mind ever since Eirlys had entered the car. Time to be a little reckless, but first . . . Lugh exhaled and let his shoulders slump.

"I'll come quietly," he said. "Just give me a few minutes. For her sake, not mine."

The wind howled through the broken windows. Sabia coughed and covered her mouth.

"I'll give you two. After that, my men will escort you." Vyzeryn nodded to her guards, then, with a sigh, stormed off.

Lugh let out the breath he'd been holding and knelt before Sabia. Her fearful expression tempted a grimace, but he forced a smile instead. She needed her big brother.

"It's all right," he said.

"They're not really our friends, are they? They're bad people."

"Of sorts. But it's okay. I'm here. We'll get out of this. Haven't we always?" When Sabia managed a smile, Lugh's heart twisted. He hugged her tightly. "That was so brave of you, standing up to her. You're so strong."

Sabia nodded, her whimpered response lost in the folds of his coat.

Lugh glanced over Sabia's shoulder, spying Eirlys and his men at the far end of the car. He caught Eirlys's eye and mouthed two words: let's deal. Then he gave Sabia every shred of his attention. He ran his fingers through her curls, remembering all the mornings he'd helped her comb it, how it would dance when she'd been healthy enough to run. "I'll find a way. And for you . . . I won't give up until you can outrun me any day of the week."

"Promise?"

Lugh swallowed hard. "Promise."

They gently butted their foreheads together, like they always used to. Sabia giggled, then broke into another coughing fit. Her sickly pallor looked even worse in the gloom. Lugh guided her back to her bed, tucked her in, made sure the misting machine was still working . . . and found himself staring at the metal stool. He'd give so much to sit at her side, to hum a lullaby until her breathing settled into the rhythm of sleep, but he had to face the music of his own devising.

"Sleep well," he whispered, caressing Sabia's face one last time.

"I love you," Sabia mumbled, already dozing.

"I love you too. More than anything." Lugh closed the door behind him, took a deep breath, and then nodded to the waiting soldiers. He sensed his Doppeling on some of their shoes and weapons, but now wasn't the time to revert it. One of the soldiers, an officer with an impressive mustache, went to restrain him. Another kept her rifle aimed at him—only for that rifle to disappear in a white flash. The soldier blinked, finding herself wielding a boot instead. Lugh's stomach dropped into his toes.

Oh shit.

And then everything reverted at once.

Rifles turned into boots and hats, and more violently, boots into rifles. The weapons flashed into existence, throwing the soldiers' balance, dropping half of them to the floor in a chaos of limbs and shouts. A few had their rifles revert vertically, ramming between their legs. One rifle, somehow ejected by its reversion, flew past Lugh and clobbered the officer who'd been trying to restrain him. It wasn't the opportunity he'd been counting on, but he had to use it. Lugh turned toward the exit, only to face a firing squad of soldiers whose weapons he hadn't Doppeled.

He raised his hands and offered a smile. "Sorry, gents. Bad timing, that."

The mustached officer, bleeding from the nose and sputtering curses, burst to his feet and brandished his real rifle this time. He drove the buttstock at Lugh's face—only for Eirlys, whistling an old Auklenn tune, to grab his arm.

"That'll do, soldier."

"Don't interfere, outlaw," the officer growled.

"*Vigilante,* my good man. There's a difference." Eirlys

gave a friendly smile. "Can't be ruining the lad's pretty face just yet, can we? Prisoners need teeth to talk, and we both know how much the Colonel dislikes wasted assets." He offered the man a cigarette. The officer sighed and took it, and Eirlys lit it with his knack. "I'll take the little shit-licker to the front. Better under my watch anyway, with all his tricks. Never know what he's hiding."

"Just get him out of my sight." The officer nodded to the others, and together they went to help with the wounded.

Eirlys grabbed Lugh's elbow. "Well then, Lugh-eee-boy. Chop, chop. Let's not keep the Colonel waiting." He guided him down the hallway, his long stride challenging Lugh not to fall on his face. When they were out of earshot from Vyzeryn's men, he hissed under his breath. "Nifty little trick you pulled there. And stupid."

Agreed. "I aim to please."

"Thought you had aversion. You been holding out on us all this time?"

"They don't call me Lugh the Liar for nothing."

Eirlys grunted. "Takes a particular brand of desperation to play this game."

Lugh put his hands in his pockets. "So you got my message?"

"Yeah." Eirlys waited until they were in the next supply car, then stopped. They were alone in the long corridor. "Came at a convenient time, seeing as the Colonel's men are busy cleaning up their own with buckets." He tapped the wall beside them, and ever so faintly, the air shimmered with residual sorcery. "You see, when you didn't die like you were supposed to, I was very disappointed. And when you showed up here and made a bloody mess of everything, I was very, very disappointed. You're like a cockroach. But since you seem to have a particular . . . effect on the good Colonel, I think I'll put you to better use. Gears are turning, and I could use another gear."

The supply car's far door opened. Dozens more of Eirlys's desperados sauntered in, armed to the teeth, kerchiefs pulled up over their noses. One gave Eirlys a nod, to which the Flameshot let out a low, serrated chuckle.

Great. What the hell had Lugh just walked into? He'd intended to work his way into Eirlys's interest to exploit the divide between him and Vyzeryn, but it looked like Eirlys was already making a move. Would it be one he could take advantage of? Or had he just served himself up on Death's dinner plate?

Only one way to find out. Lugh feigned skepticism. "So, I'm your pawn now?"

"Call it a partnership."

Lugh would have laughed had Eirlys not been a murderous psychopath. *Make him greedy. Stuff his mind with bullshit.* "You've been dealing behind Vyzeryn's back since the start."

"Old news. Your point?"

"Only a fool wouldn't. The only thing that woman wants is money, guns, and a political carte blanche to wage war. You're after bigger things."

"Godly things. Do you know why?" Eirlys rammed Lugh against the wall, knocking his breath away. He yanked the pebble from Lugh's pocket, and with his other hand sparked a twisting flame. "Revert it, kindly, or we'll see how long you can breathe with charred lungs."

Lugh didn't have a choice. He tapped into his knack, flashing the pebble back into the auto-loading rifle. Eirlys whistled and handed it off to one of his men.

"Impressive," Eirlys said at last. "I don't appreciate it when people lie to me, boy."

"W-What do you mean?"

"Don't play with me." Eirlys grinned like a jackal. "We both know you couldn't pull off that kind of magic back in Anchorshaw. I read the reports. You ought to be dead meat after that stunt. No, your knack has gotten stronger." He broadened the flame on his fingertip. "Or do you disagree?"

Lugh swallowed hard and shook his head.

"Didn't think so," Eirlys said. "Now, correct me if I'm wrong, but a nobody's shitty knack getting more potent out of the blue doesn't just happen, does it? Something changed you. Something you've only had your hands on a short while."

The Godstone. Lugh's suspicion became a certainty. It also gave him ammunition. "The Godstone. You think that did it?"

"I suspected. Now I know for certain." Eirlys fanned his fingers. The flame wove between them like a vine. "I've been around it for a moment here and there, and I've noticed some improvements as well. Enough to say it's the genuine article."

The thought of a man like Eirlys getting even more powerful made Lugh's heart race, but he tried to show curiosity rather than dread. "You want its power."

"I can only get so far as a mortal man. But as a god, well . . ." Eirlys smile grew two molars wider. "Let's just say I have ambitions."

Good. Make him want more. "That's just the start of it." Lugh glanced both ways, then lowered his voice. "I learned a lot from the savages. About the place they call Kata-Uluru. The Godstone fell there. If there's that much power in a little rock, how much do you think you can gain from the place where it was created?"

Eirlys frowned, then snapped his finger. The flame went out. "Go on."

"Vyzeryn wants to destroy it. I think we can do better."

"Harness the power of a god." Eirlys's eyebrows lifted. "That true? Or are you lying?"

"Call it whatever you want. I don't give a shit. I just want to bugger whatever plan Vyzeryn has and get out of here alive with my sister." Lugh ignored his rising nausea and put on the vilest sneer he could manage. "I don't really care about the Uluru. You know me. I lie. I act. I did everything I did for my sister. Doesn't matter whose side I'm on, as long as it meets that end. You're planning something big. I want in."

"Hmm. So the rat really thinks he can make a deal with the wolf? After you tried to get the Colonel to ice me back in the camp. You have guts, I'll give you that."

"I just want to survive."

"Of course. You're an opportunist, like me." Eirlys cocked his head, and suddenly he had a cigar in hand. He lit it with a spark of magic and puffed. If he was trying to make Lugh uncomfortable, it was working, but

Lugh didn't show it, and that seemed to butter Eirlys's mood. He smirked. "All right, kid. Here's what's going to happen. My men are dispersed throughout the train. We know where the Colonel's best soldiers are, their officers, their ammunition. We've already separated most of the essential crew from the expendables."

"You're hijacking the train?"

"Wouldn't be my first. Once the Colonel's out of the equation, everything belongs to me." Eirlys glanced at his pocket watch, then took another puff, embers flaring. "In ten minutes, my men start killing. Before then, you and I will be in the control room. All I need you to do is get in Vyzeryn's face. Give me a distraction. You're good at that."

Lugh smirked despite himself. "You're that scared of her?"

Eirlys snorted. "I'm not a fool. I can easily kill her, but I need to do it *cleanly*, up close, keeping collateral to a minimum. Especially where she'll be. I need the train's controls *and* engineers in one piece. Problem is, in close quarters, that sword of hers will be in my throat the same instant I draw. Already knows about this." He tapped his knuckles against his chest, ringing the steel plate beneath his shirt. "She's a smart lady. Never let me touch her. Shame, that."

The tingles of Eirlys's sorcery worked through Lugh's elbow. Another curse. Of course that's how this went. Lugh stifled a grimace and tried to look confidently allergic to bullshit. "So what? You'll burn me with her?"

"Heavens no." Eirlys jetted smoke from his nostrils. "You and your sister live, plus a big enough cut to retire comfortably."

Pock-faced liar. You're going to blow me up the moment I get close to Vyzeryn. Lugh broke into a cold sweat. This was already out of hand, but it was too late to back out now.

Eirlys pushed him along, four of his men shadowing behind, all with cold, intent eyes. Lugh's skin crawled. He was going to his death. A pawn's meaningless death. What could he do? He glanced for weapons, for escape routes, but there was nothing in the tight, narrow corridors. His knack was his only option. Doppel something at the right moment, and then—

"Oh, and Lugh," Eirlys nudged him with his elbow as if they were chums, "I can sense your knack before you use it, even if it's just a smidge. Try anything funny, and you'll be ash stains on my boots. Understood?"

Lugh gritted his teeth. Without Adsila's mark, he had nothing to protect him.

He'd wagered a losing bet.

Chapter Sixteen

At least a hundred Auklenn soldiers guarded the front engines. Eirlys strode on through, beaming and whistling, throwing jokes and clapping shoulders. When they stepped into the main engine, one of the desperados stopped at the door and took two stick grenades out of his duster, likely to throw into the midst of the soldiers in the corridor behind when the time was right. The other three desperados kept beside Lugh, metal clicking as they triple-checked their revolvers and shotguns.

"And here we are!" Eirlys pushed Lugh into the control room.

Lugh stumbled inside, heart jammed into his throat.

The control room was an ocean of dials and meters and switches, arranged in a semicircle manned by several uniformed engineers. It made the regular train's controls he'd struggled with so much look easy. Vyzeryn stood at the front between two engineers, gazing into the haze of blowing sand. A wide window of reinforced glass provided a commanding view. The track-setting cars blocked much of it, but the engine was far taller, the control room positioned to see overtop the whole operation. A table was bolted to the floor beside Vyzeryn, and on it lay the Godstone compass, the stone pointing forward. Eirlys stopped in the middle of the room. His desperados spread out.

"Brought the lad for you." Eirlys made a show of eyeing the controls. "Don't see why he should be here though. All this newfangled, important stuff everywhere."

Vyzeryn kept her back to them. "I don't need to explain myself to you."

"Ah, you're right. You don't." Eirlys put his hand on Lugh's shoulder, squeezing in what was evidently a signal: do it, or die.

Lugh stepped forward, eyes darting for a way out. Was there nothing he could do? He took another step, mind racing, and then an electric jolt of Flameshot sorcery flared in his elbow. Vyzeryn's hand drifted to her sword.

Oh gods, not like this . . .

Suddenly a tingling-hot pain erupted from the left side of his neck. A familiar heat rushed towards the curse on his elbow, countering it just as Lugh got within an arm's reach of Vyzeryn. Lugh inhaled with surprise—and heard Eirlys hiss a curse.

The rest happened in a blur.

Vyzeryn whirled, sweeping Lugh aside with one arm. Steel flashed. Sulfuric sorcery flared. Eirlys grunted, flames half-formed on his hands, then glanced at the sword buried in the base of his neck, angled downwards to circumvent his chest plate. He drunkenly groped at the steel, elemental sorcery flaking away from his hands like rust, then collapsed with a disappointed, gurgling sigh.

The seemingly unarmed engineering crew drew pistols and held the other desperados at gunpoint. No one spoke, the only sounds the rumble of the train and the rattle of Eirlys's dying breath.

"I had a feeling . . ." Vyzeryn walked past Lugh and yanked her sword free. "If I were a conniving, treacherous vigilante, I'd betray my employer at a time like this, too. Only I'd do it *properly*." She wiped her blade on a desperado's coat, then sheathed it. "I believed you the first time, Lugh. But it wasn't the right moment to react. If you want to defeat a clever and formidable foe, it's best to make them think they've already won."

Lugh stepped back from the growing pool of blood, relieved and yet crawling with revulsion. "He was . . ."

"Going to blow you up? No." Vyzeryn's mouth quirked. "That savage marked you with her sorcery yet again. I suspected she would, though not to your knowledge. That made you useful." Her lips stretched into a cold grin. "You were good bait. Still are."

A grizzled lieutenant stepped into the room and saluted. "Colonel, we have the rest of them rounded up and disarmed."

Vyzeryn studied her fingernails. "Good. Kill them."

The vigilantes went kicking and screaming into the corridor, only to be silenced by gunshots. Vyzeryn returned to gazing out the window. "It's just blood. Have a seat."

Lugh snapped out of staring at Eirlys's blood. Two soldiers pushed him into a chair in the center of the room, well out of reach of any important equipment. They tied his hands apart, one to each side of the chair, palms out, and then took positions at his shoulders. Their revolvers prodded his head.

"I hear your knack has changed," Vyzeryn said. "A consequence of the Godstone, no doubt. Not that it will make any difference. The outcome is assured."

Lugh glared at her as best he could. She returned it with a knowing smile.

"A shame, isn't it? That your mother didn't get to share in the stone's power."

That hit Lugh right in the gut. He knew it wasn't reasonable, that he hadn't known back then what he knew now. Not even Grandfather had known. But if he'd gotten the stone close to Mother, would things have been different? No . . . the changes had only been noticeable after he and Adsila unified the stone. Even if they'd been happening before, they were undetectable. For Mother . . . it wouldn't have been enough. He bit his tongue against a flood of grief, his body sagging despite his every effort to be strong.

"You realize how out of depth you are," Vyzeryn said. "That's the first step."

"What are you going to do with me?"

"Depends how you handle this situation."

Lugh set his jaw. "I'm not going to work with you."

"You will, regardless of what you want." Vyzeryn nodded at the bloodstains on the floor as her men dragged Eirlys's corpse away. "You were bait for him. Now you're bait for that witch. If you become problematic . . . well, I can always threaten to murder your sister and have you stab that savage in the back again, literally this time." Her voice remained level. No lies. Cold, clinical truth.

Shadows formed in the haze outside. Ancient walls and foundations, appearing and disappearing with each shift in the sands. They were close. Dormant sorcery, ancient and wild, itched against Lugh's skin, pervading every breath of air.

"You are right," Vyzeryn said. "Returning the Godstone may appease their goddess, perhaps, but for how long? And what if the savages harness her power against us? As I said, I don't deal with half measures. I prefer permanent results. So I will destroy the last tether that keeps her in this world. You can be part of that solution. Think of it as a service to your country." The iron in Vyzeryn's voice sent chills down Lugh's spine.

"All this to avenge your brother?"

"So what if it is?"

Lugh wanted to say it was wrong, that revenge was fruitless madness, but if Sabia had been murdered, he knew he'd go to extreme lengths as well.

"Understand," Vyzeryn said, "that I could not follow any other path than this. Do you know what tragedy is? The inevitable—nothing else. Part of this is indeed to light a pyre in his memory, but do not mistake me for being purely sentimental. I am also doing this for Auklenn. Tell me, Lugh, what did you find in Anchorshaw?"

Lugh shivered. "Everyone was . . . dead."

Vyzeryn closed her eyes and sighed. "So they didn't heed my warning. What you found there is just a *taste* of what's to come." Her eyes cracked open, and she slid her gaze towards the window, brow furrowed. "Long have I served for the stability and safety of the common man, woman, and child. I protected them from the likes of your father, from the likes of *you*, and I will certainly protect them from savages and their insane deity. The history is irrelevant. It doesn't matter that our ancestors threw the first blow. All that matters is victory. Not for my sake, but for the sake of the millions the Clysm will slaughter. That's the nature of war. I am merely taking responsibility—something you know very little about."

Outside the window, the blowing sands began to thin. The itch of ancient magic grew. Lugh thought he heard whispers, and he could have sworn something was prickling his open palms. Then, with the suddenness of a light switch, the view cleared into a vast space surrounded by the churning wall of the Clysm. The eye of the storm. At its heart, shaped like an enormous tree stump, loomed a mountainous rock formation. A stairway cut all the way to the mountain's summit, which was perfectly flat, and the remnants of pillared temples and walls layered around it, half buried in sand. The closest ones gleamed with amethyst veins. Lugh's jaw dropped.

Kata-Uluru. Ehekahl's origin.

"At last." Vyzeryn picked up the blood compass and detached the Godstone. "The place where this cursed rock fell. My ancestors did us a disservice by not destroying it along with everything else."

"What if you're wrong?" Lugh couldn't think of anything else to say.

A soft laugh escaped Vyzeryn's lips. "Only one way to find out now." She tapped one of the engineers on the shoulder. "Bring us broadside."

Layers of stone walls, pillars, and ruins blocked the path towards the mountain. The train adjusted course, and metallic groans echoed as dozens of heavy artillery pieces aimed. Lugh struggled against his bonds, prompting the two guards to cock their revolvers. He couldn't reach anything, and Doppeling rope into rope wouldn't work since it would appear in the same configuration. His forehead ached, as did the side of his neck where Adsila's second mark had been. The whispers grew louder. His skin itched as if something tiny and innumerable were rubbing against it. Small, electric sensations . . . like when he touched objects with his knack. What was happening to him? He looked at the Godstone, so close at hand, and could have sworn he felt its warmth from afar. No, not just warmth. A connection.

The train lurched to a halt. Vyzeryn accepted a radio transceiver from one of her men. "All guns, load explosive shells and make ready to fire." She paused, then snarled. "Fire."

The bombardment shook the train and blotted out the landscape with fire and cascades of shattered rock. Lugh felt like his brain would be rattled out of his ears. Worst of all, though, was the whispers. They rose into screams, stabbing his mind like hot knives. His headache doubled. His neck burned. He squirmed and gasped in the chair, his stomach twisting into an agonizing knot.

"Keep firing," Vyzeryn ordered, tapping her sword impatiently.

The ruins blocking the train's path turned to dust, a smoldering trench torn through the landscape straight up to the mountain steps.

"Advance," Vyzeryn said. "I want our mortars close enough to strike the summit."

The chief engineer frowned. "Colonel, that ground won't be very stable."

"I said advance." Vyzeryn gripped his shoulder. "*Now.*"

The engineer nervously scratched his forehead, then nodded to his colleagues. The *Andrasta* groaned onward.

Lugh could taste it now, the coppery tang of Adsila's lingering magic. She'd protected him again. Damnation, he refused to let that go to waste. If the stone was still changing him, maybe he *could* get out of this. He tapped into his knack, straining to sense anything to Doppel. His palms, facing outwards thanks to his bonds, tingled even more. With what? It felt as if his skin was being peppered with grit. Could he Doppel whatever that was? Was it even real? Or just prickling from the bonds cutting off the circulation? He balled his fists and felt the grit between his fingertips. It was sand and dust. Trace amounts in the air, yet his senses were so heightened, he felt it like a hailstorm. He'd never been able to Doppel something so small. Then again, he'd accomplished a lot of firsts over the last few days, and Eirlys's deduction about the Godstone's influence corroborated it.

What could he *really* do?

Time to find out.

Vyzeryn glowered at Lugh. "What are you doing?"

This better work. Lugh tapped into his knack. At the same moment he twisted one of his wrists, ignoring the stabbing pain, and groped as much of the rope as he could, contacting his bonds with the ambient sand in the air.

Vyzeryn's eyes widened. She reached for her sword. "Shoot him!"

Too late.

Power riveted Lugh in a way he'd never experienced, radiating from the Godstone itself like a miniature sun. Suddenly every speck of sand and dust in the air stood out, every impact against his skin clear. His knack connected to them all, and unlike every time before, he didn't need physical contact. Light flared, and the control room flooded with rope. It burst from thin air, every particle Doppeling. Thousands of them.

The tide of rope lengths drowned the room, muffling the curses and shouts of the guards and crew. A gunshot barked behind Lugh, but the bullet went over his head and shattered a window. Wind and sand howled in, and the Doppeling continued, taking up the grit and exploding it into more rope. Lugh fell sideways, his chair propelled on the ocean of rope like on a tide of wriggling serpents. It slammed him against a window hard enough to shatter it and spew him out. He landed on his back, and the wooden chair shattered beneath him. Rolling free, he burst to his feet, dizzy, his head so filled with sorcery it felt like it would explode. The sand beneath him began to Doppel, too, swallowing his legs in writhing rope.

He couldn't stop it.

Lugh tried to crawl, but every area of sand he touched dissolved into a loose sinkhole of rope. It spread to the front of the train, trapping the front cars and tangling the track-laying mechanisms until they shrieked to a violent halt. The track beneath shifted and groaned as it lost its support, and several sections broke, the train cars dipping inwards. Rope continued to spew from the main engines, shattering every window and spilling out like entrails.

Lugh's vision blurred in and out of blackness. Pressure mounted behind his eyes and cheekbones as if someone had shoved a fireman's hose into his sinuses. His heart palpitated. Even his lungs refused to work. Cured of his aversion or not, he was drawing too much power. Every sorcerer had a limit, and he was flying past it like a racehorse. How much longer before it killed him?

He blacked out, woke again, and then saw a wink of light from amidst the rope before him. The rope itself was coiling around it.

The Godstone.

He yanked his way free of the rope and leapt for the stone, and the moment he put his hand on it, the flow of power ceased, leaving him in a numb daze just beyond the rope, where endless sand began

What the hell was—?

A force rammed into his shoulder and drove him into the ground. Vyzeryn's sword, embedded halfway to the hilt. Lugh stared at it, too shocked to feel the pain. She bulled her way out of the rope and grabbed her thrown sword, twisting it in his shoulder. Lugh screamed and almost blacked out again.

"You little wretch," Vyzeryn hissed. "I don't care how you did that, you will reverse it."

"What makes you think I'd . . . want to?"

Vyzeryn twisted the blade harder. "Now!"

Lugh stifled a scream. "I . . . I don't know."

"What?"

"I don't know how!" Lugh couldn't revert the rope like normal. It didn't even feel connected to him, as if the Godstone itself had hijacked his sorcery and used it of its own accord. He didn't understand, but Vyzeryn's face held little patience.

"You're lying," she said.

"No I'm not!"

"So be it." Vyzeryn lifted her arm. A familiar voice cried out. Two soldiers stood at the engine's side door, holding Sabia between them. "One more chance."

"I'm telling the truth!"

Vyzeryn took a deep breath and closed her eyes. "One warning shot. Then one of her fingers."

"No!" Lugh screamed.

The soldier cocked his revolver—and then his head jerked back, blood spattering. It took a moment for Lugh to realize that it wasn't Sabia's, but the man's own blood, shot in the head. The man beside him dropped, too, as did half the other soldiers on the ground. The distant crack of a gunshot came afterwards, followed by a zipping sound. Sabia threw herself to the ground, cushioned by the Doppeled rope.

Vyzeryn hissed and reared to stab Lugh in the throat, but he slapped the blade with his palm, Doppeling it into a small rock he clutched in his other hand. Even that small use of sorcery now made his heart squirm like an eel. Vyzeryn drew her revolver instead, but then another zipping sound pierced the air, and a bullet struck the gun and ricocheted into Vyzeryn's face. She twisted with a spatter of blood and toppled into the sand like a puppet without its strings.

A rider stood on a ridge overlooking Kata-Uluru, half hidden in the churning wall of the Clysm. Lugh blinked, not believing his eyes.

"Adsila . . ."

Adsila lashed the reins and charged down the slope, dust whirling in her wake. The turrets on the train's forward cars turned. One fired with a tremendous roar, blasting the desert with a blinding detonation, but Adsila appeared through the smoke unharmed, then let her revolver sing.

Lugh barely tracked the gunshot, but the bullet zipped straight down the cannon's barrel. It must have struck a live shell while they had the breach open, because the entire car disappeared in a fiery blast that pinwheeled shrapnel across the landscape. The shockwave sent Lugh rolling. More gunfire and explosions followed. It was all he could do to crawl towards where Sabia had fallen. He'd lost track in the blast. Had the shockwave thrown her, too? He stole a glance at Vyzeryn, laying motionless in the sand.

Sabia's ragged coughing filled his heart with ice.

"Sabia!" Lugh found her curled up in the sand, hands over her mouth. Her eyes were wide and panicked, her face terrifyingly pale. He cast about, wincing as more gunfire rang, then grabbed at one of the nearby corpses. He took a water canteen and dampened a shred of cloth from his battered clothes. "Here! Over your mouth!"

Sabia nearly inhaled the cloth, then got the hang of it, her wheezes drawing out as she tried to breathe through. A terrible solution that would also suffocate her in time, but the dust would kill her faster. She had gotten a lungful of cruddy air—almost a death sentence now, or later by infection. He needed to move fast.

Lugh checked Sabia over. No obvious wounds. He

battled tears as he lifted Sabia into his arms. One way or another, he had to see her through this, even if he couldn't use his knack. Whatever the Godstone had done to him, the withdrawal from using that much power at once had left him teetering on the edge.

The gunfire intensified, but with the artillery blasts, the area had been reduced to a rusty haze of shadows. Godstone clenched in his fist, Sabia cradled, Lugh squinted until he saw the outline of Kata-Uluru. He had to get there somehow. Grandfather's words echoed in his mind.

Unite them.

Return them.

Open the eyes that bloodshed closed.

Prove.

A reckless longshot, but it was the only hand he had left to play.

"Hold on, Sabia," he said.

Movement in the corner of his eye brought him about. Vyzeryn leapt through the haze like a hound, blood streaming from a gash on her forehead. Lugh fell backwards, shielding himself and Sabia with his forearm. He had her Doppeled sword in his pocket, but he couldn't reach it fast enough, and she had a gun.

Vyzeryn cocked her revolver. "I will not let the likes of you ruin everything!"

Lugh shielded Sabia with his back.

A horse galloped through the haze, Adsila standing in its stirrups. Vyzeryn turned and fired. The horse dropped dead, but Adsila leapt free as it fell, losing her pistol in the process. Lugh acted on instinct and threw the pebble over Vyzeryn's shoulder with his free hand.

"Adsila! Catch!"

He reverted the pebble, braving another sorcerous backlash that throttled his vision with momentary darkness. His eyes cleared to see the fine sword still flying through the air, a flash between Vyzeryn and Adsila—and Adsila caught it. Fury raged across her ashen face as she drove the weapon down. Vyzeryn fired again. The bullet struck one of Adsila's braids with a burst of glittering amethyst shards, but she kept her momentum and carved the blade deep into Vyzeryn's left shoulder just shy of her neck. It all swirled in a blur of limbs and sand. Adsila crashed and rolled. The sword twirled free.

Vyzeryn stood first, left arm dangling useless. She groped at her wound, cast about a bewildered glare, and then toppled onto her side.

Adsila got to her feet with a tirade of snarled curses. She spat on Vyzeryn's body and limped towards Lugh. With every step she took, Lugh felt smaller, guiltier, all the wrongs he'd done surfacing in his mind alongside her mercies. His heart still palpitated from his overused sorcery. It took him three tries to get his words out.

"Y-You came back."

"Don't flatter yourself."

"But how did you—?"

"Found a horse that fled the camp. Dumb luck." Adsila scowled. "The stone. Do you have it?"

Lugh showed the Godstone.

Adsila nodded, then noticed Sabia still in his arms. Her face softened. "So, this is the sister you talked so much about."

Sabia was so focused on breathing that she didn't pay either of them any attention. How much longer did she have?

"We need to go." Adsila grimaced at Sabia. "This is our only shot. Come on."

Lugh hesitated, then accepted her hand. Despite everything, her strength was still impressive enough to pull them both up, and the moment he was on his feet, Adsila had a fresh set of bullets out to mark with blood. She spoke as she retrieved her revolver.

"Your sister won't last much longer out here."

"I know." Lugh bit his lip. "But if anything can save her, it's the legend that dragged me into this mess."

Adsila grunted. Shouts rose from the haze. The armored train was far from destroyed. The fire was already being doused, sparing the adjacent cars, and the garrison was rallying its numbers and bringing weapons to bear. Every second that passed let the haze clear a little more. Soon they would be easy targets.

"Hand me the stone," Adsila said.

Lugh opened his left palm, his arm still cradling Sabia. The Godstone had a glow to it and a warmth that sent tingles up his arm. He pinched it between his fingers and moved to hand it over.

A gunshot pierced the air.

The Godstone exploded in Lugh's hand.

Everything slowed as if time had gotten drunk. The Godstone went up in a brilliant burst of crimson light and flecks of sapphire and gold, struck through with transient rainbows and blood. Three amputated fingers twirled with it. *Those are . . . mine?* Time crashed into Lugh like a bull.

Agony shot up his arm. He screamed and collapsed, dropping Sabia.

"Lugh!" Adsila shrieked, the stone's final glimmers reflecting in her wide eyes.

More gunfire roared from the haze. Adsila dodged to the ground and fired back, but bullet impacts kicked up the sand around her, and she gasped as some met their mark. The haze receded further, and the silhouettes of Auklenn troops took shape. Vyzeryn stood at their forefront, covered in blood, gripping a revolver in her right hand while the left arm hung limp. Her voice grated out between bared teeth.

"You're not the only one with a knack."

An earthy odor laced the air. Vyzeryn's cloven shoulder knitted back together, and her limp changed to her usual firm stride. She flexed her left hand finger by finger.

A Regenerator, Lugh realized. No wonder she kept getting up.

"I've died more times today than I'd like," Vyzeryn said. "You, however, will only die here once. You've killed yourself and your sister. And for what? A deity you never believed in." She rolled her shoulder and picked up her sword. "And you, bloody savage girl. You shouldn't have returned. Let's see what you can do without your precious Godstone."

The Godstone. Gone. The realization finally rammed through Lugh's daze.

Adsila struggled to her hands and knees, hissing through clenched teeth, but she couldn't stand. Blood soaked through her shirt at the flank and shoulder, and her revolver lay out of reach. Sabia knelt where she'd fallen, staring with panicked eyes as she wheezed through the cloth. *Help me*, Sabia's eyes screamed.

Lugh pressed against his bleeding left hand, the stumps of his middle, fourth, and fifth finger the greatest agony he'd ever felt. Vyzeryn approached, the hellish train and an army at her back. What could he do against such relentless odds? He had nothing left. Even his capacity for sorcery had been depleted. If he used it again so soon, the backlash would surely kill him. The Godstone, and whatever advantage it gave him, was gone. Its absence left a frigid void that reached all the way into his heart.

"Your face says it all, boy." Vyzeryn gave a bloody smile. "You lose."

The *Andrasta's* heavy artillery opened fire on Kata-Uluru. Explosions erupted across the mountainside.

No! Lugh scrambled for Adsila's gun.

Vyzeryn laughed as she followed. "Run, run, little liar. You can't outpace the truth."

The gun seemed miles away. Lugh stumbled and thrashed through the sand, the jolting pains from his hand slamming through his skull, but the pain kept him focused. He had to save them. Adsila. Sabia. Everyone. Even with the Godstone lost, he had to try.

"What do you think you can accomplish?" Vyzeryn asked. "You're grasping at straws."

Lugh reached the revolver and rolled onto his back, aiming at Vyzeryn and pulling the trigger as fast as he could. All he got were clicks.

"You didn't even count how many times she fired." Vyzeryn shook her head and raised her revolver, its chrome surface agleam. "That's enough chances for you both."

Adsila gasped to Lugh's right, and he realized that they were only a few feet apart. Close enough to touch. Close enough to hold. Her emerald eyes locked with his, her mouth slightly open as if she was about to speak. Deathly pale, but she didn't look afraid, not even as she pressed her hand against the gunshot wound in her side. What he'd give for her courage. As the artillery fired another salvo, a hot, acrid breeze swept between them, moving the sands into a dance and clattering the amethyst beads in her braids. She took his hand, and the corner of her mouth twitched with a smirk.

"With me to the end, huh?"

Not this kind of end. Lugh squeezed her hand and looked past Vyzeryn to Sabia, for whom he'd give anything and yet for whom he had nothing left to give.

He prayed for a miracle.

By all the luck he didn't deserve, he got one.

Chapter Seventeen

A zipping sound pierced through the din of artillery. Vyzeryn reacted at the last second, jerking to the side and ducking her head, but the blood-magicked bullet struck her forearm anyway, throwing her aim before she could put a bullet in Lugh's heart. She dropped her revolver and staggered back, panting as her sorcery healed her wound.

The *crack* of the gunshot echoed to the east.

The rumble of hooves joined it.

"Impossible," Vyzeryn hissed.

Lugh followed Vyzeryn's gaze. The churning wall of the Clysm dominated the slopes to the east of the train. A lone rider stood at the ridgeline, cloak billowing as he lowered his rifle. More riders appeared behind him, masked and bearing the crimson-etched garb of the Uluru. Dozens at first. Then hundreds.

They must have followed the tracks.

By the gods, they're still alive. Tears blurred Lugh's vision. He wiped them away with his forearm, his throat suddenly tight with yearning. He had to *see* it! That his foolish mistakes hadn't wiped out the kindest people he'd ever met. Now even more Uluru ranged across the ridge-line. In that moment, all of Lugh's pain and exhaustion, even his shame, stepped aside for a cascade of relief.

Chaos swept through the Auklenn army's ranks as they scrambled to form a firing line, but a volley rained from the hillside, and though none of the Uluru were as strong as Adsila, their sorcery nonetheless made their aim deadly. Vyzeryn leapt for the cover of a crumbled wall, shielding her head with her forearm as shots rained down.

With a unified roar of hooves, the Uluru charged.

The speed of their small, agile horses took them half the distance in what seemed like a blink of an eye. The *Andrasta's* smaller guns rotated to engage, but they only got off a single salvo before the riders were too close, and the Uluru charged straight through the hellfire as if it were mere sand on the wind.

Lugh had never seen something so terrifyingly glorious.

Adsila's hand shook, and when Lugh turned, he saw that she was laughing and crying at the same time.

"They came," she said. "I knew it. I knew they were still alive."

Gunfire cracked around them. Sand splashed as bullets missed. Lugh grabbed Adsila and pulled her down, rolling away from the Auklenn firing line until they were behind a meager sand drift—only to curse under his breath. Sabia was still out there. Vyzeryn's voice cut over the din, barking orders, and the *Andrasta's* heavy artillery redoubled its efforts on Kata-Uluru. Lugh shoved his empty revolver into Adsila's hands.

"You have any more bullets?"

Adsila sputtered out one last laugh. "Maybe. Gotta dig around. Pockets."

"Stay here!" Lugh sprinted to Sabia's side, then carried her back. Her fingernails had turned blue, and she barely responded when he said her name, but she still kept the cloth to her mouth and nose.

"Found some," Adsila grunted, loading with shaky, bloody hands. "How's she doing?"

"Bad." Lugh laid Sabia down, mind racing. A glance at Adsila's bloodstained side only made his panic worse. "You've been shot."

"No shit." Adsila winced as gunfire tore into the drift and peppered them with sand. "Won't kill me yet. Trust me, I've been shot often enough to know. If it was a major artery I'd be dead. Worry about her, not me!"

He hardly needed to be told that, yet he didn't know what to do. Kata-Uluru was still half a kilometer away, its heights dizzying just to look at. He couldn't get Sabia up there before she succumbed to her failing lungs. The only possible refuge from the dusty air was the train, but a battlefield stood between them, and the train swarmed with Vyzeryn's troops.

A group of Uluru riders galloped past, engaging the Auklenn soldiers beyond the sand drift. A trio brought up the rear. Tahk rode at their forefront, cradling an old single-shot rifle, his blocky face partially hidden in the folds of his hooded cloak, but his grin no less evident as he neared.

"Ah, the stringy outlander still lives."

Lugh smiled despite himself, but Adsila interjected before he could speak.

"My grandfather. Is he alive?"

"Alive and pissed. Ku'Tiaman sent us to retrieve you."

Adsila breathed a sigh of relief. "I'm not going with you."

"What?"

"You heard me." Adsila elbowed Lugh. "This guy's a bullet magnet on his own."

Lugh coughed. "Adsila—"

Adsila grabbed his shoulder, her intense gaze burning away his protest. "We're finishing this, aren't we?" Her hand shook, and her expression quivered at the edges, tears shimmering in her eyes. She was barely holding on to hope, and Lugh realized, so was he. The cold pit in his stomach deepened. He put his hand over Adsila's.

"Adsila, the Godstone . . ."

"Is gone. I know! I saw it!"

The Uluru riders balked. Even Tahk grimaced. "This is true?"

Lugh barely heard the man's voice. The ever-weakening sound of Sabia's labored breaths tore him to pieces. She looked worse than ever, and there was *nothing* more he could do. Nothing! Had the stone been her only chance? His throat tightened.

"We must go," Tahk said. "If Ehekahl's Tear is lost, there isn't—"

"No!" Adsila said. "We can't give up now! Lugh!"

Lugh took a deep breath. Part of him felt like all was lost, that he ought to crawl under a rock and wait for the inevitable . . . but that wasn't the person he needed to be now. The Godstone had been destroyed. Kata-Uluru was being blown to pieces. It was madness to proceed, it could all be hopeless, but Lugh knew, as he looked at the smoking heights of Kata-Uluru, that he still believed, that he had to believe. Grandfather had given everything for this. So would he. "Adsila's right. We're going."

Adsila cracked a smile and squeezed Lugh's shoulder. Meanwhile Tahk raised both eyebrows and shook his head.

"Rabid foxes, the both of you."

"Guilty as charged." Lugh gently picked Sabia up and cradled her in his arms. "Tahk. Can you get her somewhere safe? Somewhere that's out of the wind?"

Tahk frowned. "Who is this?"

"His sister," Adsila said. "And you'll help her as you'd help me."

"We have some wagons set up behind the ridge for the wounded. Maya?"

The rider behind Tahk dismounted and pulled back her hood, the amethysts in her braid glinting in the flashes of explosions. Although Maya wore a cloak, bandoleer, and sported a rusty flintlock, her eyes still had the kind wrinkles that tugged at Lugh's memories. She took one look at Sabia and murmured an oath. "We must be quick. Yanita! Go back to the wagons and get some water boiling!"

One of the riders dashed towards the hillside.

Lugh swallowed hard. "Can you save her?"

"I will do all in my power. Ehekahl willing." Maya gently took Sabia, motherly wrinkles deepening into trenches. She gave Lugh a reassuring touch and returned to her horse, where Tahk helped her remount with Sabia in her arms. In moments she was gone, racing at a gallop for the Uluru camp. In the meantime, Adsila had taken more ammunition and a roll of gauze for her wound. She tossed the latter at Lugh.

"What's this?" he asked.

"You've been shot, too, remember?"

Lugh blinked. In all the chaos he'd forgotten about his fingers. Even when he looked at the bleeding stumps, numbness masked the pain. He wrapped them as best he could.

"You're set on this?" Tahk asked.

"We have to find out," Lugh said. "Otherwise all of this was for nothing."

Tahk grunted. "We'll see about getting you some horses and—"

The sand mound they were hiding behind exploded. Lugh found himself on his back, ears ringing as sand and debris pelted around him. Voices called out. A hand grabbed his shoulder, yanking him up to his knees. His vision blurred, but Tahk's bloodied face soon materialized, as did his gruff, commanding voice.

"Move! We'll hold them here!"

Lugh glanced around. The horses were either dead or had run off. Tahk and the other Uluru hunkered down at the edge of the crater left by the artillery blast. Adsila fired a shot towards the enemy and then grabbed Lugh by the elbow, yanking him through the chaos.

"Let's go! Let them handle this!"

Lugh swallowed his protest and raced on. She was right. He couldn't hesitate, not when others were putting their lives on the line for their sake. He would not waste this moment.

Gunfire and explosions roared behind them. Thanks to the wind and blasts, a haze had swept over the landscape, granting some cover. Not that it kept the bullets from cracking around them or the artillery from raining upon Kata-Uluru. Every shattering impact shook Lugh's teeth, and every glance at Adsila, paler and paler with every minute, shook his heart.

It wasn't long until Adsila stumbled.

Lugh went to her side. "Let me—"

"I'm fine!" Adsila got up and took a few steps, then fell again. Her bandages had soaked through. "Maybe it did hit an artery . . . shit . . ."

She's dying. Lugh swallowed hard. "You . . . you should stay."

"No. We're doing this together. I have to be there. I—" Adsila gasped as she pressed on her wound, but it was fear, not pain, that marred her face. "I have to find out. Even though the stone's gone. I have to know."

"You can't walk!"

"Just . . . just carry me."

"Carry you?"

Bullets cracked over their heads, and in the haze came silhouettes flanking from the south. Adsila cursed and fired at them, sorcery zipping the bullet with deadly results. "Just do it!"

Lugh hoisted Adsila over his shoulder like a potato sack, adrenaline helping far less than he'd hoped for. "You're heavier than I thought."

"I'll punch you for that!" Adsila fired again.

"Later."

"Oh gee, you think?"

Lugh swallowed a remark and focused on breathing. The older wounds in his thigh and forearm throbbed, and his knees ached something fierce. Nonetheless, he trudged forward, towards the burning mountain. With each step, protruding stone and weathered hunks of amethyst threatened to trip him. Shouts and bullets pursued them, Auklenn troops having gotten around the Uluru. Adsila fired back over his shoulder, stringing curse words together in ways Lugh hadn't thought possible. Something impacted Lugh's good leg, but he dared not look. He kept going, somehow, gritting his teeth until he could have sworn one cracked. Adsila fired again. Grit and sand stung his eyes. Soon the mountain steps were before him, uneven and fractured, the dark stone veined with amethyst. The first step alone was enough to make him fall to one knee.

How could he make it all the way to the top like this?

How could he give up?

"Adsila," Lugh rasped. "You still with me?"

"Yeah." Adsila coughed. "Still here, hanging like a crap sack."

Lugh set his jaw and rose. Another step. Then another, and another, until he stopped counting. His head spun, and when he glanced back, he realized he'd gone a third of the way. The train lurked far below, smoking from a dozen fires, and the ruins around it flashed with gunfire as the Uluru riders skirmished with the infantry. The fighting had reached the base of the steps, a platoon of infantry contesting an Uluru counterattack as more began the ascent. Vyzeryn led at the front, coat billowing, rifle aimed. Her bullet struck the wall to Lugh's left, dicing his cheek with fragments. He staggered, but kept climbing. Adsila returned fire. Another shot answered, closer this time.

Keep going, Lugh.

Lugh wasn't sure if it was his own thought or something else. He couldn't feel his left hand anymore, or even move it, and the cuts on his cheek kept soaking his lips with blood.

Keep going.

"One bullet left," Adsila grunted.

"Save it."

"For who? Us?"

Lugh winced as he took another step. "Don't talk like that."

"Heh." Adsila nudged him with her knee. "When this is over, you owe me a drink."

"As many as you want."

"I'll hold you to it."

Lugh fell to his knees again. More than halfway now, yet it felt like an eternity remained.

"And maybe," Adsila went on, "you can show me around Auklenn sometime."

"Why are you saying this now?"

Adsila coughed. "I'm delirious and losing a shitload of blood, asshole. I'm not thinking straight." She fired her last bullet, sorcery zipping. "People say weird things when they're dying."

Lugh surged to his feet. "You're not dying!"

Adsila laughed weakly. "Sure motivated you though."

Artillery shells exploded on the mountainside around them, too far from them to kill, not far enough to spare them from the blasting heat and deafening noise. Lugh felt Adsila flinch. The warmth of her blood soaked through his shirt.

"Adsila?"

A weak punch in his flank sufficed as her reply.

Lugh focused on the steps. They blurred together. He wanted to collapse, to rest, to breathe. He resisted the urge again and again. Blasts shook him. Heat scalded his face. Shrapnel stung his back. He lost count of the times he stumbled, but he never once let Adsila go. It was as if her weight was giving him strength enough to push through layer after layer of the desire to stop. Gods . . . was this what Grandfather had meant on that mountain hike all those years ago? Was this the feeling? So much pain, so much weariness, yet at the same time, unstoppable.

Grandfather was right. This whole journey had been his mountain to climb, his burden to bear. No matter how it turned out, it was his heritage to face it with courage. To the end.

And suddenly, with a gust of wind in his face, he reached the summit.

A vast bowl of glassy black stone loomed before him. Webbed cracks emanated from the center, like a punched window.

"We made it," he breathed.

Adsila coughed. "The center. Get . . . to the center . . ."

Lugh stepped onto the glassy rock. The air became heavy and electric. *Alive*, just like before, when he'd walked the Clysm alone. Or was it just in his head? Doubts mounted like corpses in the battle below. The

Godstone was gone. How would this work without the Godstone? He walked as fast as he could, the center close, the thick, electric aura doubling with every step.

"Almost there," he rasped. "Hold on."

"Damn . . ." Adsila hacked again and spat blood. "You're . . . stronger than you look."

Lugh managed a grin—only for a high-pitched shriek to split the air. Adsila shouted and shifted her body, forcing Lugh to the ground and piling her weight on top of him. A split-second later, a blast pulled the world out from beneath him. Fire. Red. Winks of amethyst. Then darkness, and the numb flicker of dreams and memories. Father's harsh voice as he wielded a cudgel. Mother's gentle whisper as she lay on her deathbed. Grandfather's intense gaze as he handed Lugh the tin containing the Godstone. The bracelet Sabia had given him, crusted with ash . . .

He came to with a gasp and inhaled blood. Coughing wildly, he rolled onto his belly and got on his elbows. More blood ran hot down his scalp. Adsila. Where was Adsila? He groped around, eyes stung by smoke and flame. His hand brushed something wet. Blood. A pool of it, accumulating from a river that led to . . . Lugh found himself staring at Adsila. She lay on her side, facing away from him. Her hat had fallen off, and her amethyst hair beads were scattered amidst the thickening crimson of her blood.

"Adsila?"

She remained still.

"Adsila!"

Lugh crawled to her side. Her blood was pooling

right in the heart of the crater, flowing through the intricate web of cracks. Dried marigold petals, torn from her necklace, bobbed in the frothy red. Lugh skirted around to face her. Still she didn't move, not even with a single breath. Tangled, blood-soaked hair covered her eyes. He brushed it aside, but her eyes stared right through him, half closed, pupils dilated. His voice caught in his throat.

She's dead.

How could Adsila be dead? It felt impossible. Of all the people he'd met . . .

Dead.

Lugh waited for reality to hit him. Surely he'd scream, cry out, do something. Instead, silence. A hollow, numbing silence where his heart used to be.

Artillery hammered the glassy plateau. It sounded distant. Even the shockwaves were like mere puffs of air compared to the absence that dawned before him. "Adsila . . ." Lugh took her hand. So cold already. "I'm . . ."

What? Sorry? Ridiculous to say that now. She'd pushed through so much, only to lose. The cruel unfairness of it baffled Lugh . . . and he couldn't help but think about the drinks he'd promised her, and a wish for her to get to know Sabia. That he couldn't show her the better side of Auklenn, that he couldn't make things up to her, that he couldn't sit back with her one day and laugh about this whole ridiculous ordeal.

A future. Gods, he'd seen a *future* with her.

And here he was, just as the Drunk forewarned. Alive despite everything.

Lugh the Liar.

"No," he whispered under his breath. "Not her, too."

The heavens churned over him. Rusty, impenetrable cloud, perpetual sand. Roiling thunder and rumbling artillery. The world was deaf. Was Ehekahl deaf, too? He refused to believe that no one was listening, that it was *hopeless*. The weight to the air had reached a pinnacle, its heaviness pressing on his mind, the static riveting his body and making his hairs stand on end. Even as more artillery fell and the crack of gunfire grew nearer. Even as Adsila's lifeblood flowed before his eyes. Even as everything seemed lost . . .

I'm not done.

Lugh brushed Adsila's hair further aside, taking in the face that had always been so strong and beautiful. "I'm not done," he whispered. "I'm not done, Adsila . . ."

Not while he still breathed.

Lugh squeezed her hand, and then crawled to the center of Kata-Uluru. The pool of blood and marigold petals mirrored his face and the troubled sky.

"Ehekahl. I might not be one of your people. I'm just a down-and-out rag from the backstreets of a place that doesn't believe in you. A liar and a fool. But if you can still see . . . if you can still hear . . ." He put his hand in the blood and pressed against the smooth stone beneath. "If you can still *feel*."

A shell struck the plateau nearby. A moaning whoosh of shrapnel sped through him. He collapsed, then pushed himself back up with his submerged hand, gasping as his own blood dripped into the pool. He didn't know where one pain ended and another began. His chest rattled as he forced out his words.

"If my word amounts to anything, please . . ." He tapped into his knack, the click in his brain louder than ever before. He didn't Doppel anything, but he let his sorcery hang there, pooling hot at his palm. "Save her."

The blood shifted, a lacey pattern expanding from the marigold petals. The edges crystalized with ice, and a feminine voice whispered from everywhere and nowhere at once, joined by the same presence he'd felt in the storm.

"You wish for her to live?"

Ehekahl. It had to be. Lugh coughed up blood. "Yes . . ."

The air shifted in a dance of embers and smoke.

"Life is saved through truth and truth alone."

"I'm telling you the truth," Lugh rasped. "I want her to live!"

"And what is your truth, Lugh Ahearn?"

The blood crystalized into a mirror.

Lugh flinched, staring at his own reflection. Battered, coated in blood and grit, hair wild in the fiery gusts. A face he had hated for so long, belonging to a man who'd always lied, cheated, and crawled through the filth for the sake of—Lugh blinked, a knot twisting deep in his heart, worse than all the pains combined. "For the sake of others . . ."

The chaos muted even more. Suddenly Lugh heard the sounds of Auklenn again. The bustling streets. The belltowers in the evening. Rainfall against the bedroom window. The noise of the life he'd lived. A life he hadn't chosen, a life he wasn't proud of . . . and one he'd always thought made him a wretched son, a terrible brother, and a coward. Yet a wretched son would never have buried himself in crime to support his mother. A terrible brother wouldn't have gone through so much to care for a sister all the doctors had given up on. A coward wouldn't have tried time and time again, faced the powers and armies of Eirlys and Vyzeryn, and chosen to side with Adsila and the Uluru in a hope against hope. He had changed.

No, not changed.

Lugh looked himself in the eye. Lugh the Liar . . . wasn't the man in that reflection.

He never had been.

Tears brimmed and rolled down Lugh's face. Another blast hammered him, yet it might as well have been a flick. He didn't care anymore. All that mattered was the twisting ache in his heart. The pain of a truth he'd pushed away all his life: that he wasn't all those terrible things. So much had broken him, and he'd chosen not to see the goodness in his own heart. A lie. All this time, the biggest lie of all was the one he'd been telling himself. And the truth . . .

"I was wrong about myself," he whispered. "I'm more than my past mistakes. Despite everything . . . I'm a *good* person. Deserving of forgiveness . . . even love."

That was his truth.

The voice laughed. A singsong so much like Mother's.

My truth. Lugh shuddered as the pain in his chest lifted, a weight vanished into thin air. He felt so light, so different, and when he focused on his reflection, he realized he was smiling—a smile that reminded him of Grandfather's atop that rainy mountain. Here he was, having climbed his own, arriving at the same conclusion: that it was worth it in the end.

Even if that end was death.

He looked to Adsila, and the voice whispered all around him.

"What will you give for her?"

Lugh breathed in and poured all his strength into his knack, offering his sorcery, his life. Blood rattled in his lungs. He gurgled out his last word. "Everything."

And he meant it.

The voice didn't laugh this time. Instead, something flashed in the blood's mirrored reflection. A wink of light like a star. Lugh's world blurred, and he found himself lying on his side, but the light remained, falling from the churning cloud.

A teardrop of the purest light.

Chapter Eighteen

"I love you," Mother whispered. "Don't forget."

Lugh squeezed Mother's emaciated hand. She lay in a hospital bed, a husk of her former self, surrounded by the flowers he brought her, now wilted. Lump in his throat be damned, he'd say it. "I love you too. And . . . gods, Mom, I'm so sorry . . ."

"Sorry?" Mother's eyes cracked open. "Why?"

"For . . . for *everything*." Lugh knew the specifics, but he couldn't stomach them. Not here. Not now. He knelt at her side, adding his other hand to hers. "Just . . . for not being better. I'm never been—"

Mother shook. At first Lugh thought she was having another seizure, but then he realized she was laughing. Despite her weakness, she managed a ghost of a smile.

"You don't see it. Who you are, and who you can become."

Lugh's voice caught in his throat, and before he could speak, Mother raised her other hand, brushing the hair from his face and resting on his tearstained cheek. Her eyes shone brighter than all the altars in Auklenn.

"I still see it," she whispered. "A mother always does . . ."

The memory fragmented in agony and fire.

Lugh watched the teardrop of light strike the pool of blood dead center.

Light erupted from the impact, brighter than the sun. It slammed into Lugh, but it didn't hurt or even push him, passing through him like air through a veil. The marigold petals erupted into vines, bursting forth in a green tide that swept over the dead stone like centuries passing in the blink of an eye. Flowers. Grass. Life. Wetness fell on Lugh's cheek, cold and gentle. The sky was no longer crimson. The Clysm's rusty gloom collapsed in on itself, and instead of sand, rain fell.

Washing away the blood and ashes. Glittering on the petals of marigolds and a thousand different shades of green.

Was this real? Lugh's eyelids went heavy, then fell like curtains. He dreamed of Sabia, of Mother when she'd walk him home from school, of the rare days he'd spent listening to Grandfather's tales, of the rarer days when he'd see Father's smile, and of Adsila laughing as she danced. When he opened his eyes again, blue sky and golden sunlight greeted him. He reached towards the sun and realized his left hand was whole. The pain was gone.

It was real after all.

Adsila! Lugh sat up with a gasp, only to find Adsila still on her side, soaked through from the rain and washed free of all the blood. Leafy vines and marigolds had grown over her, lush and aglitter with raindrops, and her scattered amethyst beads had become intertwined with green.

The entire plateau glowed with new life, but there was no life where Lugh wanted it most. Hadn't his truth been enough? What more could he have said? Why had Ehekahl saved him and not her? This wasn't what he'd wanted! He looked away, eyes burning. A lump formed in his throat. "Forgive me, Adsila."

The wind blew over the plateau, rustling the flowers. In that sound, he almost didn't hear the whisper. *"Help."*

Great, now he was hearing things.

"Lugh, you dunce. Help me!"

Lugh whirled. "A-Adsila?!"

"Yes." Adsila's chest rose. "These bloody vines are pinning me down!"

Oh. Lugh scrambled over and pulled at the vines, swinging between laughter and tears. The plants relented, and Adsila rolled free. She patted her shrapnel-tattered clothes, but her wounds were gone. Only then did she appear to notice the wonder all around them. Her hands froze, and then drifted, shakily, to where her dried marigold had been. Tears ran down her face and winked as they fell to the verdant ground.

"This . . . am I dreaming?"

"I wondered the same thing."

"That's not very convincing. Can you punch me?"

Lugh sputtered at the request.

"Just kidding." Adsila stared at the beauty around them. Her lips parted, but she remained silent for a long moment—long enough for her tears to dry. "It worked. We . . . actually did it, Lugh. We did it!"

Lugh glanced around at the beauty, the myriad plants glittering with sunlit rain. He'd accomplished what

Grandfather had yearned for all his life. Lugh touched his chest, over his heart, feeling different. He had also done the one thing he had always needed yet had denied himself for so many years: he had forgiven himself. "Yeah . . . we did."

"I never thought . . ." Adsila blinked rapidly. "Thank you, Lugh. Thank you."

"You made it possible."

"*We* made it possible." Adsila touched the nearest marigold. Her voice shook. "I was dead, wasn't I?"

Lugh's voice caught in his throat. He nodded.

"So that wasn't a dream, either." A sad smile bloomed on Adsila's face. She brushed her tangled hair from her eyes, then picked up her battered hat. She gently ran her thumb along its rim. "I saw my mom and dad. They were . . . happy for me. I wanted to stay, but this . . ." She looked to the heavens, sunlight bringing out every ashen freckle. "What did you do?"

Lugh glanced where the teardrop had fallen. The pool of blood was gone, overgrown with marigolds. "I told the truth."

"And proved that we're still worthy of this life." Adsila grabbed his elbow, pulling him close. "Ehekahl saw it in you, despite everything that happened. And she . . . did this . . ." Adsila looked around again, blinking rapidly as she spoke. "The Clysm . . . it was all there, hidden away, wasn't it? The rains, the fertility, the life, waiting to be reborn. Waiting for hope." She smiled and wiped her eyes. "That's it. My father . . . he was right."

Lugh glanced around, but the teardrop that had fallen from the heavens was gone. No Godstone. Was it not needed anymore? Was the real tether between this world and the divine somewhere else? Or maybe it rested in every human heart . . . including his own. Lugh shrugged and stopped wondering. He put his hand against the small of Adsila's back. "Let's go look, shall we?"

Adsila donned her hat. "Hell yes."

Together they navigated the plateau, careful not to step on the flowers. They gasped when they reached the edge. What had once been a barren land glowed with life, soil, and grass and meadows and rivers having formed where there'd once been sand and rock. Ivy and flowering vines had grown up all over the armored train, wreathing its artillery in blooms. No gunfire sounded in the distance. The battle was over.

"It's beautiful," Adsila breathed.

Grandfather would have loved this. Adsila punched Lugh in the shoulder. Lugh winced. "What was that for?"

"For calling me heavy." Then Adsila grabbed him by the collar and hauled him into a kiss. When they pulled back, breathless, she winked. Sunlight glittered in her emerald eyes. "And that's for coming back."

Lugh's head spun, but he still managed to grin. "And for carrying you up all those damn stairs?"

"That too. Shit, this place is high up." Adsila laughed, but quickly sobered up into a pensive frown. "Let's go. This isn't over yet."

Lugh tensed. Adsila was alive and well, but he still had someone to save.

Sabia.

They descended the battered steps as fast as they could, but the overgrown vines and patches of flowers and small trees made it slow going—as did the people trapped in the wild growth. Vines and roots had curled up around the Auklenn soldiers, locking them in place but not wounding them. Frozen in the poses of combat, some with weapons still shouldered, they were a glimpse into the final moments before Kata-Uluru's power had unleashed. The Auklenn forces had broken through the Uluru skirmishers. At least a hundred had pressed up the steps, grim, battle-hardened men and women of Vyzeryn's elite—undoubtedly to ensure that Lugh and Adsila were removed from the equation.

"Holy shit," Adsila said as they walked through the forest of trapped soldiers. She touched the stock of a rifle, whose wood had sprouted little pink flowers and leafy fronds.

Lugh met the eyes of the men and women he passed. None of them spoke, fearful awe and resignation written across their faces. Despite their loyalties and their experience, they knew it was over, and he silently thanked Ehekahl that she'd spared them. Most of the trapped soldiers reminded him of everyday folk he'd known back home. Not evil people, but misguided and stubbornly following orders. Of that, Lugh had committed his fair share.

They were near the bottom when one of the entrapped bodies muttered.

"You were right."

Lugh froze. Vyzeryn was stuck in a commanding pose, sword in one hand and rifle gripped mid-stock in the other. Ivy laced her blade, and roots had twisted through the action and out the barrel of her rifle, but her eyes were as sharp and able as ever, locking onto him with the precision of a sharpshooter. Lugh swallowed his instinctual fear and stood taller.

"Colonel."

Vyzeryn snorted. "Not for much longer. After this failure, I doubt I'll have rank at all."

"You would call this a failure?" Lugh approached her, jaw tense. "It's over."

"Not in the way we wanted."

"The Clysm is gone. There's no more threat. And this . . ." Lugh gestured around them. "What is this but a miracle?"

"A miracle?" Vyzeryn's expression soured. "You forget how steeped in pride we are, Lugh Ahearn."

"And what would your brother think of that pride?"

Vyzeryn grimaced. She closed her eyes. "That's enough. Let me wallow in defeat. I'm sure you have someone better to see. For what it's worth, I hope your sister is all right."

"You threatened to *shoot* her."

"A bluff." Vyzeryn's lips quirked. "And a rare half measure on my part."

Lugh's chest burned with all the vitriol he could say, but as sunlight glittered on the rain-damp vines imprisoning Vyzeryn, he felt his anger cool . . . and knew this, too, was his chance to be the better man. He swallowed hard. "Thank you."

"Spare me your sarcasm."

"If you'd left her in Anchorshaw, she'd be dead. So . . . thank you, Colonel."

Vyzeryn's eyes blinked open, surprise flashing across her face like the brief shadow of an overflying hawk. Then she grunted bemusedly and closed her eyes again. "She was worth saving."

She is. Lugh turned away, letting the last shards of anger slide off his heart.

Adsila stood by, red in the face but restraining herself. She had her revolver out, and had stolen bullets from soldiers as she went. She opened and closed the cylinder moodily as they continued down the steps. "I'd have punched her at least once. She blew your fingers off, remember?"

"My mother said that blood for blood only makes things worse." Lugh flexed his healed hand finger by finger. "I think I'll listen to her. Heaven knows I didn't do that enough."

Adsila grunted and stuffed her revolver into its holster.

A group of Uluru soldiers appeared through the green, moving cautiously up the steps with weapons ready. A hulking man at their forefront lowered his weapon and lifted a hand.

"Ku'Adsila! Outlander!"

"Tahk!" Lugh gripped the other's hand, and nearly passed out when the bear of a man yanked him close and clapped him hard on the back. Tahk's laughter shook his bones.

"You two bloody did it," Tahk said, releasing him. "For a moment I thought we were all dead and traversing the afterlife. Could have sworn I took an artillery shell to the skull. Hah!"

Lugh caught his breath and smiled. "I'm glad you didn't."

"And I'm glad we were right about you." Tahk clapped Lugh again, but when he turned to Adsila, he became solemn and formal. The other warriors had gone to one knee. Tahk did likewise, bowing his head. "Thank you, Ku'Adsila. You saved us all."

"Thanks to this city rat." Adsila nudged Lugh.

"And thanks to him as well." Tahk lifted his eyes. "What shall we do now, Ku'Adsila?"

"Isn't my grandfather in charge?"

"Yes, but after what you did, your word carries Ehekahl's divine will."

Adsila exchanged glances with Lugh. He nodded. Adsila licked her lips, thumbing her holster. "Spare the outlanders and see to the wounded. This battle is over, and we must be the better of both sides."

"Understood." Tahk waved to his comrades, and they carried on, disarming the Auklenn soldiers as they found them.

Lugh caught Adsila's eye. She smiled and shrugged.

"I'll need one hell of a stiff drink later, but your mother sounds all right. I'll take a page from her as well."

They reached the bottom to find the overgrown battlefield awash with Uluru and disarmed Auklenn soldiers, and to their surprise, they could find no dead or wounded. Men and women walked about in the verdant green, staring in awe at their tattered clothes where bullet, shrapnel, or blade had pierced. The same power that had healed him and revived Adsila had reached everyone else as well. A miraculous mercy that set his heart racing. What about Sabia? He opened his mouth to call her name—and heard her voice calling to him from the direction of the entangled train.

Lugh burst into a sprint. He tripped and fell over debris and roots, bruising his arms and legs, an electric, overwhelming heat blossoming in his chest and drowning out every insignificant pain. Uluru and Auklenner alike stepped out of his way, and before the flower-dappled wreck of the *Andrasta*, he found her—and she was *running*. Petals scattered around Sabia in the brilliant sunlight. Her pale face was flushed from the effort, but there was no cyanosis, no weakness, only the vitality he'd prayed she'd one day receive again. She tripped a few times, but she came up laughing, a beautiful light in her eyes that made Lugh want to fall to his knees and weep—but nothing, not this feeling or all the armies in the world, would keep him from closing the distance between them.

They embraced at the edge of a crater overgrown with fragrant lavender.

"Sabia!" Lugh lifted her under the armpits and spun her around. He didn't know what else to say, but her laughter sufficed to make him break out as well, and laughter said more than enough. He settled down at last and went to one knee, looking her over carefully. "How do you feel?"

"Great!" Sabia grinned ear to ear. "You made me better, didn't you? I knew you would!"

"I . . ." Lugh's voice cracked, and his eyes burned. He pulled her close and ran his hand through her golden curls. "Yeah. Just like I promised. You're okay now. Everything's okay."

Sabia hugged him back. "Are you okay, too?"

"More than ever." Lugh looked over her shoulder. Adsila stood by, smiling. "And there's someone I'd like you to meet."

It was well into the evening before Ku'Tiaman found them.

Nightfall swept over the land with a gentle breeze, and with the moonlight bright overhead, the dewy landscape glittered in unison with the star-jeweled sky. Lugh and Adsila sat around a cooking fire, joined by Tahk and many others. No celebrations, but rather a calm, almost reflective air as everyone came to terms with what had happened. The Auklenn soldiers had been rounded up but treated fairly, and the battered war train had proven full of supplies. Its rear engines, unscathed, would still serve well. As for Eirlys and his men who had died before the train had reached Kata-Uluru, they remained dead, as did all those who had lost their lives in the sands beyond, the good and the bad. Lugh could only accept that reality like a bitter medicine. There was a limit to all things. Victory and loss came hand in hand. Now it was up to the living to set things right.

Lugh warmed his hands on a mug of spiced tea. Staring into the fire reminded him too much of the horrors he'd seen, but he stared anyway, facing it. No more running away.

"She asleep?" Adsila asked.

Sabia lay partly on Lugh's lap, curled up and thoroughly exhausted from playing in the meadows with Adsila and the Uluru children, who'd arrived from the camp set up before the battle. Lugh smiled as he brushed her wild hair. She groaned and shifted, but her eyes remained closed.

"It's been ages since I've seen her play like that," Lugh whispered.

"And she's just getting started. Imagine when she gets all her strength back." Adsila swigged from a whiskey bottle she'd stolen from the train. She'd found her machete, too. The blade lay across her lap, freshly cleaned and mirroring the moonlight. "I can see why you did all this. What drove you. For someone like that, well . . . I'd do anything, too."

Lugh smiled, then gave a grateful nod to Maya, who sat across from the fire with several other older Uluru women. Maya dipped her head in return, the wrinkles by her eyes deepening. Sabia's memory of the battle had been spotty, but she could never say enough about Maya's comforting voice.

Grass rustled as horses came up behind them. Ku'Tiaman rode in the lead. Only a ghost of his frailty remained. Ehekahl's power hadn't just revived and healed, but had mended the ills of the body, even the time-garnered troubles of age. Although still elderly, Ku'Tiaman looked like a new man. Only his eyes were mostly unchanged. No longer rheumy, but still as piercing and resolute as ever, albeit with an unguarded tenderness that came out when he looked at Adsila.

"Grandfather," Adsila said, smiling.

"Adsila." Ku'Tiaman returned the smile. "It looks like I owe you an apology and my eternal gratitude. To your father as well. I . . . was wrong. About both of you."

Adsila had taken her hat off. Her hand drifted to its weathered brim. "Thank you."

Ku'Tiaman looked to Lugh. "And you as well, young Ahearn. Despite all the trouble you brought us, you have also given us a great blessing. My stubbornness almost ruined all of it. I was a fool to lose my sight as I had."

"I was an even greater fool," Lugh said. "Thank you for giving me a chance even though I . . . didn't deserve it."

"Do you really still believe you were not deserving?"

Lugh flinched, remembering what had happened on Kata-Uluru. He stared into the flames. "I'm sorry. I've seen myself a certain way for so long, it's . . . difficult to change. But I understand now. The lies I told myself. And the truth."

Adsila gently punched Lugh in the shoulder. "Say it."

"I deserved a chance." Lugh chuckled and ran a hand through his disheveled hair. "Gods . . . I never expected things to turn out like this."

"That makes two of us," Adsila said, raising her bottle and taking a swig.

"Ehekahl works in mysterious ways," Ku'Tiaman said. "Your grandfather must be smiling in the afterworld."

Lugh looked down at his hands—hands that had deceived so many . . . yet hands that had also toiled to protect those he loved, and in the end, hands that had set things right. He remembered Grandfather's deathbed, how Lugh had held his wrinkled, arthritic hands in those final moments. The intensity in Grandfather's eyes, and then the absence. Perhaps everyone's hands were stained, and what mattered was whether you had the courage to wash them clean. Lugh breathed out slowly. "Yes. I know he is."

Ku'Tiaman nodded solemnly. "I would like to stay and hear the whole story from you two, but I've got to be off. Uluru's resurrection has given this old man a lot of work to do."

Lugh glanced towards a ring of nearby fires, where the Auklenn prisoners ate in silence. "What will you do with them?"

"They will return home in peace. Of that I am already certain. There is no more fight left in them, not after what they've seen." Ku'Tiaman frowned, eyebrows knitting together. "But it is troubling. There will be a need to communicate with Auklenn on equal and honest terms. Otherwise they will never recognize us. We cannot have this cycle repeat. Not only for our sake, but the world's. Vyzeryn has offered to help in that regard."

Adsila choked on her whiskey. "She has?"

"I don't like her any more than you do, nor have I forgiven her. But it is interesting, Adsila, seeing what changes people." Ku'Tiaman nodded towards one of the fires. Vyzeryn sat amidst her troops, leaning on her empty scabbard, food uneaten as she stared into the flames. "And we will need help from people like her. People who have seen the truth, and whom truth has changed. It will take time, but we will rebuild and foster a new era. Perhaps, one day, Auklenn and Uluru can be friends. It won't come easy, but it is worth trying. The alternative is a poison I have tasted too much of . . . had almost lost myself to, just as that woman did."

Adsila nodded, then took another swig, wrinkling her nose as it burned down.

Ku'Tiaman turned his horse around. "I also look forward to your help, Lugh. We can always use someone like you on our side."

Lugh pondered that as Ku'Tiaman and his men rode off. *Someone like me, huh?* He sipped the tea, savoring the warmth as it worked through his chest. He had changed the way he saw himself, but it felt . . . odd. He wasn't used to it. Like wearing a second skin, one that wasn't weighed down by so many fears and regrets. What did that make him now? Not a new man. He didn't need to be someone else, he just needed to be the Lugh who'd made it all this way. That was his task: to learn to live with his true self. It felt like sweeping aside old foundations and starting anew . . . but he knew he was starting with something good, something that had always been there, beneath the lies. Someone Mother could be proud of. Someone Sabia could depend on. A good man . . . and the man he'd choose to be going forward.

A nudge from Adsila snapped him out of his reverie.

"So, city rat," she said, face rosy from drink. "What happens now?"

Lugh chuckled. "I suppose we'll have to find out. Start by living on."

"Sounds about right." Adsila brushed dust off the brim of her hat. "My dad said something like that, too. We live on. Learn to be better, despite everything.

That's how he lived. I think that's how I'll live, too." She hunched forward, grimacing at the moonlit reflection in her blade. "I . . . killed a lot of people, and not all of them were bad, yet I'm the one who was given mercy. Bloody as I am . . . I'll make what I become next worthy of the gift I've been given."

Lugh raised his eyebrows. "That's . . ."

"Poetic, coming from me?"

"I was going to say eloquent."

"Yeah, right." Adsila sheathed her machete, then took out her revolver and opened the cylinder. She stared intensely at the casings. After a long moment, she tipped the gun over. The bullets sang against the rocks and disappeared amidst grass and marigold blooms. "Maybe it can really happen."

"What?"

"The kind of life where I won't have to use one of these."

Lugh smiled and held her hand, taking the weapon. With his knack, he Doppeled the revolver into a marigold. "I think it already has."

Adsila laughed. "That's pretty damn poetic for a city rat."

"What can I say?" Lugh put the marigold in Adsila's hair. "A liar gets a lot of practice."

Epilogue

The passenger train rumbled into the station with a hiss of steam and a squeal of metal on track. Lugh covered his face as the wind of its arrival kicked up dust and dried leaves. The two-tracked train station, still resplendent with colored streamers from a festival, bustled with Auklenner and Uluru travelers alike, chatter rising as people queued up to board or to meet arrivals. The peaceful sounds reminded Lugh of simple days, when Mother had taken him on trips to the countryside. He still remembered the awe he'd felt at his first train ride, how everything had seemed so large, so grand, so curious.

Those were good days. Yet he didn't wish to be anywhere other than where he was now.

Kata-Uluru loomed with blue sky at its back and midday sun as its crown. The town in the plateau's shadow by the same name, established after the battle, had drawn Uluru from all across the continent, becoming a small city in its own right. Laden with green and surrounded by fields, it reminded Lugh of the undulating countryside Mother had always loved. It smelled of clean air and freedom, rather than the Auklenn routine of coal fires, manufactories, and dominion. Kata-Uluru's rolling fields and lush forests were in autumn's sway, harvest green peppered with the myriad shades of red, orange, and yellow. And alongside the train station, on rusted old tracks, the *Andrasta's* wreck rustled with fronds of ivy and autumn blooms, a monument to troubled times past.

Remarkable what three years could do. Remarkable that he was lucky enough to be part of it. Vyzeryn had been true to her word. Auklenn, at last, had opened its eyes. The west had returned to the place Grandfather had dreamed about: a land of beauty and peace.

To think it all started with me gambling. Lugh chuckled. He'd played his hand, and it had been a good one after all.

Sabia tugged at his arm. "Lugh. The train's here!"

"Oh! Right." Lugh shook himself and hefted the suitcase, only for Sabia to take it from him. At twelve years old, she'd grown taller and stronger than he once could have dreamed. Her lungs no longer bothered her, and her days were filled with adventure and life . . . but she was also growing up. She yearned to become someone, to embark on the journey that would lead her to herself. One of the best boarding schools in all of Auklenn had accepted her application. She wanted to become a physician to help sick people like herself. Lugh's chest ached as he watched her carry her suitcase toward the train. Her blue peacoat, polished boots, and trousers went oddly well with the Uluru charms she wore around her wrist and neck. Her golden hair, braided with amethyst beads, glowed in the sunlight, but her smile still outshone everything.

He wondered just how much Adsila had rubbed off

on her. Maybe more than Lugh himself, at this point. The two were like sisters.

"Come on!" Sabia called. "It's leaving soon!"

Lugh realized his legs had locked. Damn, he was afraid. He forced himself to follow her to the train's door. The conductor, an old Uluru man with whimsical eyes, nodded and waved for the engineer to hold the train. Lugh grabbed Sabia by her shoulders. His voice shook. "Be sure to write home every week."

"Of course," Sabia said.

"Don't let anyone bully you, but don't get into too much trouble either."

"Got it."

"Get enough sleep. And be sure to eat—"

Sabia punched him gently in the chest. "You worry too much. I'll be fine." She grinned. "Adsila's been teaching me."

Lugh suppressed a groan. "What, exactly?"

"Oh, nothing." Sabia's smile grew wider. "Just a few life skills."

Gods have mercy on anyone who messes with her. Lugh laughed despite himself and pulled Sabia into an embrace. His throat tightened when her arms squeezed him back. So strong. Growing like a weed. "I'll miss you."

"Me too."

"Go on, then. Make me proud."

Sabia jumped onto the train and twirled to face him. "Aren't you already?"

Lugh wiped his eyes. "Of course I am."

"Good." Sabia's mischievous smile faded, and a hint of apprehension wrinkled her brow. "I love you."

"I love you too. Always."

The train howled, and with a hiss of steam began to move. Sabia blinked rapidly, wiped her eyes with her sleeve, and smiled anew. Shoulders back. Eyes forward. Ready to face the world. The train gained speed, its thrum of machinery rattling Lugh's teeth. He forced a smile as he waved Sabia off. The other train cars passed, the polished windows mirroring his reflection—a reflection he no longer flinched away from, belonging to a man he'd always been wrong to hate. The last few years had held much healing for the land, but also for himself.

When the train disappeared down the bend in the track, between rolling hills of wheat and corn, he lowered his hand and took a long, shaky breath. Letting go. One of the hardest things he'd ever done.

"She's growing up so fast. Crazy, isn't it, Mom?" Lugh looked to the clear sky, to wherever Mother rested. In the silence, he could imagine her smile. He wasn't ashamed anymore, but the old ache remained, and he knew it always would. So be it. He'd carry it in his heart, and be the son she'd always believed he could be. Until they met again.

Still, to let Sabia go into the world, to be so far away from her, chilled him to the bone. He stared down the track and shivered.

A hand gripped his shoulder.

"She'll be all right."

Lugh nodded, putting his hand on Adsila's. "You're late."

"I got caught up with something. Grandfather's still as overbearing as ever. Besides, I already said my goodbyes."

"Good. She looks up to you, you know."

"How can she not? I'm looking-up-to material."

Lugh chuckled and turned at last. Where Sabia had changed so much, Adsila remained like a stubborn rock against the currents of change. She still wore a long brown duster, spurred leather boots, and buttoned undershirt overlaid with charmed necklaces, all topped with her father's hat. Revolver and blade still hung on her belt, as much a part of her as her freckles, but they hadn't been used in years, and she no longer carried herself like someone always expecting a fight. Neither did her eyes have the burdens he'd seen when they'd first met in Capstone. Even her drinking habits had changed, dwindling until she only drank on special occasions. They both had the silent wounds of what they'd been through together, but so, too, did they have the lessons that helped them bear them.

And they also had each other.

"What are you staring at?" Adsila asked, arching a notched eyebrow.

"You, of course." Lugh kissed her, then clapped her shoulder. He loved that smile of hers, and how her freckled nose wrinkled when she faked an inquisitive look. "Sorry. I'm just . . . getting over this. Sabia's never gone off on her own before."

"The boarding school literally has an *entourage* waiting for her."

"I know, but—"

"I also have Tahk and four of his best on the train. They're armed, of course." Adsila's brow furrowed. "How's that? Enough for you, worry wart?"

"I *know*, it's just . . ." Lugh sighed. "You know how it is."

Adsila's face softened. She took off her hat, running her thumb along the rim. "Of course. That's part of life. Learning to let go. But it's a good thing, having something to let go of. It sure beats having nothing."

"Poetic," Lugh said.

"Just the truth."

They stood side by side before the empty track. The station was emptying, and soon only the wind and the whispering ivy on the nearby wreck broke the silence. A goldfinch flitted overhead and landed on the barrel of one of the *Andrasta's* heavy guns. Still aimed at Kata-Uluru, but never to fire again. Three other goldfinches joined the first, and with a flurry of chirps they flitted toward the cornfields. Woodsmoke and soil hung on the breeze.

"Thank you," Lugh said at last. "I'm not sure where I'd be without you."

"Same place I'd be without you." Adsila hooked his arm. "Dead."

"Nothing like a little morbidness on a sunny day, huh?"

"It's also the truth. Come on, let's get out of here." Adsila pulled him along the platform and onto Kata-Uluru's bustling streets. Wagons and pedestrians flocked this way and that, while Uluru lawmen joked amongst each other while on patrol. Somewhere in the distance, a group of children shouted and laughed at play. It was hard to imagine that the ground it all stood on had once been rife with blood and sand. People waved and called out to them, honest smiles joining honest words. Lugh was still getting used to that. Adsila loved it. She waved and shouted retorts to their friendly banter. Lugh scanned the busy street as he walked. Shops open. Signs freshly painted. Markets overflowing from the bountiful harvest. It filled him with an urge to laugh. He smiled instead, turning his gaze forward—only for a familiar face to snag his eye.

A bearded man leaned against the wall outside the bustling post office. His weathered cavalry jacket swayed in the breeze, and his brimmed hat was tilted back in a casual disregard for fashion. Lugh froze mid-stride. The Drunk smiled and touched the brim of his hat, but when Lugh blinked, he was gone. Only a few errant autumn leaves danced in his place.

"What is it?" Adsila asked.

Lugh blinked several more times, then fished through his pocket until he found the blue poker chip he made a point of carrying everywhere. A reminder, and a lesson. He turned it over, thumbing its smooth surface. "Thought I saw him. That man I told you about."

"Maybe you did." Adsila guided him back into a walk. "Many spirits haunted this land after the war, but now they can rest. Thanks to this."

Lugh nodded and stowed the chip away, allowing himself to bask in the town's peaceful wonders once again, in the beauty that thrived despite the troubled past. Damn, it felt good, and in more ways than one. His sorcery aversion had never returned, although his knack had regressed into its modest capabilities. The power, like the Godstone, had been fleeting. But he didn't feel shortchanged. There was more to life than power. So much more.

"How's the business coming?" Adsila asked.

Lugh chuckled. "Grand opening is tonight, actually. I was going to surprise you."

"Consider me surprised." Adsila elbowed him and grinned. "So, a saloon eh? And here I thought you'd had enough of those places."

Building a saloon hadn't been Lugh's first idea, but it had been the first to stick. In all the towns he'd been in, good and bad, there'd been a place where people could leave their troubles at the door, sing and dance, and live on in a world that sometimes got tired of living. The Frontier, Uluru, needed a place like that. Not a gambling den. Not a grungy oasis for outlaws. A place where friends could gather and celebrate life and the lives of friends no longer around. That's what the new Frontier needed to be. A land built on understanding, friendship, shared ground, and faith.

A home worth staking a future on.

Lugh closed his eyes as Adsila led him along. He focused on her strong arm in his, the warmth of her presence, her dependable smell of leather and woodsmoke, and the way her just being there gave him all the reassurance he needed. "I was having a hard time deciding on a name, but I finally figured it out."

"Oh? What is it?"

"The Marigold."

"That's a good name. Reminds me of a saloon I shot up a few years back." Adsila pulled Lugh a little closer and winked. "Then let's go drink the Marigold dry, shall we?"

"I thought you called quits on drinking like a horse."

"I did!" Adsila kissed him on the cheek. "With special

exceptions for special occasions with a certain special someone. On the house, of course."

"Still holding me to that promise, are you?"

"Wouldn't dream of not doing so."

"That's so like you, Adsila." Lugh put his arm over her shoulder, leaning his head against hers. "Though, I wouldn't have it any other way."

"Really?" Adsila arched an eyebrow, her lips curling beautifully.

"Really." Lugh looked towards the clear blue sky. "And that's the truth."

When Spencer Sekulin isn't on the road as a paramedic or studying, he is most likely writing. Born and raised in Ontario, Canada, Spencer fell in love with books at a young age, with authors like Terry Brooks and Eoin Colfer giving him an appetite for speculative fiction. Though he didn't begin writing until university, he quickly discovered that it was just as fun as reading. The rest is history. His passions include emergency medicine, voice-overs, homemade coffee, travel obscura, and of course, writing.

www.ingramcontent.com/pod-product-compliance
Lightning Source LLC
Chambersburg PA
CBHW020138310726
48970CB00006B/1925